"It'll take you federal boys months to sneak around the back way on these guys, if you ever do," said Hank Yarborough, scratching his chin. "Remember, the others may have no prior connection to Lennart and Thorton. Hell, they could've met at Disneyland. Bennie here is our shortcut."

"Shortcut?" said Gibbs.

"He means bait," Benella said.

The sheriff: "It's quite likely that the only thing keeping them close by is the desire to clean her clock, if you'll pardon the expression."

"Then I want in," Havershaw said.

"In?" Connor shouted. "What, you guys plan to sit around waiting for the T-rex to come after the sacrificial goat?"

"Connor," said Yarborough. "The situation's gone critical. We'll cover Bennie like Saran Wrap, with the FBI's help, of course. She'll be safe as Tinker Bell, I guarantee."

But, as Connor knew all too well, in situations like this, there were no guarantees.

MORE MYSTERIES FROM THE
BERKLEY PUBLISHING GROUP...

THE HERON CARVIC MISS SEETON MYSTERIES: Retired art teacher Miss Seeton steps in where Scotland Yard stumbles. "A most beguiling protagonist!"
—*The New York Times*

by Heron Carvic
MISS SEETON SINGS
MISS SEETON DRAWS THE LINE
WITCH MISS SEETON
PICTURE MISS SEETON
ODDS ON MISS SEETON

by Hampton Charles
ADVANTAGE MISS SEETON
MISS SEETON AT THE HELM
MISS SEETON, BY APPOINTMENT

by Hamilton Crane
HANDS UP, MISS SEETON
MISS SEETON CRACKS THE CASE

MISS SEETON PAINTS THE TOWN
MISS SEETON BY MOONLIGHT
MISS SEETON ROCKS THE CRADLE
MISS SEETON GOES TO BAT
MISS SEETON PLANTS SUSPICION
STARRING MISS SEETON
MISS SEETON UNDERCOVER
MISS SEETON RULES
SOLD TO MISS SEETON
SWEET MISS SEETON
BONJOUR, MISS SEETON
MISS SEETON'S FINEST HOUR

KATE SHUGAK MYSTERIES: A former D.A. solves crimes in the far Alaska north...
by Dana Stabenow
A COLD DAY FOR MURDER
DEAD IN THE WATER
A FATAL THAW
BREAKUP

A COLD-BLOODED BUSINESS
PLAY WITH FIRE
BLOOD WILL TELL
HUNTER'S MOON

INSPECTOR BANKS MYSTERIES: Award-winning British detective fiction at its finest... "Robinson's novels are habit-forming!"
—*West Coast Review of Books*

by Peter Robinson
THE HANGING VALLEY
WEDNESDAY'S CHILD
INNOCENT GRAVES

PAST REASON HATED
FINAL ACCOUNT
GALLOWS VIEW

CASS JAMESON MYSTERIES: Lawyer Cass Jameson seeks justice in the criminal courts of New York City in this highly acclaimed series... "A witty, gritty heroine."
—*New York Post*

by Carolyn Wheat
FRESH KILLS
MEAN STREAK
TROUBLED WATERS

DEAD MAN'S THOUGHTS
WHERE NOBODY DIES
SWORN TO DEFEND

JACK McMORROW MYSTERIES: The highly acclaimed series set in a Maine mill town and starring a newspaperman with a knack for crime solving... "Gerry Boyle is the genuine article."
—*Robert B. Parker*

by Gerry Boyle
DEADLINE
LIFELINE
BORDERLINE

BLOODLINE
POTSHOT
COVER STORY

Dead
Run

Leo Atkins

BERKLEY PRIME CRIME, NEW YORK

DEAD RUN

A Berkley Prime Crime Book / published by arrangement with the author

PRINTING HISTORY
Berkley Prime Crime edition / December 2000

All rights reserved.
Copyright © 2000 by Clay Harvey.
This book, or parts thereof, may not be reproduced in any form without permission. For information address:
The Berkley Publishing Group, a division of Penguin Putnam Inc.,
375 Hudson Street, New York, New York 10014.

The Penguin Putnam Inc. World Wide Web site address is
http://www.penguinputnam.com

ISBN: 0-425-17777-7

Berkley Prime Crime Books are published by
The Berkley Publishing Group, a division of Penguin Putnam Inc.,
375 Hudson Street, New York, New York 10014. The name
BERKLEY PRIME CRIME and the BERKLEY PRIME CRIME
design are trademarks belonging to Penguin Putnam Inc.

PRINTED IN THE UNITED STATES OF AMERICA

10 9 8 7 6 5 4 3 2 1

Acknowledgments

Christopher's mom, Barbara, a principal principal, confrere, and who still looks very much like she did at nineteen, which was, ah, several years ago.

Wanda Faye Hiatt, dear friend, supporter, source of inspiration.

My sister Anne Tyler Ashley, and her brood: Sandi and Corey, Ty and Heather, Michael and Maraline, Rikki and Jeff, listed chronologically, of course, to keep me out of trouble.

Nancy Fleming, Pennsylvania pixie, whose children's stories touched a generation.

Ruby Hawks, who reads everything I write and exhorts others to do so; is she great or what?

Gentle Pal Mike Holloway, and his wife Nancy and daughters Courtney and Rachel; they epitomize "family."

Debbie Ortiz, close friend for more than twenty years; a jewel indeed.

Buddy Jim Roberts, man of iron will, iron scruples, and a mean beef stew.

Susan Cooke, reader, critic extraordinaire, maybe Mom of the Year.

Ed Humburg, who guides, informs, prods, proselytizes.

Pals Andy Riedell and Andy Riedell, father and son, soldier and policeman; a quality pair, that.

As always, Emma Lee Laine, nurturer, confidante, lady.

Jim Rosso, Vietnam vet, training partner, good friend.

Former coworkers Angela Cloninger, Gina Brown, Jeff Fenn, and Art Leak; an eclectic array of humankind.

Tom Colgan, my editor; obviously a man of taste and vision, and a wonderful griot in his own right.

And last but emphatically not least, my Wilmington friends and fellow writers Sharon Hartung, CarlaGay Higgins, Martha Howell, Marj Zepernick, and Andrea Young; look for those names on book covers.

To Christopher, soon to be thirteen(!).
You just keep getting better, Son.

"Murder's out of tune,
And sweet revenge grows harsh."

—Shakespeare, *Othello*

"Folly is for mortals a
self-chosen misfortune."

—Menander

Prologue

Aт 9:13 A.M. ON THURSDAY, APRIL 2, A BANK NEAR THE outskirts of Richmond, Virginia, was robbed of an undisclosed quantity of money by two men wearing full body armor, dark ski masks, helmets, gloves, and army boots; one man was carrying a Bulgarian AK-47 rifle, the other a Benelli twelve-gauge riot shotgun. They also wore sidearms (two each—one concealed, one exposed), and razor-sharp tanto fighting knives strapped to their legs. No alarm was sent by any bank official, at any time, because a female teller was taken hostage when the holdup men exited. She was subsequently set free, unharmed and unmolested, just mildly dehydrated from six hours of midday sequestration in a black SUV, bound and gagged. She recovered in time to peddle her story to a national tabloid, for a bundle.

Also at exactly 9:13 EST that same sunny morning, a bank in Knoxville, Tennessee, was being knocked over by a similar pair of body-armored gents with masks and gloves and helmets and carrying a shotgun and an assault rifle and handguns and tantos. (And two packs of Juicy Fruit, though the FBI report fails to mention the latter.) No alarm was triggered by a bank official at this location either, until a phone call was later received from Betty Mavis, a teller kidnapped by the robbers upon their retreat and held captive for several hours in a stolen Audi's trunk. (The all-wheel-drive version; nice car.) The miscreants did give Betty a magazine to read and a container of bottled water, but it was too dark inside the trunk to read and the water was stale. Grateful nonetheless, she sang quietly to herself to keep her spirits up. After being released in a mall parking lot, Betty immediately sought mall security to report the incident. Security, mildly skeptical, called the bank. The bank officer who took the call confirmed her story then called the FBI.

Neither were Georgia banks immune on that sparkling spring day, for when their synchronized Seikos agreed that it was precisely 9:13 A.M., a stubby stupid monolith and his much brighter cohort (identically armed and attired as their more northerly comrades, except for the addition of one ice pick) made a request for withdrawal from a suburban Atlanta branch—large bills only, please. When one of the bank managers showed sufficient gumption to protest, his cheek was laid open by the front sight of an assault rifle. No further objections were forthcoming. This pair of thieves also took a hostage, though said lady did not fare as well as her counterparts in Richmond and Knoxville. She was constantly threatened by the stout, swarthy one; only the restraining presence of the second, less nefarious robber enabled her to escape serious harm.

An hour later the leader of the Atlanta heist liaised by telephone with the orchestrator of the Richmond job. They laughed and patted each other on the back—metaphorically speaking of course, since one was in South Carolina, the other in West Virginia . . .

Three robberies, *three* cities; same time, same MO! What a hoot! Fame and felicity would soon be theirs!

Well. Fame, anyway.

Chapter 1

IT MIGHT NOT HAVE BEEN SUCH A DISASTER IF IT hadn't been Friday night with the place chock-full of diners. Two strangers had just come in and the tall guy wasn't bad looking in a macho go-to-hell sort of way, and Arlene couldn't help but glance in the mirror behind the counter for a quick self-appraisal. *Good grief, talk about a bad hair day,* she thought. *Oh well, he needs a haircut himself, and a shave, and* two *baths, and his nose could be an acre or two smaller, but who's perfect, besides me of course.* She smiled at her own self-deprecating humor, still evident despite the late hour and a sore bunion.

"What's the special tonight, darlin'?" the tall drink of water interrupted Arlene's reverie by placing a toothpick on his lower lip and moving it from one corner of his mouth to the other provocatively. She decided to play coy.

"My name ain't darlin'," she corrected. Then: "Ham hocks with greens, four ninety-nine; country-style steak with rice and gravy, five forty-nine; baked chicken and dressing, five ninety-nine. You get one extra vegetable— the list's on that blackboard, same every night—and either corn bread or dinner rolls—which we don't bake, but we do the corn bread—and your drink, either tea or coffee. Dessert's extra and we're out of everything but blueberry cobbler." She took a well-deserved breath.

"The cobbler good?" the tall man asked, toothpick bobbing.

"Not 'specially. The banana pudding is, but it's all gone. Y'all are pretty late. Been to the movies?"

Her left hand lay on the counter. He placed his right one atop it and massaged her wrist with his middle finger. She didn't pull her hand away, despite the dirt under his fingernail. "No, but I can take you when you get off," he said.

"Don't get off til after the movie house closes."

"Can we get the food to go?" the shorter one said, putting in his two cents. He wasn't really short, just thick, like a weight lifter, but not fat, either. And sandy-haired, near as she could tell, what with the buzz cut.

"Sure, if you like plastic plates and cutlery, got them little compartments in them so the gravy don't mix with the pole beans." She cackled at her levity. The two strangers did not. Yankees, probably. Everybody knew Yankees were humor deficient.

"Give us two of each, and I don't give a hoot what the extra vegetable is. Mix the bread, too, half and half. And six cobblers," instructed the lofty one.

"Don't know if we got six cobblers left, but I'll check. What if we don't?"

"Then don't charge me for them."

"Tea or coffee?"

"Split it up."

"Okay." She took the order to the kitchen.

The two guys sat at the only vacant table and casually looked around. Pine-paneled walls with four large posters, one per wall: Ronald Reagan, John Wayne, W. C. Fields, Franklin Pierce Adams shaking hands with someone unidentifiable, all black-and-white. Coffee urns in the corner, and one for iced tea; big old Wurlitzer jukebox spinning some Patsy Cline ditty; eight square tables covered with red-and-white-checkered oilcloths and sided by wooden straight-back chairs; twenty-foot-long Formica-topped counter with six rotating stools, each having a single stainless-steel tube for support; woodstove near the far end of the counter, not lit. Decorative or functional?

In through the screen door—letting it go *whack* behind them—came two sheriff's deputies, obviously on duty, decked out in rural-ranger garb: Smokey bear hats, tan uniforms, Sam Browne belts with cuffs and Mace and radios and sticks and handguns—identical Smith & Wesson .45 autos, big ugly stainless-steel things with black plastic grips—and a belt holder for two extra magazines just in case Carl Drega was alive and well and loose in North Carolina.

The tall stranger—whose given name was Jacoby Lennart—said, *sotto voce* to his partner, "Check out the county mounties."

Amos Thorton, not being dead, and having been alerted by the slamming door, was already checking them out. He responded with equal quietness: "No bulges at the ankles, on either of them, so no backup guns. No vests, neither." Both he and Lennart did have vests. Under lightweight cotton jackets. The vests were not for adornment.

Lennart climbed to his feet and walked over to the jukebox, boots clocking on the hardwood floor, just as if he might actually play something on it—Ferlin Husky or some-fucking-body else that would make him sick to his stomach. ("On the wings of a snow . . . white . . . dove . . . " Gag.) As he adopted the appearance of perusing the selections (three for fifty cents), he was actually scoping the parking lot; only one patrol car, so the county cowboys were together. Odd; he'd thought all these bumpkins were lone wolves. He tried to look bewildered by the array of choices in, uh, music, as he went back to his table and sat, obviously fraught with indecision.

Sure he was.

•　　•　　•

Across the room a very attractive, very tall, very astute, very *aware* lady took note of Lennart's act and didn't buy it. She was seated at a table with her sister, Katelin Stuart, her sister's husband, Damien, and the couple's daughter, four-year-old Mary Leigh. Damien had served as a marine, and currently spent part of each weekday evening teaching martial arts to local cops and their spouses, and to the attractive, tall, astute, aware lady beside him, whose name was Benella Mae Sweet and who was saying to him: "Damien, take Mary Leigh to the bathroom. Right now."

Damien was perplexed. "Why?"

"I don't have to go to the bathroom, Aunt Bennie," Mary Leigh protested.

"Please, honey," Benella insisted. "I'll buy you a new Beanie Baby if you do."

"Which one?" the pragmatic child wanted to know.

"Bennie," Damien said. "What's going on?"

Benella Mae looked her brother-in-law in the eye. "Just take her. Now, Damien. And lock the door behind you. Then get in a stall and lock that."

"But—"

"Just do it!" she sibilated, a bit harshly. "And don't come out till I call you. Me, no one else."

Damien knew his sister-in-law well, thus he knew that she not only meant what she was saying, but had a good reason for saying it. "Come on, honey," he said to his daughter. "We'll decide what Beanie Baby to get." And they went.

Katelin had been observing all this without comment. She, too, knew her sister very well, and was waiting for whatever came next. Here it came. "Kate, come with me." The two of them headed for the ladies' room.

Occupied.

So they waited in the narrow hall.

Not long.

One of the deputies, after ordering his coffee and cobbler, noticed the strangers. He didn't like what he noticed:

one had too much hair, the other not enough; one looked like he needed a hosing, the other like he'd just had one. City boys. *Inner* city. Dope and stuff. Or maybe ex-gyrenes, tough guys. He elbowed Elmo, his partner. When Elmo gave him a look and said, "Wha'smatter, Stew?", the first deputy pointed with his lantern jaw. Elmo followed the pointing chin, observed the pair of nonlocals, and observed the nonlocals observing them. "Ol' boys ain't from around here," he said.

"Man, nothing gets by you," said Stew Blaisdell. "Notice they're wearing jackets?"

"I ain't blind."

"It seem cold outside to you?"

"Come to think on it, I reckon not. But them jackets look pretty lightweight."

"They also look kind of bulgy to me," Stew allowed, just as Arlene carried an armload of plates from the kitchen over to the nonlocals, then went in search of bags big enough to put them in. "And that's too much food for them to eat by theirselves," he continued.

"So they got friends. No law against it," from Elmo. His coffee and cobbler had arrived and he'd abruptly lost interest in the pair of out-of-towners. "Thanks, Carrie," he said to the other night-shift girl, who was seventy-four and sported a large facial mole and a discreet nether tattoo. Of a nasturtium.

"You're welcome," Carrie acknowledged, and disappeared into the kitchen, the aroma of inexpensive cologne in her wake. Elmo didn't seem to mind; he dug right into his victuals.

Stew did not. He ignored his coffee and ignored his cobbler, and stood up from the stool to make himself more imposing than he was sitting down, which at six-three and two-forty was pretty imposing. He tilted the hat back off his forehead, John Wayne style, and looked hard at the interlopers.

The interlopers looked back.

• • •

Out of one side of his mouth, Amos Thorton said, "Either they've made us, or that jerk's real unfriendly to passers-through."

"How the hell'd they make us, stupid? We're not wanted for anything," Jacoby said, and spat out his frayed toothpick.

"It's all over the news about the bank—"

"How could they connect us with that? We wore masks and gloves and long coats. No one can identify us, so forget it. Once we got out of Knoxville, we were home free."

"What if one of the others got caught, and ratted—"

"I won't tell them you said that," Jacoby gritted. "No, this jasper wants a pissing contest, and since we sure as hell can't stand no pat-down, if he makes a move, we gotta take him out. Him *and* his partner. Be ready to scoot for the car."

"Jacoby, I—"

"Just be ready."

Amos nodded just as the deputy made his move.

"Okay, hon, what's going on?" Katelin asked Benella.

The two women had finally gained the bathroom, which in a way was unfortunate because the last patron had obviously sampled the pintos and they'd disagreed with her.

"Did you notice that tall, grubby guy who just came in? Had a buzzhead companion, only shorter, both of them wearing ugly cotton jackets?" Benella queried.

"No, I didn't. Why?"

"The tall one went over to the jukebox, as if to pick out a tune. But he didn't. In fact, he seemed more interested in the parking lot, and it was right after Stew and Elmo came in."

"Maybe they're expecting someone."

Benella shook her head. "I don't think so. And why the jackets? It's at least seventy outside."

"Maybe they're cold-natured."

"One of them, perhaps. Not both."

"Don't you think you're being a little paranoid?"

"Okay, I'm paranoid. So humor me. Stay in here until I can check things out. I'll go talk to Stew, see what he thinks."

Katelin sighed theatrically. "If it'll make you feel better."

"It will. And be sure to lock the door behind me."

"All right, but there's no way I'm going into that stall. I'd rather get shot."

Benella grinned. "You got a point. Back soon."

And she slipped out the door.

Stew was still playing stare-down with the tall guy when Benella stepped up beside him. "I see you've noticed our odd men out," she said.

"Yeah," Stew acknowledged, "and I'm about to go dance on that tall one's greasy head if he don't soften his look."

"Then you better send Elmo over by the door. Let them see they're flanked."

"Who you giving orders to, lady? You been hanging around Connor Gibbs too long."

"I'm not trying to tell you how to do your job, Stew."

"Yeah you are. Trouble is, you're right." Stew turned to Elmo and whispered into a hairy ear. Elmo mopped blueberry juice from his mouth, put on his hat, stood, hitched his belt up over a bulbous belly, sidled toward the door.

While Blaisdell's right side was turned away from the pair of nonlocals, he thumbed the retaining strap off his pistol, readying for trouble.

"It's going down," Lennart said. "The big motherfucker just flipped off his strap. You face fat boy—*casually!* Let's don't start nothing. We're just pleasant vacationers, two guys passing through that stopped for a little grub. Soon as I open up on Gunsmoke over there, you drop His Lardassness."

"He's good as dead already. Let's just do it and get the hell out," from Thorton.

"Here y'are, gents," Arlene said, walking over to slap

two paper pokes filled with provender on their table, startling them. The drinks were in a spill-proof cardboard box. "That'll be thirty-nine dollars and twelve cents. Oh, and we didn't have but four cobblers left. They're the bag with the big *X* on it."

Lennart palmed a pair of twenties with his left hand, handing them to Arlene. "Keep the change," he said absentmindedly.

Arlene made a face. "Sure you can spare it?"

"What?"

"Eighty-eight whole cents. Maybe you'll need it to gas up your Mercedes."

As Lennart turned his head to dispose of this picayune annoyance, Stew Blaisdell made his play. He took two long strides; five more and he'd be chest to chest with the tall one.

Across the room, Deputy Elmo Floyd had been awaiting his cue; Blaisdell's sudden move was it. As Elmo reached to unstrap his piece, all hell broke loose.

Amos Thorton sat with both hands in his jacket pockets, watching the overweight deputy like a cobra watches a mongoose. As soon as the fat man's hand moved toward his gun, Amos drew from one of his pockets a compact pistol of his own and shot the deputy in the navel, the liver, the neck, and the face, all in the span of two seconds. The large deputy crashed into the Wurlitzer (causing Hank Williams to skip a couple of grooves), sagged to his knees ponderously, then fell over onto his side. His handgun never cleared its holster.

Deputy Blaisdell's did, across the room. He was a firearms aficionado, a gun freak, a shooting buff, and he was fast as lightning, having spent his formative years playing quick draw with toy pistols. BOOM! his .45 roared, slamming his ears, but he was so focused, so gripped by tunnel vision, that the blast didn't even register on his mind, though he did notice his bullet pucker the tall guy's jacket—

dead center over the heart—and he watched the man spin half around at the impact, and he felt good about himself, and his ability with a gun—revered by his law enforcement peers—and his coolness under pressure . . . but wait, the bastard was turning back toward him, no way after a FUCKING PINWHEEL, but there he was, gun in hand—A GUN IN HIS FUCKING HAND—muzzle rising toward HIM, and Stew's .45 bucked again, BOOM!, its bullet missing this time to strike an elderly man over in the corner with his wife, still eating, not even looking up as the big .45-caliber slug took him, and Blaisdell refocused on the tall perp's gun—pointing straight at him now—and BOOM! went his .45 yet again, the big Smith jerking in recoil, but that bullet missed, too (HOW THE HELL?), blowing a dime-sized hole in the pine paneling across the room, then BAM! BAM! BAM! the tall guy's gun was talking . . . and all three sank home, center hits, and Stew's heart went erratic and his sternum splintered and he was going down and there was the ceiling, and then the leg of a chair, and then the underside of a table—moving, overturning, crashing to the floor—and there was the ceiling again . . .

Then there was nothing.

Because he was dead.

When the shit hit the fan, Benella Mae Sweet dove over the counter, landing hard on the floor on the opposite side, then scrambled like a coyote on ice to get into the kitchen and out of the line of fire, BAM! BAM! BAM! BAM! Buzz Cut's gun had said as she was going over the counter, then BOOM!—BOOM!—BOOM! Stew's gun had said as she'd scrambled for the kitchen, then BAM! BAM! BAM! the tall guy's gun had said as she scurried for the shotgun that Hollis Bernharte—the restaurant's owner, off tonight watching his daughter sing "Oh, What a Beautiful Morning" at a nearby high school—kept in the pantry, loaded, for when stray cats plundered the garbage. *Cats.* Shit, the gun would be loaded with birdshot! But Benella grabbed it anyway, it being better than nothing, and jacked a shell up into its chamber, then headed into the fray.

A blood lust was upon Amos. When an old woman screamed, he turned and splattered the wall behind her with blood. Her blood. It took four shots because the stupid old biddy wouldn't just stand still and be shot, she had to keep *jumping around,* so Amos wasted two on the wall, and that made eight, so his K-9 was empty, its slide locked back. He slammed in a fresh magazine, hit the slide release, sought another target. None upright. Amos thought: *Look at 'em scattering, diving to the floor, as if I can't hit 'em when they're lying down—BANG!—take that you ignorant piece of—*

"Get the car!" shouted Jacoby Lennart, over by the big deputy—not so big now with his sorry self on the floor faceup and holes all in him. Lennart had the cop's .45 in one hand, his 9mm in the other. Suddenly a man (well, a teenager) made a break for the door.

Can't have that, buster, thought Amos, and nailed him once, miss, miss, twice, miss, miss, then the kid fell out the door and sprawled on the porch.

"GET THE FUCKING CAR!" Lennart yelled.

So Amos went to get the fucking car.

Lennart couldn't believe that damned Amos Thorton. What'd he think, they'd just whistle and the car would come zooming up like in some Indiana Jones flick? BOOM! *There goes that smartmouth waitress.* BOOM! *Have another one, bitch, you wanted a tip.* The cop's gun felt good in his hand, it had some heft, not like the little Kahr, but hey, a .45 was harder to hide, BOOM! *There goes the jukebox. This cop's boomer is gonna run dry any second now . . .*

Arlene grabbed her leg and screamed when the first bullet hit her, but her cry was cut short by the next one, right through her chest, front to back, spackling the coffee urn with scarlet droplets. Benella thought, *You sorry son-of-a-*

bitch, and came through the kitchen door to let the tall guy have a dose of eights right in the middle of his lanky bod, and at close range, too, where they'd still amount to something in a cluster, and El Lanko hit the deck, writhing, but abruptly sat up and fired—BOOM!—taking out a sugar bowl not far from Benella's left ear, then—BOOM!—through the counter, down low, not far from her knee, where it ricocheted off the floor to splatter a number-ten can of green peas, and she stuck her pump gun around the corner and pasted him again, catching some of his leg with the pattern this time, drawing a little blood, then—suddenly remembering he probably had on a vest—she aimed for his head, but he rolled and she missed him entirely, instead taking out a napkin container where it had fallen to the floor, creating instant confetti that fluttered in the air like snow. Then she was jacking the slide, praying that Hollis kept the gun fully loaded . . .

Man, that hurts, thought Jacoby Lennart when the tall woman with the scattergun blasted his calf. *At least it's small shot, not double-ought,* he thought, rolling again. The slide had locked back on the .45. "Damn!" he expleted, and cast it from him, just as he heard the squealing of Goodyear rubber out front.

Amos coming.

Tossing two throwaway rounds toward the big bimbo with the riot gun, Lennart climbed to his feet and limped toward the door. A man grabbed his gimpy leg as he passed, a halfhearted attempt at stopping him. Lennart paused long enough to shoot the guy twice—BAM! BAM!—in the face, then he thought about shooting the woman beside him— lying there screaming, her head covered by her arms, the boyfriend's fresh blood all over her—and he pointed the gun at her head, but the shotgun roared again, impacting his vest, knocking him askew, making him drop the Kahr, but he drew a second one from his left jacket pocket and fired BAM! BAM! BAM! at the Amazon with the shotgun—*who the hell's she think she is, Annie Oakley?*—one

of his bullets bursting a pepper shaker, he didn't know
where the others went, but he knew where he was going.

Out the door.

When Lennart's shot shattered the pepper shaker, pepper flew everywhere—onto the counter, onto the floor, into
Benella's eyes, and up her nose. Sneezing, eyes watering,
she nonetheless managed to pump the shotgun once more.
Different feel this time. She pressed the release and half
opened the action. Empty. Hearing the front door slam, she
risked a watery peep around the counter corner. El Lanko
was gone.

Stew's .45—discarded by the lean, frenetic asshole—lay
on the floor not ten feet from her. She retrieved it, dumped
its empty magazine, grabbed two loaded ones from the
downed deputy's belt pouch, slammed one of them home,
and thumbed the slide release to chamber a round . . .

Then headed for the door.

Jacoby Lennart was hobbling right along, in pain but
bearing up, not fifteen feet from the car in which Amos
Thorton waited—gunning the motor, raring to go—when
he heard a feminine voice shout, "Hold it!" He turned,
9mm in hand, to confront the lofty shotgun-toting wench
on the porch behind him. Only now not a shotgun but the
deputy's big .45 in hand, her feet planted, weak-side foot
leading Weaver style, looking at him over the sights, wisps
of golden hair spilling over her forehead, clumps
of . . . what? . . . *green peas* clinging to her pant's leg. She
looked like an ad for Orphan of the Year.

This couldn't be happening.

"I'm leaving now," Lennart shouted over the engine's
din. "Consider yourself lucky I don't kill you and screw
the remains."

"Consider yourself lucky I don't shoot your nose off!"
Benella yelled back, though later she couldn't imagine why
she'd goaded him. Runaway adrenaline maybe.

Lennart roared something incomprehensible and up came

his gun. Because of his vest, Benella would have to make a head shot, from twenty yards, in poor light; all Lennart had to do was shoot her anywhere in the body and *bingo,* dead meat. She remembered what Connor Gibbs had drilled into her about confronting a body-armored antagonist: *Watch the front sight, aim for the head.*

She did . . .

. . . as Amos Thorton sat gunning his engine and Jacoby Lennart was raising his pistol, seeking its sights, with one eye on her and one on his gun . . .

. . . for a second, anyway . . .

. . . because the very next second Benella's gun discharged, its bullet impacting the bridge of his nose, and one of those eyes splatted onto the side of the Firebird with a liquid *plop,* then slid wetly, redly down, trailing goo like a garden slug.

When Amos Thorton peeled off in panic—the rear end of his car fishtailing back and forth—the eye fell to the pavement. Six minutes later, the first ambulance on the scene squished it under a tire.

Chapter 2

THE SCREAMS WERE HORRIBLY UNCEASING—
DADDEEE! DADDEEE! DADDEEE!—over and over.
Benella Sweet could hear them clear out into the parking
lot despite the muting effect of several walls, considerable
distance, and the tintinnabulary aftereffects of all the gun-
shots pounding her ears. There was no need to check for
a pulse on the slime at her feet; her bullet had entered his
nose high near a tear duct, to the left of the bridge, blowing out an eye and much of the back of his head. El Lanko
lay faceup in a spreading pool of warm fluid, some of it
gray, some a deep, glossy purple in the dim light of the
single streetlamp. Nothing needed here but a body bag . . .

She went to the screams.

A new one as Benella burst through the screen door—
from Katelin, near hysteria: "Mary Leigh! I'm coming,
honey!" Mary Leigh was well past hysteria; her ululating
screams had become nearly subhuman. Katelin made it to
the little girl first, kicking in the bathroom door and scooping her up to stroke, hug, caress—bypassing the bleeding
body on the floor, as if ignoring the untenable might make

all this go away. It wouldn't, of course, but people deal best with one catastrophe at a time. So Katelin consoled Mary Leigh—or tried to—while Benella saw to Damien Stuart.

There was little to see to, at least in the sense of administering aid. Damien was dead, from a bullet to the temple. No suffering; he'd been covering his precious daughter's body with his own when a 9mm slug had tunneled its impersonal way through pine paneling and drywall to find his brain.

Mary Leigh hadn't known anything was amiss with her daddy until her slight body had been pinned to the linoleum by his abrupt inertness. She had wriggled desperately out from under and tried to rouse him, ignoring the signs of immobility, incoherence . . .

. . . death.

When the awful fact finally registered, it rent her tiny heart and exploded from her throat: DADDEEE! She tugged at his arm, tried her panicky best to lift his curly head, shift the muscular shoulders she had so often ridden with her little legs gripping his powerful neck. Damien, the proud father, hoisting his daughter high for all to see . . .

Never again.

Benella hustled mother and child from the bathroom to a pair of empty chairs in the kitchen, then sought a phone. Mary Leigh continued to wail, robbing Benella of the ability to swallow, to speak, nearly to breathe.

Oh, God! Please help me. Help us all.

And He did. Otherwise, chaos would have prevailed.

Chapter 3

CONNOR GIBBS, HIS ELEVEN-YEAR-OLD SON, Cameron, and Cody Wainright "Blister" McGraw, also eleven, were at Connor's office, despite the late hour, viewing *Men in Black*.

"This is my favorite part," claimed Blister. Will Smith was about to shrink the pawnbroker's head.

"Mine's when the baby alien is born in the car," Cameron countered.

"Popcorn anyone?" Gibbs asked, swinging his long legs off his desk.

Before "anyone" could answer, the phone rang. Gibbs, six-feet-seven and just under 250 pounds, reached to answer it: "Quixote Enterprises."

"Get over to Bernharte's right now!" A strident Benella Mae Sweet. "And call Holmes!"

Gibbs said, "What happened?"

"The end of the world!"

"The boys are here with me."

"Don't bring them! Just hurry."

He hurried. First a call to his dad, for permission to drop

off the boys; granted. En route, he phoned Attorney Holmes Crenshaw. Not home. Gibbs left a message, relayed the boys to his dad's house, then was on his way. Benella Mae was seldom distraught. On the phone, she had been.

The hot Mustang ate up the miles.

The small parking lot was full—of sheriff's department Chevies, highway-patrol cruisers, SBI sedans, a crime-scene van, an FBI Ford, three ambulances, and a fire truck, not to mention scads of onlookers' vehicles. Gibbs parked a quarter mile down the road and hoofed it back. A highway patrolman stopped him at the edge of the parking lot, but Deputy Sheriff Mike Everette jogged over to run interference.

"Bennie's inside and okay," Mike told Connor after steering him away from the trooper. "And responsible for that." He pointed to a blanket-covered body that lay in a sticky pool of fluid.

"What?"

"Yeah, she snuffed the scumball before he could make it to his car. But a partner got away. The bastards killed Stew Blaisdell and Elmo Floyd, plus four bystanders. And wounded Barly Franks, poor kid. He might croak yet."

"What the hell happened?"

"Way I get it, two rough-looking dudes came in and ordered takeout. Stew didn't like the way they shaped up and went to brace them. After that the story gets hazy, but one thing's for certain sure, the foxes got loose in the henhouse."

"Leaving *six* people dead? Some foxes."

"Yeah, especially with Bennie blasting away at them with Hollis's old scattergun."

Connor said, "Let me go check on Bennie. She sounded crazy on the phone."

"Sure. I'll be out here if you need me. The feds and staties are taking over anyway."

They parted.

•   •   •

Inside the restaurant, bedlam lurked. Benella was over by the jukebox, sitting on the floor beside Katelin, stroking her sister's hair. She glanced up at Connor's entrance and smiled weakly, motioning him over with a lift of her chin.

He knelt and kissed her worried brow. Twice. "What's doing?"

Benella glanced down at her sister, lying there on a blanket, calm and serene and under the influence of a very powerful sedative, then whispered, "Damien's dead."

Gibbs was shocked. "How?"

"Stray bullet. He was in the bathroom covering Mary Leigh with his body. A bullet went through the wall. At least he didn't suffer, thank God."

"Where's Mary Leigh?"

"They took her to the hospital. She was hysterical. Worse, really. They had to sedate her. Katelin, too. She was almost as bad. She had to kick in the bathroom door to get to Mary Leigh, who was screaming 'Daddy' over and over . . ." Benella paused, reliving the terror. "I've never been so scared," she continued. "And there on the floor . . . Damien . . ." Couldn't go on. Tears now, not torrential, but steady. Gibbs had never seen Bennie cry. He didn't know exactly what to do, so he emulated her consoling of Katelin; he stroked Benella's hair gently.

After a couple of minutes, she said, "I'll be okay. Go talk to Hank."

Hank Yarborough was the county sheriff, a small man with a sharp mind, a keen wit, and a tough job. He was over at the bullet-splintered counter, drinking coffee and conferring with a suit. Probably a Fibbie; too clean-cut and arrogant for a state man. State men accepted the fact that they were fallible and human; feds did not.

Connor drifted over, but stopped short of joining the pair, not wanting to interrupt. Yarborough held out a hand for shaking. Gibbs shook it.

The suit, a gray forty-four regular, wide through the shoulders, glanced dismissively at Connor and said, "We're talking here."

"I noticed. I also noticed Sheriff Yarborough offering a hand," Gibbs returned.

The suit, though tall himself, had to look up at Gibbs, and he didn't like it. He squared himself and growled, "Beat it."

"I think not," said Connor quietly.

Hank Yarborough was content to sit back and enjoy all this, but the suit turned to him and said, "Sheriff, if you don't do something about this oversized chowderhead, I will."

Connor said, "And what will you do?"

"Toss your big butt out on an ear," quipped the suit.

"Now, that's an interesting juxtaposition, sort of like the Chris Tucker line in *Money Talks*: 'I'm gonna kick your ass in the head.' Are you a Chris Tucker fan?"

"Sheriff? Me, or you?" said the suit, getting angrier by the second.

"This is between us," Gibbs said. "Me and you, just a couple of good old boys. If you're federal, and my dough says you are, then you've got no jurisdiction here. Therefore, if you try to 'toss my butt out,' it will constitute assault, and I'll resist."

The suit looked at him hard.

"In fact," Gibbs went on conversationally, "I'll resist vehemently."

The suit walked away in disgust.

Hank said, "Never seen anyone who can talk someone into submission like you can. I'll give you the match on points, but what would you have done if he'd tried to take hold of you? You can't smack a fed."

"I was a fed once. I got smacked a time or two."

Yarborough looked at Gibbs, who was only slightly smaller than Mount Everest. "Bet the smacker didn't fare so well immediately after. Besides, the CIA don't count. You spooks aren't real law enforcement."

The sheriff, suddenly serious, looked around at the bullet pockmarks, the overturned chairs, the drying blood. "This situation is messy."

"I know, but officious jerks like that stick in my gorge."

"Mine, too. Still, I try to be diplomatic to the Fibbies. Is Bennie all right?"

"About whacking the guy or about losing a family member?"

"Either, both."

"No problem with the former, and we haven't talked about the latter. But she's tough. And she's done it before. She'll handle it. I'm more concerned about exposure. I don't want her on television, or having her picture in the paper. She's a private person."

"I'll do what I can," promised Hank.

"Any clue who the dead guy is?"

"No, and the FBI is mum on the subject. Which is odd. They sure got here fast enough. And like you said, if this is a local matter, why do I have them tramplin' my begonias in the first place?"

"'Tramplin' my begonias.' You're so colorful."

"And don't forget it. I'm going to talk to the medical examiner. I expect you'll be here awhile. Might as well have some coffee. It's lukewarm and it's old and it's too damned strong, but at least it tastes bad," the sheriff informed, and walked away.

For several hours, guns were recovered, bullets were dug out of wood and plaster, blood was mopped up, survivors were debriefed, and the press was kept at bay. Eventually, it was time to leave. Benella, dodging the press, was hustled out to a squad car, which took her home on a roundabout route. No one followed.

Gibbs didn't have it so easy when he left; after all, he was a well-known private detective. But he made it to his car without too much commotion. The head Fibbie watched him leave without affection.

If Gibbs was bothered, it didn't show.

Chapter 4

A T THE RESTAURANT, IT HAD COME RUSHING back, her seemingly irresistible tendency to protect all those around her, regardless of personal danger. Benella finished stacking the bras, all neatly folded and arranged alphabetically according to color: blue against the front of the drawer, champagne next, then periwinkle, tangerine, and white (all Victoria's Secret, big bucks); some of them lacy and feminine (how could a bra *not* be feminine?), others practical and supportive Olgas, mostly from Belk and easier on the budget. (As she'd matured, support had begun to take precedence over frill—gravity, you know—and it didn't seem to matter to Connor, just so long as they were easy to undo.)

When Benella Mae Sweet was upset, depressed, or despondent, she would often rearrange her lingerie. For hours. As she was doing now . . .

. . . *She and her younger sister had lived most of their early years in an orphanage. Bennie, always the jock, had played soccer beginning at age four. She even loved to watch it on TV. Maybe it was because her dad had supposedly*

*played soccer in college; it was in her genes. All the way
through age eleven she played, with defense her preference.
(Which suited the coach just fine, since he'd always proclaimed that, "If you can stop the other team, you're never
going to lose.") And her team didn't lose, at least not much.
Benella was often the only one playing back (except for a
sweeper, the last line of defense before the goalie) and many
a breakaway did she stop. Despite reaching five-feet-six while
still in elementary school, and 120 pounds, she had lightning reflexes and a fearlessness that couldn't be taught . . .*

. . . How had she accumulated so many panties? And why
did so few match her bras? (Because sets cost an arm and
a limb, that's why.) She sorted the panties now—lime and
redwood and pale pink and navy. (Navy? What could she
wear those with?) Florals next, and the lavender pair with
the white polka dots. JoAnn (her soul mate, her married
significant other) loved those . . .

*. . . After New Orleans, and the unspeakable horrors she
had gone through there, Benella tended toward activities
that didn't require relying on others, since she'd learned the
hard way that others couldn't be relied upon. Except for
Connor Gibbs, her best friend and only male lover in all
her adult life . . .*

. . . Benella had forgotten the camisole; Connor had given
it to her one birthday, along with an ivory bustier. (She
smiled remembering the first time she'd worn it; Connor
nearly had apoplexy trying to remove it.) Teddies next, her
weapons of choice since they made Connor virtually paw
and whinny. (Who said long-term ardor was difficult to
maintain?) In a different drawer, nightgowns—silk and flan-
nel and satin—and a few garter belts (she *hated* panty hose).
That reminded her, she needed new nylons . . .

"You okay?" said Gibbs, coming up from behind to slip
an arm around her slender middle as she folded the last
item into place and closed the drawer. He rubbed her temple lightly with a forefinger with his extra hand.

Still facing away, she rubbed his chin with the top of

her head. He inhaled deeply and kissed her hair. "I love the smell of you," he said.

And that, of course, was that.

Afterward, she felt better.

Chapter 5

"SON-OF-A-BITCH! SON-OF-A-BITCH!" AMOS Thorton kept repeating, in Room 218 of a Wendover motel. "She just nailed him, bang, one shot and down he went, like a sack of compost."

"And who was this bimbo?" asked Marvin Delaney, sitting on the bed across the room, his red beret tilted jauntily.

"How the hell do I know?" said Amos. "I didn't notice her while I was inside the restaurant. Maybe she was in the can, or the kitchen or something. While I was on the way to the car, I heard a shotgun cut loose inside, and I said, 'What the fuck was that?' but kept right on humping. Soon's I got cranked up and headed for the door, out pops Jacoby, limping like hell but making good time, so I stopped right in front of him and suddenly there she was, this big tall bitch, on the porch."

"With a shotgun?"

"Hell, no. A big pistol. Anyway, she yelled to him—I don't know what, 'cause I was revving up the motor—and he stops. Then he said something back, and then she did, and next thing I know she's shot his ass and he's going down. I vamoosed."

"You left a buddy in enemy hands. Did you do that in the Gulf?" asked K. K. Kapatchnik, on the bed beside Delaney, munching Pringle's potato chips, one-third less fat.

"This was different, this wasn't war. Besides, that big sharpshooting gash would've had me dead to rights if I'd climbed out of the car. I ain't looking to die no time soon, K.K."

"How far was she?" K.K. pressed.

"From the car?"

"From Jacoby."

"Twenty, twenty-five yards, why?"

"How many outside lights?"

Amos tried to remember. "One. I think."

"So," K.K. went on, "the range was twenty meters, with an iron-sighted handgun, in poor light, and you claim she had you dead to rights? Is that your story?"

"She'd just dumped Jacoby with a head shot! You think that was luck?"

"That's what I think," said Delaney.

"Me, too," Kapatchnik agreed. "Besides, you left a man down, Amos. We don't do that in this outfit."

"Outfit!" screeched Thorton. "We're freakin' bank robbers, not a military unit!"

Delaney stood to look Amos Thorton eye to eye, then said, "Sit down." Thorton sat. Delaney moved closer. Real close. Leaned forward. Nose to nose. "And Amos?" he said ominously.

Thorton swallowed hard. "Yeah?"

"Don't ever raise your voice to me."

"I'm just excited, is all," Thorton averred.

"Because if you do, I'll slit one of your nostrils, like they did to Nicholson in *Chinatown*. You dig?"

"Okay, okay."

"And Amos?"

"What?"

"Don't ever leave a man down, even if it means getting your own balls shot off. Understand?"

Amos swallowed again. "I understand."

Marvin Delaney straightened, turned, surveyed the room and its occupants. Aside from the three above-mentioned, also present were Matt Bachison and Jim Bobb, the latter seated in a chair with its back against the door, the former settled cross-legged on the floor. Delaney said, "We all agreed from the get-go that we were doing this for money, excitement, and glory. We netted plenty of cash on this first series, nearly three mil, and had a little excitement. Now we're going to have some more. And glory as well, because before we're done, this burg is going to witness a veritable·horde of hearses, and all on that bimbo's head."

Murmurs and nods of expectation.

"Okay, then. And Amos?"

"Yeah?"

"In the morning, buy up all the different newspapers you can find, and tonight, glue yourself to the TV. You've got a room all to yourself now, so it shouldn't be a problem. I want to know who this sharpshooting gal is, and I want to know pronto."

"You got it, Marv," from the sycophantic Thorton.

The meeting was adjourned.

Chapter 6

MARVIN DELANEY HAD BEEN A STAFF SERGEANT *during Desert Storm, in a hell-bent-for-leather artillery outfit. As a forward observer, he'd had plenty of chances for action. Once, he called in a strike on an old man at a waterhole. The old man was no soldier, was unarmed, and even worse, he had only one leg. Nevertheless, Marv nailed him good, then carried back a severed hand for show-and-tell. His compadres were impressed and Marvin began to develop a reputation of sorts.*

In those days, Delaney bunked with a called-up National Guardsman from Dallas named K.K. Kapatchnik. K.K. had flunked out of law school, dropped out of Ranger school, but had graduated cum laude from the school of hard knocks. And K.K. was vicious. He and Delaney amused themselves by starting fights at the PX, or outside the NCO club, or in civilian hot spots after returning stateside. They won some, lost some, but mostly triumphed, since they were as mean as wharf rats.

Both were streetwise and entirely bereft of scruples. Since petty thievery wasn't beneath them, the duo always pos-

sessed pockets full of money, leading-edge sound systems, TVs the size of drive-in movie screens, and an arsenal of uncommonly lethal, extremely expensive firearms. Dope peddling fretted them not, so each afforded five-liter Mustangs. (K.K.'s was a convertible.) With moral turpitude their bent, they offered an eclectic array of whores to horny Fort Bragg soldiers, the profits from which provided them with 2,115 square feet and a gabled roof in a tony Fayetteville neighborhood.

Then that roof fell in: Crime-stoppers' tips brought the duo prospects of serious jail time; tons of bucks went to high-profile lawyers; ultimately, dishonorable discharges ensued. With their tails between their legs and their numerous bank accounts scraping bottom, the boys dissolved their partnership, with K.K. going home to Dallas and Delaney back to Roanoke. Being masters of the con, they quickly sought and found wedlock, and resultant fat-cat jobs with disapproving but loyal fathers-in-law. There followed prosperity, kids, church socials, mortgages.

And boredom. Restless, gut-churning, hand-wringing tedium. After eight years of such domesticity, life sat not lightly upon Delaney and K.K.

The result was a meeting at a waffle eatery near Charleston, South Carolina, in July of '99. Those present included Jacoby Lennart and Amos Thornton, two former Gulf War comrades-in-arms. Lennart was six-two, dark-haired, built like a Slim Jim. Thornton was shorter, heavier, sandier, and nappier, when he let his hair grow, which wasn't often. He wore sandals in winter (no socks) and sunglasses indoors, even on rainy days. Formerly a high-school all-star wide receiver, he still moved like an athlete at thirty-five, still pumped iron, and ran five miles daily, sandals and all.

Also present was retired Sergeant First Class Matthew Bachison, Vietnam veteran, three-time Purple Heart awardee, holder of the Silver Star for valor. (He was awarded the Purple Heart so often because he was absolutely fearless, not to mention reckless; he snagged the

Silver for dragging his wounded CO—an idiot shavetail fresh from the Point—to safety during a mortar attack.) Military-trained as an armorer, Matt knew weaponry inside and out. He stood five-ten and scaled 220, could toss the shot put fifty-eight feet and deadlift 585 pounds. Though never married, he had four children in Saigon, none by the same mother.

Rounding out the clique was James Bobb, born in Oklahoma thirty years before, to an itinerant fruit picker and a professional wrestler. Built like his mom, but without her body-slamming ability, he'd worked beside his father in watermelon patches and peach orchards throughout the South until joining the army at eighteen. There he received his GED, then advanced infantry training, then tutelage as an APC driver at Fort Knox, where he met Sergeant Bachison. The pair had come through the Gulf unscathed, except for a mild dose of clap acquired from the same source.

Marvin Delaney had opened the waffle-house summit thus: "Anybody at this table got baggage they can't bear to leave behind if this thing turns sour?"

Five head shakes.

"Do we all agree that we're bored to death, and that anything would be better than what we got now?"

Five head nods.

"And we agree up front that we partner until we each acquire one million, then we head our separate ways?"

Five more head nods.

"Is anyone hurting for cash right now?"

No hands were raised, despite the fact that Jim Bobb didn't have a hundred bucks in assets, unless he counted his collection of Batman comic books.

"We further agree that we ain't like those two L.A. fruit-loops, wandering around with automatic weapons, blasting this way and that, just asking to be offed by some blue uniform thinks he's Rambo?"

Everyone laughed, except Matt Bachison. But even he smiled a little.

"Okay then," said Delany, and laid out the plans, right

there in front of the group, in a waffle restaurant in Charleston, South Carolina.

"Wow," said Bobb, awestruck.

"Shades of Coffeyville, Kansas," Kapatchnik commented historically.

"Bob, Grat, Emmett, and the boys'd be proud," opined Matt Bachison.

"Yeah, well, we're gonna do it right," asserted Marvin Delaney.

Then they brainstormed long into the night. The results, some months later, were three simultaneous bank heists executed without a hitch.

After Thorton's chewing-out, the others left for their own rooms. K.K. Kapatchnik lit up a stogie and said to Delaney, "You serious about this retribution crap, or was that just for morale?"

"Both. It feels wrong letting that gal get away with whacking one of us. And like I said, putting her under the ground will have a strong deterrent value. It'll be like an advertisement in the paper: 'Amateurs Beware.' "

K.K. puffed heartily. "Maybe. But as far as the public is concerned, bank robbery is one thing, murder's another. Especially when a broad's involved. Right now, mostly we have the FBI on our ass. Grease this woman and every deer hunter in the state will be looking to pop us."

"Another reason to go after the bimbo. It lets the populace know that not only are we intolerant of interference, but we will go out of our way to be vengeful."

Kapatchnik lofted a smoke ring. "That's one way to look at it."

"Besides," Delaney submitted. "There's the challenge."

"Ah. You're affronted by how easily she took Lennart out." The room was filling with cigar smoke.

"Not affronted, intrigued. Who is she, an IPSC competitor, an Olympic marksman, or just a whiz at winning teddy bears at the carnival?"

"When we catch up with her, how about we rumple her

a bit. I mean before offing her." K.K. launched another diaphanous ring.

Delaney grinned. "You horny bastard."

K.K. grinned back. "Poontang rules," he said.

Chapter 7

"Is she down?" Benella asked Connor, referring to Mary Leigh. The two of them were at Benella's house. Cameron Gibbs and Blister were outside playing Frisbee, in case Mary Leigh wanted youthful playmates.

"Yes, but it was slow going. I had to read six stories before she winked off." He shook his head. "Poor thing."

"This is really going to be hard on her."

"Don't I know. You going over to Katelin's?"

Benella shook her head. "Damien's parents are there, and who knows who else. I'd be in the way."

"But—"

"I'd be in the way, Connor. Take my word for it. I don't do this kind of thing well. I never know what to say, and I won't spout platitudes. I'll go to the funeral, and I'll be here afterward, when everyone else has deserted Katelin."

He nodded.

"As for right now, I need to work for a while," she concluded.

"I'll keep an eye on Mary Leigh."

And Benella went upstairs to her studio.

• • •

Going for an eggshell gloss the old-fashioned way, one coat of paste filler first, matching the color of the mahogany, then a light application of orange shellac. Sandpaper next, light and deft and mindless, so she could drift . . .

Images, of *that distant wedding day—Damien so handsome, Katelin so innocent and expectant and beautiful, all awhite, (justified), and Connor coming down the aisle, smiling from cheek to cheek, to give Katelin away . . . Damien and his best man (what was his name?) flush with the metallic sheen of nervousness . . .*

Benella blinked back the tears herself, remembering. In the background, muted Yo-Yo Ma from the stereo, not invasive, allowing her to hover above and within as the sandpaper worked its magic and dust fell to the newspapered floor . . .

. . . The just-marrieds, off to Williamsburg for a starry-eyed honeymoon—only five days, though, Damien couldn't miss more work than that—and then in ten months, Mary Leigh, all seven pounds of her, and Benella was an aunt (who was ready for that*?). Damien and Katelin remained starry-eyed, the perfect couple, even after the blush of newness was gone, still held hands and went on "dates," leaving the baby to steal Benella's heart, until they moved to Richmond . . . Then occasionally bringing Mary Leigh to visit . . .*

Well, no more long weekends for Katelin.

Widow's weeds instead . . .

More waterworks (*damn,* she hated to cry) as Benella forsook the sandpaper for haircloth, rubbing, rubbing, with more intensity than intended. Pumice on the final coat, her tears in abeyance now, and no more trips down memory lane . . . just tune out and do busywork, encompassed by that silken cello, while across town her beloved sister was being given Valium in heavy doses.

• • •

Blister and Cameron came in from the yard to find Gibbs reading the paper, one ear peeled should the little girl awaken. The boys plopped on the sofa across from Connor and Blister said, "I feel really bad for Mary Leigh."

Connor looked up from his paper.

"I know what it's like to lose a father," said Blister.

Gibbs nodded encouragingly. Blister had said very little about it since his father's murder, nearly two years before.

"And what it's like, being young and not having one," Blister went on.

Another nod from Gibbs.

"Mary Leigh's in for a tough time," Blister concluded.

Cameron's turn: "My mom took me away from him"— he paused to point his chin at his dad— "when I was just a kid. When we moved to California, I used to lay awake nights, crying. Sometimes I'd wake up calling to him, then couldn't go back to sleep. I played ball without being able to look up and see him watching every move I made, like he always had before . . ."

He paused again, to swallow a lump, then continued, voice husky: "Yeah. Mary Leigh's in for it."

Connor, speaking around a lump of his own, said, "We'll see that she has a lot of help, the three of us."

"And Bennie," added Blister.

"Yes," Connor agreed. "She's worth her weight in platinum."

Little did he know.

Chapter 8

ALL MORNING AMOS THORTON HAD KEPT HIS eyes glued to local TV stations or tiptoeing through newsprint, but naught had he found except mention of an "unidentified" woman who had "thwarted a massacre" at Hollis's Roadside Eatery. Not only no name, but no pix, no video, no *nada*. "Shit!" Amos expleted, and threw *The Charlotte Observer* across the motel room, where it fluttered to the floor like a vapid gull. "Shit!" he said again, and went to take his lumps.

In the Coffee Shoppe, Delaney and K.K. were scarfing up breakfast viands when a disgruntled, discouraged, and disaffected Amos Avery Thorton III joined them. "There's nothing, just nothing, not a freakin'—"

"I get the point," Delaney interrupted. "So, go snoop."

"Snoop?"

"Dig, ask around, you know? Be a sleuth, a hawkshaw, a shamus."

"What are you talking about?" from a bewildered Thorton.

K.K., around a mouthful of French toast, said, "He wants you to go out into the world. 'Seek and ye shall find.'"

"I don't get it." Amos, alas, was no giant intellect.

"*Talk* to people," Marvin elaborated. "Someone around here knows who that sharpshooting woman is. There were lots of people in that greasy spoon when you and Jacoby shot it up. Find one of them. Butter them up, pay them something, but"—and he grabbed Amos's arm—"get a *name*. Now go away, I'm trying to enjoy my food."

"And coffee," Kapatchnik reminded.

Delaney snorted. "Right. You call this coffee? Remember that little place outside Tel Aviv? Now, that was coffee."

Amos left. To seek.

And seek he did, but didn't do much finding. If any of these suburbanites knew the identity of this mystery woman, they weren't divulging. A few demanded to know why he was asking, which made him nervous; the last thing he needed was suspicious attention. So he made up a story about being a journalist from Nashville. Of the dozen or so people he spoke to, none bought that story, perhaps because he resembled a journalist about the way Mike Tyson does.

He did find one thing, though, or it found him: a small black dog with splayed front feet and a face like a baby seal. The mutt was obviously on its own, so Thorton adopted it, buying it two hamburgers and naming it Buster. After two hours of being snubbed by the locals, Amos felt like Buster was his only friend in this rotten town.

He was right.

Back in Room 218, a dispirited Amos Thorton informed his cohorts of the fruitlessness of his search. "The fuck's that," asked Jim Bobb after Amos had finished, pointing with his chin.

"My dog, Buster," said Amos.

"What, you've had him in your carry-on bag?" prodded

Bobb, lying on a bed dressed in casual attire: Mötley Crüe T-shirt, cutoffs, flip-flops, and size-forty-two khaki boxers that showed at the bottom of his pants, like a slip. No gun; he'd left it in his room. Which didn't matter; there were guns aplenty in *this* room, most of them under the bed where a maid wasn't apt to spot them.

"I found him during my search," Amos said.

"Search for what?" Bobb picked at a scab on his knee.

"Truth," Delaney interrupted. "So what'd you find out, Amos?"

"Nothing. Not a freakin' thing," Thorton complained.

"Why not, Amos?"

Whining: "Nobody would tell me nothing. It's not my fault. The whole freakin' community's clammed up."

"So what do you plan to do now, Amos?" Delaney pressed.

"How do I know? You and K.K. are the brains of this group."

"And ain't it a good thing," Kapatchnik concluded. "You're the only guy I know whose brain surgeon is a proctologist."

"Hardy-har," grunted Matt Bachison, from over in the corner, where he sat trimming his nails with his tanto.

"Here's what you do, Amos," Delaney instructed. "I hear they're burying those two deputies tomorrow. Chances are the bimbo'll be there. Well, so will you, Amos, watching for her. You dig?"

"Yeah," said a very unhappy Amos Thorton. "Who else is going?" he asked the room at large.

"Take Buster," Kapatchnik said.

"You don't suppose having a dog at a funeral might draw attention, do you?" from Bachison, sarcastically.

K.K. tossed him a look, which Matt ignored.

"Leave the friggin' dog, Amos," Delaney said.

So Amos left the friggin' dog and went to the funeral alone.

Chapter 9

HOLMES CRENSHAW, FORMERLY WITH THE CIA, currently an attorney-at-law, and for three decades Connor's closest male friend, and who had several times saved his life, said, "Bennie doing okay with all this?" He sipped, then placed his coffee cup beside him on the couch.

Gibbs, seated in a floral-design wing chair that would barely contain his bulk, said, "Define 'this.'"

Crenshaw was tall and lithe, immaculately three-piece-attired, soft-spoken, black as a moonless night. He said, "All of it. Acing the mug outside Hollis's place, dealing with Katelin's loss—not to mention Mary Leigh's."

Gibbs shrugged. "She says she is."

"So what do you think?"

"Hard to tell. Bennie keeps things in. You know her history. This is nothing by comparison. Her discomfiture is directed toward Katelin, who I understand has always had it pretty good, at least for an orphan."

Holmes sipped his brew for a moment. "I can stay, if it's necessary."

"You've already been granted a continuance."

"Twice," Crenshaw agreed.

"This is a murder trial, right?"

"With three of us defending."

"You sure the guy didn't do it?"

"Absolutely. All the evidence is circumstantial."

"But?"

"But he's a brother and the victim wasn't and the trial is in South Carolina."

Connor sipped his own drink; tea, now tepid. "Bennie will be fine. You go to South Carolina, knock 'em dead."

"How about you? Will you be fine?"

"You bet," said Gibbs affably.

How wrong, how wrong.

Three hours later, Connor was lying beside Benella on her antique four-poster bed. Their combined weight was nearly 420 pounds. The bed creaked and groaned in protest. He said, "That's crazy."

"Sugar pie, those two men died trying to protect a whole restaurant full of people. And they didn't have a chance. Stew shaded the tall one by a half second, I saw the strike, dead center. If the creep hadn't been wearing a vest, Stew would have taken him out."

"I acknowledge that, but what if the second man's still around, and wants a piece of your hide? The media hasn't been able to latch onto your name, but it's only a matter of time till silver crosses a knowing palm and they will. And what if this guy has friends?"

"You'll protect me," she said, snuggling closer.

Detecting something in her tone, he looked at her. "What have you found out?"

"Nothing."

"Bennie."

She climbed out of bed in search of *USA Today*. "Did you read about these bank robberies?" she said, coming back with the paper.

"The simultaneous ones? In Atlanta, Knoxville, and . . . where was it?"

"Richmond."

"Yes, indeedy," he affirmed.

"The descriptions of a couple of them, such as were given, match our two bad guys."

Connor read for a moment. "These profiles are a bit vague, don't you think?"

"Why do you think the FBI showed up? And so suddenly? This is local jurisdiction. But not if . . ." She paused.

". . . some of those bank robbers were involved," he finished her thought.

"Bingo."

"That's all the more reason not to go to the funeral service. Wendover is geographically central to those three cities. What if all six—well, five now—of those guys are here in town, holed up somewhere? The article made them sound pretty competent. Furthermore, what if some camera person pans their Sony at graveside and your face winds up on CNN?"

"And it's spotted by a Hollywood talent scout?"

Gibbs brushed the levity aside. "I'm serious."

"I'll wear a disguise."

He snorted. "Glasses and a Groucho mustache?"

"You'll see," she said, because she wasn't joking at all.

Hank Yarborough was on one side of his messy desk, Mike Everette on the other, seated, hat in hand. In front of Yarborough was a set of latents. Fresh ones. *Very* fresh ones.

"Anyone give you a problem?" asked the sheriff.

"I had Pickle sneak me in."

"He still the janitor over there?"

"Custodial engineer."

"Right."

"Pickle" was Dan Pickeral, an employee at the county morgue for nearly fifty years.

Everette shook his dark head. "Cost me four tickets to *Riverdance,* though."

Yarborough arched a bristly brow.

"For his wife," the deputy explained.

"And old Pickle will keep quiet?"

Mike sniffed disdainfully. "He wouldn't tell the feds who shot Kennedy."

"Does he know?"

"About Jimmy Hoffa, too."

They both grinned.

"I'll run these through," Yarborough said. "Thanks for the help, Mike. I'd promote you if you deserved it."

"Let me grab a few keys of smack out of the evidence room, call it even."

"For sale to affluent kids only."

"Right," Everette agreed. "Then no one would care."

And the two went back to crime-busting.

Chapter 10

ALL OF WENDOVER'S 162,000 RESIDENTS DIDN'T show up for the funeral, but several hundred of them did, including so many law enforcement uniforms it gave Amos Thorton pause just to be there. It helped that he was incognito, having somehow acquired a garish red wig, a sweeping fake mustache, and a black, broad-brimmed, outback-style leather hat, with chin strap. From a local Goodwill store he'd purchased an ill-fitting beige shirt, a two-sizes-too-large brown suit, worn-out wing tips (black, to match the hat), and a burgundy tie with mallards on it. With the hat, he looked like the proctor at a Ducks Unlimited meeting, but at least no one was scrutinizing him, so his disguise must be working. He leaned against a Dutch elm and scrutinized everyone else.

He saw not one familiar face.

"There. How's that?" Benella said.

Connor tilted his head back to examine his companion critically. Heavy eye shadow, ruby lipstick, unflattering navy suit (borrowed from Pearl across the street), small black hat with veil, black pumps that made her even taller than her six-one, rimless glasses from Eckerd's, *sans* lenses. "Gorgeous," he allowed.

She socked him in the stomach, hard as a rock from five hundred crunches a day. "Oomph," he said, feigning hurt.

"Will anyone know me?" she pressed.

"No one will even look at you twice. They'll simply take you for a modestly upscale bag lady."

Benella slugged him again and said, "Let's go."

Although early morning had been beautiful, by the time the funeral service ended and the procession was en route to the cemetery, clouds threatened. Amos joined the queue of cars, driving a rental gained with a stolen Visa the owner of which would be in Mexico for at least another week. He listened to a Dead tape and worried about what Marvin Delaney would say if he didn't come up with a face.

Glistening with drizzle, the crowd was somber, befitting the situation. Two more funerals today; even more tomorrow. All because of two guys. Shaking her head in disgust, Benella scanned the crowd. Was Number Two here? Or any of his friends? (If indeed he had any.) Katelin Stuart, under the influence of Valium, stood next to her. Benella had tried to talk her out of this, but here she was, swaying from grief and exhaustion, showing her support for the fallen officers. Mary Leigh stood beside her mom and held her hand tightly; the child hadn't let Katelin out of her sight since . . . well, Friday.

The minister droned, the rain fell, the earth moved.

Soon someone else would die.

Someone present at this service.

The death would be neither quick nor pleasant.

Now, *there* was a face Amos thought he recognized, the woman holding the little girl's hand . . .

Hey! That's the lady in all the newspapers because her husband was killed.

Amos remembered spotting her when he'd first walked into the diner, this foxy chick sitting with some nerdy guy and another looker, a tall one, and . . .

A little girl.

Gotcha.

Sheriff Yarborough motioned to Gibbs as the assembly began to break up. Connor walked over. Yarborough said, "I've got some information for Bennie. Ask her to call me. Soon."

"Want her to phone from the car on the way home?"

Yarborough shook his head. "I'm making my widow's rounds, pay my respects personal like. Give me a coupla hours."

"Okay," Connor agreed, and they each decamped to his own unpleasantness.

Gibbs was waiting at the car with an umbrella when his ladies arrived. He helped Katelin and Mary Leigh into the back, then escorted Benella around the front, opened her door and held it until she was seated, then got in under the wheel. "Where to, ladies?"

"Home, I suppose," Katelin said.

"What about some lunch?" Connor suggested.

"I doubt I'll ever eat out again," Katelin murmured as Mary Leigh leaned against her arm.

"I meant over at my house." Connor didn't want Katelin and Mary Leigh to be alone right now. Benella squeezed his hand.

"I don't think so, but we do appreciate the offer," Katelin demurred.

"If you change your mind, I know how to make a U-turn," Connor insisted, and headed for Katelin's house. He was so concerned about Katelin that he didn't notice the rented Dodge behind them. It followed all the way to Katelin's at a discreet distance, and whipped into a drive-way four houses down when Gibbs pulled into Katelin's driveway. There it sat idling until Gibbs had ushered his two backseat passengers safely inside the house and come back out, backed into the street, and tooled off in the opposite direction. Then the Dodge parked alongside the curb outside the Stuart home, its engine stilled.

Inside the Dodge, Amos Thorton was thinking, which didn't come easy. As if to prove it, his mind maundered: *So who's the tall bitch in the veil? The one who shot Jacoby? Never mind. The pretty lady who just went into that house can tell me for certain sure.*

He was right.

Chapter 11

MARY LEIGH'S FACE WAS FLAT WHEN SHE SAID, "Mommy, I'm hungry." Emotionally drained, obviously. Alive, though. Not like her daddy . . .

Katelin teared up again, turning quickly away so her daughter wouldn't notice.

"Mommy?"

"I heard you, honey. I'll fix us a tuna sandwich."

Mary Leigh shook her head, becurled and pink of cheek. "I'm more hungrier than that."

Katelin was so tired she could scarcely stand. She didn't need this. She needed twelve hours sleep. And Damien. A fresh gushing followed the thought, salty, coursing onto her lip.

"Mommy?"

She turned tiredly toward her child. "What would you like, sweetie?"

Mary Leigh pondered, little brow knitted from the effort. Her eyes lit; retrieval: "I want some Bunsrick stew," she announced.

"Let me check," said Katelin. The pair moved down the

hall to the kitchen. There on a shelf, the requested item, in a sixteen-ounce can. "Got some." Katelin stretched a weary hand up, up, to snare the item. "And spinach?" she asked, seeing the Del Monte right there.

"Yuck," was Mary Leigh's opinion.

"You need your greens."

"Broc'li's green."

"And somewhere else."

"What?"

"We don't have any."

"Not even frozen?"

"Not even."

"Well, sa'sparilla," Mary Leigh commented, her favored expletive.

"Ditto," her mom agreed, placing the Brunswick stew on the counter, above the knife drawer. She stood there for twenty seconds, leaning. *Why am I so drained?* she thought. *Why indeed.*

"Mommy?"

"I'm okay, honey."

"Can I open it?"

"No. I've told you, it's dangerous. The top might cut you."

"But I'm *four*."

"Even so."

"How can it cut mè?"

"Here, I'll show you."

Katelin turned to the counter behind her—beneath the window that provided a view of the backyard—and removed the cloth cover from the electric can opener. She placed the can against the magnet, under the cutting edge, then *zzzzzzz,* the task was done. Normally, Katelin stopped the can's rotation just before total severance; that way she could tuck the top back into the can once it was empty. Her mother had taught her it was safer that way; no loose, sharp edges in the garbage bag. This time, for the benefit of her daughter's education, she let the can complete the circle, removed it, then peeled the top from the magnet.

Mary Leigh was watching closely as Katelin held up the lid, its keen edge glistening wetly. "You see how sharp it is?"

Mary Leigh nodded, reached out an inquisitive index finger.

"Careful," Katelin warned.

The little girl was indeed careful; she barely touched the lid before quickly withdrawing the extended digit. "I think I won't need to do that till I'm eight or seven," she decided.

"You're probably right," agreed Katelin, too fatigued to smile as she placed the lid on the counter beside the opener, messy side up. "Have you made your bed today?"

Out sneaked Mary Leigh's lower lip; just a bit, not full wattage. "No, ma'am."

"Go do that while I fix supper."

Mary Leigh skipped down the hall and up the stairs to do so just as the front doorknob was turning silently.

Amos Thorton could hear voices—female voices, little-girl-and-helpless-gorgeous-widow voices—as he stood there on the porch with one hand on the doorknob and the damp wind whistling down his neck. There certainly was a "gnnip" in the air, as his Celtic granny would say as she drew her shawl close about her. He shivered involuntarily, not just from cold.

Should he go fetch the others? No. Better that he took care of the problem himself. The lady inside knew that sharpshooting bimbo, and after a little slapping around—and maybe a pinch or two, here and there—she'd tell Uncle Amos everything she knew.

Damn right she would.

He turned the knob.

Katelin dumped the contents of the can into a saucepan, spilling some corn and a small chunk of chicken breast onto the stovetop, which she tiredly but promptly mopped up with a paper towel, being a very neat person. Flipping the dial to low heat, she stood looking out the window at the gray, gray day, thoughts drifting, her pulse at a snail's pace.

Not for long.

Amos Thorton eased the door closed, latched the dead bolt, divested his big feet of the sandals anyone else would have been embarrassed to be seen in, and removed his sunglasses, opaque with rain. He wiped the lenses on his shirtfront, shrugged his thick shoulders, replaced the shades, and tiptoed down the hall.

Toward the kitchen.

Mary Leigh had made her bed as well as she knew how, which was surprisingly good for a four-year-old. Though hunger tugged at her, so did her favorite doll Winkie, over in the corner. Winkie won. She sat on the floor and began talking to her dolly as downstairs a man with incredibly dark intent came silently to stand behind her mother.

Katelin worried the stew with a wooden spoon; the mixture was still clumped and globular and clinging to the bottom of the pan. She poked at it absentmindedly, then looked again out the window.

And her breath caught.

Amos Thorton could smell her. Some sort of soap, not perfume. He inhaled deeply. Maybe he would take longer than he'd originally figured. Have a little fun, maybe. Listen to her scream. He liked that. The screaming. And especially the pleading: *I'll do anything you want, just don't hurt me anymore.* He *loved* that. He inhaled again, all the way to his toes.

She looked *fine* in her black dress, its stiff collar still turned up against the outside cold, her neck long and pale and graceful, soft brown curls brushing the nape, one or two awry; he felt like reaching out and prodding them back into place she was so close, little more than an arm's length away as he stood there, barefoot and turgid, waiting for her to turn, to see the surprise on her face . . .

Delicious.

Oh, God! It's him! Tired no more. Petrified instead. Where was Mary Leigh! Still upstairs. Katelin had caught the man's reflection in the windowpane, and was unsure whether he knew she had. *Oh, God!* What should she do? The knife drawer was behind her. Behind *him!* The only thing the drawer in front of her contained was dish towels and pot holders and a box of toothpicks.

Pot holders . . .

Amos closed his eyes briefly, sucking in a draft of her, like fine, heady wine. His tumescence was becoming unbearable, borne on the combination of illicit entry, her lack of awareness of his looming presence, and his prurient nature. He breathed again, silently, deeply, and reached for her.

Katelin slid open the drawer, slipped in a hand, lifted out a pot holder, folded it in half against her right palm, and with her other hand placed the tin-can lid inside it, one half of the raw edge protruding from between her clasping fingers.

God, please help me! she prayed.

And spun.

Mary Leigh was skipping lightly down the upstairs hall humming to herself. When making the right-angle turn at the head of the stairs, she stumbled, falling forward toward the stairwell, reached a desperate hand toward the banister to keep from tumbling down, missed her grasp, went to her knees, lost her balance, and rolled downward.

"MOMMEE!"

His hand was almost upon her vulnerable arm, her slim, pale appendage, the goose bumps working along his spine, mouth dry with anticipation, when he heard the child scream and reflexively turned his head toward the sound. At that precise, fortuitous moment, Katelin twisted her lithe, strong, terrified body counterclockwise, brought her left elbow up sharply against his reaching arm, deflecting it away from herself, and sliced the Brunswick-stew lid across Amos Thorton's throat with all her strength, will, and fear.

The pain was immediate and intense and disorienting and debilitating. Amos Thorton's erection went south; his attention shifted from arousal to survival; and blood left his body in long ropy gouts, spraying the walls all around as he staggered and stumbled in a circle. The woman ducked under his outstretched arms to scamper out of reach, then down the hall and up the stairs as he followed, his left hand futilely attempting to stem the spurting exodus of fluid from his wound, the other beckoning to her for help, as if pleading, *I'll do anything you want, just don't hurt me anymore,* and he sank to his knees on the bottom step, peering upward in a gathering haze . . .

But no one was there.

And then he no longer was.

Chapter 12

CONNOR GIBBS AND BENELLA MAE SWEET were a half mile from the Gibbs home when their cell phone sounded. Connor picked it up and said into it: "Change your mind about lunch?"

Katelin's panicky voice screamed, "Come quick!"

Gibbs slid into a barely controlled U-turn—taking out Mrs. Smitherman's mailbox (*Oh shit!*)—and hit the gas. Upon their arrival at Katelin's, no one answered the door, despite their ringing and pounding. "Kick it in!" Benella shouted.

Gibbs kicked it in. There before them, in the hall not far from the stairs and thoroughly bled out, was the corpse of Amos Avery Thorton III.

"KATELIN!" screamed Benella, running to the bottom of the stairs. Mary Leigh appeared at the top, looking bewildered.

"Step back, honey," Benella ordered so the child wouldn't see the gore down below.

Mary Leigh stepped back.

"Is your mama up there, sweetheart?"

"Yes," was the thin reply.

Benella pounded up the stairs. Still at the bottom, Connor didn't bother to check for a pulse. He'd seen similar sights before. The ghostly pallor left no room for ambiguity; this guy was dead. Gibbs was covering the body with a throw rug from the den when the first squad car arrived.

"You coulda messed up the crime scene with that rug, mac," said a huge deputy sometime later. The man was nearly as big as Gibbs.

"At least I didn't hose him off."

"You getting smart?"

"One of us needs to. You seem ill equipped."

The deputy stepped closer to Gibbs just as Hank Yarborough came through the front door. "What's up, Greeson?" he barked.

"This bad boy's being flip with me."

"Who, Connor? You can't mean it. What kind of grief you giving him?"

"I told him he shouldn't have covered up the stiff."

"Right. He should have left it alone in case the little girl came down. Give her a good look at the hard side of life."

The big deputy, embarrassed at Gibbs having witnessed his chastisement, mumbled, "Sorry, Chief. I didn't think."

"Your primary shortcoming," Yarborough pointed out.

"But not the only one," added Gibbs.

Greeson gave Connor his steely-eyed cop stare. Gibbs looked back at him, seemingly bored.

The sheriff said, "Greeson, go fetch Everette. Then direct traffic or something. I don't want to see you again till you're thirty."

"Hell, Chief, I'm thirty-four."

"Forty, then. Scat."

Greeson scatted.

Hank Yarborough shook his small, tightly coiffed head. "Guy's dumber than a hyena. How're things upstairs?"

Gibbs shook his head. "Katelin's being sedated. Again. She was nearly over the edge. Bennie's with Mary Leigh."

"Katelin gonna be okay?"

"Too soon to tell, if you mean mentally. Physically, the doc says she tore a ligament in her right palm, but not too seriously. She was smart to use a pot holder. If she hadn't, she might've sliced her hand pretty bad."

Hank nodded, then said, "Benella look at the body?"

Connor's turn to nod. "It's the one that got away, all right."

"Why you reckon he came here?" from Hank.

"Maybe he was at the funeral and recognized Katelin from the restaurant. Then maybe he followed us, intending to put the squeeze on her to get to Bennie."

Hank nodded his concurrence.

"Then that ties it up, with a bow. Two up, two down." Gibbs swiveled a thumb for emphasis.

"You think?" said the sheriff.

"Don't you?"

Hank rubbed his pointed chin. "I might if it wasn't for them Fibbies. Disturbs me, them sniffing around."

"Nosy, you suppose?"

"No. Feds never show up without a reason. Maybe not a *good* reason, but a reason. They're onto something, and they won't let on what. Makes me want to scratch my bum in befuddlement."

Connor smiled at the locution.

"Any coffee around?" the sheriff asked.

"I think so."

"Let's have some while I enlighten you."

Katelin was asleep. Mary Leigh was asleep. Benella Mae *wished* she were asleep. But she wasn't. She was sitting in a rocker in her sister's living room, worried sick about Katelin, dreading Damien's funeral, sipping fetid coffee dregs, and watching Mike Everette trying not to smoke a cigarette. "Light up, Mikey," she insisted. "It's okay."

Everette's appreciation was palpable as he stroked his Bic and inhaled. Gibbs winced at the noxious exhalation. Benella tossed him a preemptive look, so he kept his counsel.

"So we're in agreement that this was self-defense," Benella began. "That putz of a DA's not going to try prosecuting Katelin, is he?"

"After she just lost a husband to this guy or his pal? I think not," Yarborough said.

"Well, he's a political specimen with an eye on the governor's mansion." Benella sighed from fatigue and frustration. "So who knows?"

"I'll call Holmes, get his take on it," Connor suggested.

"No need," Yarborough said. "I'll talk to the man if it seems called for."

Two EMS people came down the hall ferrying a body bag on a stretcher. "Pretty grim business," Hank offered after the remains of Amos had passed.

"For *Katelin*," Benella snapped. "She didn't invite the jerk over for lunch, Hank."

The others were silent, allowing her to vent, but after a moment, she said to Yarborough, "Tell me what you have on the perp from the restaurant."

From memory, the sheriff recited: "Jacoby NMI Lennart—"

"NMI?" Benella interrupted.

"No middle initial," from Hank, then continuing: "DOB 8/29/64; from Ridgefield, New Jersey; dropped out of high school after being accused of burning up a chemistry lab; went back to school in New York City, finishing in 1984; joined the army, served in the Gulf; made it to SP/4, but got busted for assaulting an NCO, a woman; no criminal record as a civilian, except for eleven speeding violations spread over six years; spent some time in the Michigan Militia, playing soldier; works as a welder in Springfield, Illinois, or did until eight weeks ago, when he turned up disappeared along with some welding equipment. His ex-wife wants her back dough, his ex-boss wants his sorry hide, and it looks like both of them are in for disappointment. Hey, wait a minute." Yarborough rubbed his chin in thought. "Maybe the reason the Fibbies are so interested in Lennart is that they suspect he's one of those six bank robbers that have been all over the news."

"Bennie suggested that this morning," said Gibbs. "But how did the FBI make the connection? I understand the robbers wore masks and long coats."

Everette jumped in. "I heard the guns the robbers carried were distinctive in some way, easily recognizable, and that they worked in pairs. Since there were two guys at the restaurant, maybe the feds are taking a long shot, but it seems reasonable. Besides, they doubtless have information not released to the press."

"You can count on that," Connor agreed. "And speaking of the feds," said Connor, "where are they right now? I'd have expected them to be here, in everyone's face."

"We kept this off the radio," Everette said.

Connor smiled. "Won't they be pleased when they learn that."

Hank grinned in return. "Tickled pink."

"Forget the FBI," Benella said. "My concern is whether the recently departed was hanging around on his own, or whether some of his cohorts might also be in town."

"That's a possibility," Hank consented.

"Couldn't these two creeps have been en route to a meeting with the other four? I mean, the robberies were in three different states," Connor asked.

"Yeah, and Wendover smack in the middle," Benella said.

"Could be," said Yarborough, "that this sextet pulled off the robberies, then departed for a neutral zone to divvy up the spoils."

"And sent two of their number for takeout," Gibbs said. "Yep."

"So now we may have to worry about four more trying to find Bennie?"

"It's more likely that they'd not want to stick around. Too much heat," was Yarborough's opinion.

"So what are you going to do about this?" asked Benella.

"Try to find them before they find you," Hank said, climbing to his feet.

"And if you don't?" Benella pressed.

Yarborough shrugged. "Let's just hope we do."

"How reassuring."

"Don't worry, we'll take it from here, babe," Connor said.

"Nothing's guaranteed," said Hank. "Well, take care of Katelin. She's got a load to bear with all this. The little one, too."

And the parley ended.

Benella was sitting by Katelin's bed, reading, when Gibbs came in. Katelin's breathing was heavy and regular. Connor stood behind Benella and stroked her cheek with a forefinger. She reached around and patted his leg, then looked up into his worried eyes.

"This is something you and I will have to handle. At least for now," he stated flatly.

She nodded. "If you need me to, I'll put Lyn in charge at the club."

"I think that's wise. And you better stay away from there completely. No need taking trouble there."

"Okay."

"I'll ask Braxton Chiles to see what he can dig up about our new friends. He has conduits Hank Yarborough doesn't."

"I'll say."

"As far as Katelin's concerned . . ." he began.

"Yeah?"

"Sometimes in life bad things just happen, and you either deal with them . . ."

"Or?"

"They deal with you."

Chapter 13

"THE POOR DUMB BASTARD," OPINED JAMES Q. Bobb, standing in front of the television with a chicken wing in each hand. He took a bite out of one of them and chewed noisily. A poor likeness of Amos Thorton's face smiled up from the screen. High-school picture, no doubt. "Ugly, won't he?" Bobb critiqued. "When he was a yonker, I mean."

"Look who's talking," K.K. Kapatchnik said under his breath as he lay supine on the bed, arms behind his neck to support his shaved head so he could see the TV.

"What was he doing at this lady's house?" queried Matt Bachison from the bathroom.

"Who the fuck knows?" from Jim Bobb as he walked over to the wastebasket and tossed the sundered wings, then wiped his fingers in his profuse chest hair. Licking his chops, he made another dip into the Kentucky Fried bucket, this time selecting a drumstick. He bit into it, smacking juicefully. "This gonna bring the po-leece knockin' on our front door?" he asked the room at large.

"Don't know how," K.K. responded. "We're not connected to Amos in any obvious way, recently anyhow, though if they dig deep enough they might trace us back to Fort Hood."

"Yeah, well, if the boys in blue come around here, such a shellacking they'll get. For good old Amos. He wasn't a bad guy." Bobb wiped his mouth with the back of a sweaty hand, belched, and scratched his belly.

And with Amos Thorton's eulogy having been delivered, the boys trotted out the brew and held a wake.

Special Agent Tattersall wore a charcoal suit, a robin's-egg shirt, a canary cravat with black polka dots, cordovan wing-tips, and a raspberry face. Hank Yarborough—seated behind his messy desk with his feet up, cool, calm, and collected, or at least presenting that appearance—wore his Stetson, his Colt, and a Cross pen in his left shirt pocket.

Tattersall was saying: "Tell me where the body is, Sheriff," inflecting the last word contemptuously.

Hank tilted the hat back. "Last time I saw it, two EMS guys were toting it out to their truck. Guy was dead, so they prob'ly took him to the morgue, you know?"

"We checked," hissed the FBI man, ferretlike. "It isn't there."

"Isn't, or wasn't? If it *wasn't,* then it might be now."

Tattersall stamped a wing-tipped foot. "Don't play games with me!"

Yarborough tilted his hat forward. "Or what?"

"Or you'll think Beelzebub has descended upon you."

Yarborough produced a toothpick, looked at it a moment as if deep in thought, then popped it in his mouth. "He a linebacker for Dallas?"

"You fucking *rube*! You think I won't slap you with an obstruction charge?"

"Oh, I know you would. If you could."

"I CAN!" Ever redder, Tattersall's face.

"Then do it."

"WHAT?"

"Like we used to say when I was a kid, do it, then talk about it."

Mired in frustration, wroth to the gills, FBI Special Agent Clifton Lewis Tattersall stormed out, slamming the door so hard one of the sheriff's bowling trophies fainted and fell from its shelf with a thud. "Well, shoot," lamented Yarborough, picking it up. "Dented the floor."

Everette knocked and came it. "You cowed?" he said.

"I woulda been if he'd stomped his foot one more time."

Everette exited laughing.

In a dark, nondescript automobile outside the sheriff's department sat three dark, nondescript males dressed in dark, nondescript suits. Obviously federal employees, networking. Dialoguing. Plotting.

"I want to nail that sucker's *cojones* to the WALL!" said the one in back, who looked remarkably like C.L. Tattersall.

"He's got jurisdiction. You bulldozed him after the restaurant shooting, but he jumped first on this one. He's probably got the cadaver home in his freezer, next to the venison," said the front-seat passenger.

"I want a tap on his home, his office, his 911 line, on the PAY PHONE IN THE LOBBY!"

Ib Blankenship looked at Web Tyles, over behind the wheel, and grimaced. "No judge will sanction that."

"Bugger the judges!"

"Now wait," calmed Tyles, in his deep, bass voice. "Let's think a minute. We're operating under the assumption that some—maybe all four—of the bank robbers are in the area, correct?"

"Well aren't you clever," Tattersall grated.

"Then we don't need a tap, on anyone. What we need is bait."

Tattersall's vulpine ears perked. "Bait?"

Tyles rubbed where his rug itched. "They've been protecting that woman's identity like she was royalty."

"The one that shot Lennart?" Blankenship clarified.

"Yep."

"So?" said the backseat.

"So what if we let her name slip? To the media," Tyles suggested.

"Whoa. It would be open season on her," Blankenship assessed.

Tyles just smiled. "Then all we'd have to do is wait, and watch, and be there when it goes down. Or soon after."

"Might be rough on the lady," Ib said.

"Hey, nobody asked her to butt in. Besides, she's so big and tough, let her take the heat."

"I like it," from Tattersall. "Do it."

"Seen this?" Benella said, holding up the newspaper, where her picture appeared, and her name, and lots more.

Gibbs said, "I'll call the paper."

"I thought we had an agreement," Connor Gibbs said into the phone.

The editor of the local daily said, "I thought so, too, but I was overridden. It was dumped in our laps, Connor. Three wire reporters got it first. It's in *USA Today,* for Pete's sake. If we'd sat on it, we'd have looked like bumpkins."

"What about Bennie? What happens now? You plan to sit on her front porch with a twelve-gauge!"

"Yarborough ought to."

"I'm not talking 'ought to.' I'm talking 'what if'?"

"What can I say? I had no choice. It was out of my hands."

But Connor didn't hear him. He'd already hung up.

Hank Yarborough next, at whom Gibbs railed profanely for perhaps a minute.

"You done?" said Hank.

"Just tired. Give me a minute."

"Connor?"

"What?"

"Let us reason with one another."

"Go ahead."

"Who stood to gain the most from tossing Bennie to the sharks?"

"How should I know? Anybody who needed pocket change."

"Then why wait? Why not give her up earlier?"

"Maybe they had to convince themselves to do it."

"Or maybe no one local gave her up."

"Then who?"

"You know I shut the feds out of this one, right?"

"Yes."

"I hid the body, withheld Katelin's identity, the whole nine yards."

"And?"

"And one fed in particular was mad as a wolverine deprived of a caribou haunch."

The dawn of comprehension.

"This is a big collar," Hank continued. "They'd be mopping up after three bank heists, and nailing all the perps. That could mean lots of ink, airtime on CNN, maybe a promotion, change of station, dinner with the director, a date with Madonna."

On his end, Connor Gibbs was silent. "Who's in charge?"

"Guy named Clifton Tattersall, but you'll get nowhere yelling at him. Fibbies are used to it. Everybody wants to yell at them. They're less popular than the IRS, and they know it and don't care."

"So what do I do?"

"Move like you're barefoot in a chicken coop."

"Maybe I can think of something better," Gibbs surmised.

"Walk careful."

"Indeed."

"Give Bennie a piece, have her start wearing it. Bring her into the office, I'll issue her a carry permit. And you, you big, mean, private dick, you hang close."

•   •   •

"Hank wants you to come in for a concealed-carry permit," Connor told Benella.

Sitting on his lap, she said, "And you told him?"

Priapically, "I told him sure, fine, okay."

She allowed a hand to roam. "I see you have your gun. Pretty long barrel."

He moved a thigh reflexively. "You developing Restless Leg syndrome?" she teased.

"This is serious," he rasped.

"No," she whispered, grasping, tugging, kneading. "*This* is serious."

And so it became.

An hour later, with Benella fast asleep in his arms, Connor stared up at the ceiling. He was worried, about four faceless men and what they might do ... to Benella, to Katelin, to Mary Leigh ...

Hank Yarborough would do the best he could, within the confines of the law.

And the feds could luck up; they certainly had the resources. But ...

Maybe it was time to circle the wagons.

Chapter 14

"SHE SHOULDN'T GO."

"Bennie . . ."

"She *shouldn't*. She's so drugged up she can barely make it to the bathroom."

The doctor interceded: "Ms. Sweet, I appreciate your concern for your sister's condition, and I'm certain she will not insist upon going if you resist, but how will she feel a month from now, a year, if she fails to attend her own husband's funeral? And what will she tell her daughter?"

Benella sighed.

And they all went to the funeral.

It was awful.

"You spot her?"

"Yep," said K.K. Kapatchnik.

"Give me the glasses," Delaney ordered.

Through the Zeiss ten-power binoculars, Benella Mae appeared virtually at arm's length. "Not bad looking," Delaney observed.

"I know, you want to poke her in the whiskers," said K.K.

"No, in the mouth."

"Mighty pretty mouth, too. Be a shame to waste it."

Delaney glanced at Kapatchnik. "I don't plan to waste it."

"Whoopee."

Delaney returned to the Zeiss. "What we ought to do is take her to the Charlotte Metro Zoo. Feed her to that lion we read about."

Uh-oh, thought K.K. *He's loony enough to do it, especially if he sees it as a challenge.* "Whatever turns you on," he said, and popped some spearmint into his mouth. "But if I remember right, tabby only chewed the guy's legs and the back of his head."

"Hell, the cat was playing. The owner pulled it off the jerk's back. If old Leo had been serious, they'd've both been dead."

There's entirely too much seriousness to this discussion to suit me, Kapatchnik thought. *Delaney could fool you that way.*

The bad part came when he wasn't kidding.

"I feel really exposed here, like we're taking a bath outside Graumans's Chinese Theater," Connor whispered.

"How about a little reverence?" Benella chastised.

"I liked Damien, but I'm more concerned about the living, specifically you and Katelin."

Benella looked over at her sister, sitting palely graveside while the minister intoned. "God, she can't take any more."

"Agreed."

"So what next?"

"I've been thinking about it."

All the visitors, thoughtful and generous and well meaning, had gone, and the house was still. Katelin was upstairs asleep, exhausted from her ordeals. Mary Leigh slumbered beside her, clutching a Barney blanket. Connor and Benella were downstairs with Hank Yarborough. Coffee flowed.

Hank was saying, "Guy I know in Maryland has, ah, *access,* if you know what I mean. We may soon have an ID on some more of these hotshot bank robbers. And pictures we can use. They have to show their faces sometime."

"Unless they hire someone to go for food, toilet paper. Then they can lay low until it's time to strike," Benella said.

"That cheers me up," Gibbs said wryly.

Benella patted his hand. "Be prepared for what your adversary *can* do, not what he might. Who taught me that?"

Connor just grinned. "More coffee, Hank?"

"You bet."

After the hollowware was refilled and Gibbs was reseated, Benella changed the subject. "I've been thinking we should go away."

"Who's included in *we?*" Hank asked.

"Me, Katelin, and Mary Leigh."

"Where to?"

"I've been considering that," was her noncommittal answer. She didn't elaborate.

"Can Katelin get off work?" Hank said.

"She can take medical leave. I'm sure the doctor will back her up."

Hank thought about it. "You understand that I can't cover you if you aren't close by."

Benella nodded. "But Connor can. For a while, until there's a break in the case and we can come back."

"Maybe," from the sheriff.

"The feds will be working it, too. Surely these creeps will surface somewhere," Connor surmised.

"I'm sure they will," agreed Yarborough. "*Where* is what nettles me."

Down the street tooled five pairs of eyes in a van. "Keep moving," said K.K. Kapatchnik. "Don't want to linger. The walls have eyes."

"I believe that's ears," Delaney corrected.

"Little play on words, Marv."

Jim Bobb toed the throttle, increasing their progress to perhaps forty miles an hour.

"But take it easy," Delaney reminded, "this is residential. We don't need some uniform out to fill his speeding quota sniffing around this truck."

"Yeah, especially with that stupid fucking Buster in here." griped Bobb. "They can prob'ly smell him clear up in Staten Island."

"How could they tell? But you do have a point," said K.K., looking over his shoulder at Matt Bachison, who had taken it upon himself to adopt the dog after Thorton's demise.

"He reminds me of my sister's dog, that's why I keep him around," Bachison explained. "You got a problem with that, K.K.?"

Kapatchnik turned in his seat. "I might at that."

Delaney said, "Cut it out. The dog hasn't been a problem so far, and Matt has as much say as anybody in this group. Except me. He wants to keep the mutt, it's his decision, unless there's a problem. Then I'll punch its clock myself. Jim Bobb, you can get a pet possum if you want."

Kapatchnik snorted, but left his hard stare on Bachison, who was unimpressed.

After they had negotiated several streets and turns to determine that there were no feds in the weeds, Delaney said to Jim Bobb: "Come back when it's dark. See if you can find a house within sight of the target that shows signs of absence. Papers in the yard, a light on and nobody home, something like that. Break in the back. No light of course, and turn off whatever's on. Neighbors will think the bulb blew."

"What if I can't?" from Bobb.

"Can't what?"

"Find a empty house close by?"

Delaney glanced at K.K., who rolled his eyes. "Then pick out one with a good view and wax the owners when they come home."

"Yeah?" Bobb grinned, liking it.

"But remember it has to be nearby, not two blocks away."

Jim Bobb, ever the fainéant, had mixed feelings about his assignment. "What if I'm seen?"

"Don't be."

"What if there's a whole family?"

"I'll send Matt to help. That make you happy?"

"Don't need Matt. Just want to know if I can crunch a whole family."

"Your choice. But don't wake up the neighborhood. When you get it all set up, call us."

"Okay."

And it came to pass.

Hank was gone and Benella and Connor were talking and he said, "Where did you plan for us to go?" They discussed their options at length, then Benella retired to Katelin's bedroom for the night and Gibbs took a couch downstairs. Before going to sleep, he called his father.

"Y'ello," said Walter Gibbs.

"Hi."

"I talked to Hank. He says things aren't going so well."

"Seems not."

"Says you and Bennie might hie off somewhere."

"Might."

"You tired, or just cross?" from the elder Gibbs.

"Both. Will you and Cameron take care of Oreo?"

"No, son, we planned to let her starve."

"Don't forget the litter box."

"How the hell could we forget?"

"I love you, Dad."

A pause, then: "Things must be worse than I thought."

"Tell Cameron . . ."

"Tell him what?"

"Never mind. I'll talk to him in the morning."

"Sleep light."

"Ever vigilant."

Another pause. "You need company?"

"No, I'm not dragging you into this. You just look after Cameron."

"Why don't you get the McGraw woman to drop Zep over. You could use a dog's ears and nose right now, what with all the shadows stirring."

"I'll think about it."

"Holmes out of town?"

"Yes."

"Well . . ."

"Good night, Dad."

And they hung up.

At one o'clock, the phone.

"Sorry to wake you," said the voice.

"Evening, Mr. Chiles," Gibbs responded. "What have you uncovered?"

"Zip. Of course they could be in a motel room somewhere, holed up and sending out for eats. But no one seems to know anything, has heard anything, or has seen anything."

"Thanks anyway. You on a cellular?"

"Yep. Just down the street."

"From where?"

"The Stuart residence."

Connor walked to the window, looking out onto a Ford station wagon way near one end of the street.

"You in the Taurus?"

"And listening to Debussy. Sleep well, your back door's covered, too. My second cousin."

"Thanks."

"No problem, my man."

So Connor went to sleep.

Chapter 15

CONNOR GIBBS LAID A SLICE OF HOMEMADE whole-wheat bread on the surface of a cutting board, used a butter knife to spread upon it a layer of cream cheese, then a lavish slather of kudzu jelly. A second slice of bread went on top, making a sandwich of sorts. One-handed, he broke an egg into a shallow bowl, added a teaspoon of milk, and used a wooden fork to whip the mixture to a soupy consistency. He carefully dipped the sandwich into the concoction and let it set until the bottom piece of bread had soaked up most of the liquid, then turned it over to let the top side absorb what was left. A tablespoon of unsalted butter went into a frying pan, preheated on medium. When the butter had melted, he placed the saturated sandwich into the pan and fried it for about two minutes. When the underside—tested with the edge of a spatula—had lightly browned, Connor turned it over to darken the other side. Benella came in, hair freshly damp from the shower, as he slid the French toast onto a plate, ladled some kudzu jelly on top, and put the plate on the table. As she sat to eat, he bussed her crown.

"Morning," he said, and set about preparing another serving.

"Yum," Benella said after taking a bite. "What a treat. Where do you get this jam again?"

"Jelly, and I order it from Thomas Gourmet Foods in Greensboro. So far as I know, nobody else makes it."

"Anywhere?"

"Anywhere. How's Katelin?" he asked, cracking another egg.

"Still asleep and still as a mouse," Benella answered as he whipped the mixture, frothy bubbles rising. The kitchen smelled of fresh coffee and essence of vine.

"And Mary Leigh?" The bread was soaking now.

"She's in her room with Winkie. She seems okay, but . . . I don't know."

Gibbs stared out the window at the bright spring day, then flipped the toast. "She hungry?"

"I asked her and she said no."

Since Benella never ate unless she was hungry, and didn't understand why other people did, she never encouraged anyone to eat unless they were cadaverously gaunt or fresh off the desert. Mary Leigh was neither, so Benella had left her to play with her doll, figuring that when hunger pangs struck, the child would come in search of sustenance.

Connor, on the other hand, encouraged *everyone* to eat (including himself), so long as there was food ready, waiting, and hot. (Which was why he ran five miles a day, did crunches and push-ups and jumping jacks by the thousands, and regularly pounded the heavy bag into submission; if he hadn't, he'd have weighed four hundred pounds.)

"I think I'll go check on her," he said, and bounded up the stairs. Benella smiled to herself, got up, checked the still-frying toast (almost done), then removed it from the pan. On top went a double dollop of jelly, for her an incredible extravagance. In a minute, Mary Leigh was downstairs and ravenous. Gibbs, too, eyeing the empty pan.

"Mice," he said, and cracked an egg.

Breakfast proceeded apace.

• • •

Dr. Sorenson came at ten and was displeased. "Katelin's too hard to rouse," he informed. "She's not that heavily sedated."

Instantly worried, Benella said, "What now?"

"Let her sleep another few hours, then try to get her up and walking. Encourage her to eat something. I'll look in on her this afternoon," he said.

"Had breakfast?" from Connor.

"Yes. At six," claimed the doctor, and departed.

"Was he implying sloth?" Gibbs asked Benella.

"Probably," she replied, and went upstairs to Katelin.

Mary Leigh's mouth was smeared with jelly. Fingers, too. "This is gooood stuff," she heralded. "Can I have some more damorrow?"

"Whenever you want to, sweetheart," Connor said.

That pleased her. "Have I had it before?"

"The French toast? I don't know, but probably not. I never knew anyone outside my family who made it."

She licked a finger. "It's a old fambly recipe?"

Gibbs smiled. "That's right."

"I love those, don't you?"

"Yes, but I especially love *you*." He laughed, scooping her up for hugging. She hugged him back, very tightly.

And then the tears came.

Connor washed Mary Leigh's face after the catharsis, and the child was now in front of the TV sucking a thumb, when upon the door, a knock. Gibbs peeped through the peephole. On the threshold stood a very, very diminutive man with a mop of hair, dressed in a mauve T-shirt, gray trousers, scuffed Nikes, and a light blue jacket. Beneath the jacket, Gibbs knew, lived a pair of Colt .357 revolvers. The two guns weighed nearly as much as their bearer.

Connor opened the door. "Mr. Chiles," he greeted.

"Good morning, my man. Just checking in before I check out. Did you slumber peacefully?"

"As if on a melatonin bender. And you?"

Braxton Chiles shook his shaggy head. "No rest for the wary. Cousin Ab says you had a troller last night, a van with privacy glass. Up and down the street several times, not too slow, not too fast, then off it went."

"You've a relative named Ab?"

"An abridgment of Absalom."

"Of course. Is he taking off, too?"

"If you can spare him. Has an exam today."

"Exam?"

"He's a student at Wake Forest."

"And he was up all night?"

Braxton shrugged elaborately.

"Can I pay for this one?"

"Not me. Ab can use it, though. Burger King tends to parsimony."

Gibbs extracted five hundred-dollar bills from his wallet and passed them to Chiles.

Chiles handed three back.

Gibbs cocked a quizzical brow.

"Wouldn't want to spoil him. Next thing you know, he'd quit flipping burgers and hire out as a watchdog for Boz Fangelli or his ilk," from Braxton.

"You know not."

Chiles shrugged again. "There have been overtures."

"Based on his relationship with you, I trust."

Again a modest shrug. Braxton Chiles was one of the deadliest gunmen alive. And one of the most storied.

"Well, I hope he stays in school," Connor said.

"So does Aunt Flo."

"Ab's mama?"

"Um-hmm. I'll continue to keep an ear to the pavement. Nighty-night," said Braxton Chiles.

It was nearly nine in the morning.

Chapter 16

Eight hours before the previously mentioned conversation between Connor Gibbs and Braxton Chiles took place, Purley Faber had been in a terrific mood. After three days of isolation at the ocean, in a rented condo, walking the beach, nobody but him and his cat, Jerico, filling up on clams and scallops and red wine, watching the ball games on ESPN, slipping over to Myrtle Beach for a carnal visit with an old flame, Purley was on his way home. What a vacation. He sang along with the Drifters as he drove, "Under the boardwalk . . ." He waved to Lonnie Wycomb, walking her Cairn in the late night air. "Out of the sun . . ." Trying for falsetto, though he couldn't sing a lick and knew it and didn't care. No one complained when he sang raucously in the shower, since he lived alone, except for Jerico of course, snoozing there beside him on the seat. He stroked the black fur. "We'll be having some fun . . ." he warbled as he pulled into his driveway.

Matt heard the car outside and shucked his SIG. Jim Bobb went to the window. "A Renault," is all he said.

• • •

Jerico entered first, through his little, swinging cat door, and was instantly alarmed. Back through the door he went.

Purley Faber saw, but took no cue from kitty. "Going to see a girlfriend?" he said, chuckling.

No.

Jerico wasn't.

As soon as Purley walked through the door, Jim Bobb grabbed him from behind, clapped one callused hand over Purley's mouth, and inserted the point of an ice pick into one ear.

Then pushed.

When Purley screamed, it was into the clasping hand, although the sound still seemed loud in the quietude, at least to Jim Bobb, close as he was, and he rapidly rotated the ice pick to scramble the simp's brains and shut him up.

It worked, In seconds, the house was silent once more, except for the sound of Purley Faber's heels drumming the floor.

Jerico adopted a family down the street.

Chapter 17

"THOSE STUPID FEDS. THEY'RE DUMBER'N DIRT," Jim Bobb said around a bite of PBJ, washing it down with a swallow of milk. His thick Adam's apple bobbed as he drank.

"Um-hmm," said Matthew Bachison, freshly into his toilette: tan Dockers, a red Einstein T-shirt tucked in under black galluses, Weejuns, no socks. Suburban camo.

Two houses down, a dark, nondescript sedan had pulled up to the curb, depositing a dark, nondescript man dressed like an aerobics instructor. The man—tall, athletic, square-jawed, and forthright—walked purposefully to a side door of the house (a beige-shingled Cape Cod), knocked, and was admitted as the sedan pulled off. Five minutes later, a middle-aged couple emerged through the same door, baggage in hand, and stood on the small porch uncertainly until the dark, nondescript sedan reappeared (from the opposite direction, to fool chance observers) and turned into the driveway. In jumped the couple, up backed the sedan and off down the street they went.

"Gee. Who'd have noticed that?" Bachison commented.

"I told you. Dumber'n dirt. Richard Jewell was safe as eggs."

Bachison snorted and snapped a suspender just as the phone rang.

"Yo," Bobb said into it.

"What's cooking?" asked K.K. Kapatchnik.

"The feds have arrove," Jim Bobb reported.

"Where?"

"Two doors down. This house with dormer windows and a stupid birdbath."

"And the fake geese. Don't forget to tell him about the fake geese," from Bachison, now rooting around in the fridge.

"Shut up. I'm trying to talk, here," Bobb insisted, hand over the mouthpiece.

"You guys in tight like a tick?" queried K.K.

"Plenty of grub, though not much stuff I like. There's a box of persimmon seeds. Now, I ask you—"

"Jim?"

"Huh?"

"Shut up."

"Well, you asked if—"

"Jim?"

"What?"

"Has anyone come to the house yet?"

"This one, or the one the feds—"

K.K. took a deep, deep breath, and said, "The one you're in."

"Yeah. Last night. I put him on ice," he said, and snickered. Bachison was arraying lettuce and tomatoes and Dijon on the counter.

"On ice?"

"I stuck an ice pick in his ear."

"He's dead?"

"As my uncle Earl."

"Where's the body?"

"In the family plot in Oklahoma City. On his gravestone it says—"

"The guy at the *house,* Jim." *Give me strength,* thought K.K. Kapatchnik.

"Oh. In a broom closet. We had to kinda fold him."

Bachison was spreading mustard on a slab of rye bread. He grimaced at the memory of placing poor Purley into his own closet.

"In a day or two, he'll start to smell," Kapatchnik advised.

"He *already* smells. He shat his britches when I skewered him."

Bachison said, "Hey. I'm trying to eat," and took a big bite of his sandwich.

"You boys need anything?" K.K. said in preparation to signing off.

"I reckon not," from Jim Bobb.

"Keep an eye on the feds. And remember, either one of you leaves, it has to be after dark, and out the back."

"Gotcha," said Jim, nodding his head in agreement.

And they hung up.

Dr. Sorenson was seated on the couch in Katelin's living room, sipping coffee and rubbing his bum knee. (Old football injury. Harvard.) Across from him in the floral-print chair sat Benella Mae Sweet, with Connor standing beside her for support. Katelin's prognosis was not good.

Sorenson was saying, "She will not get out of bed except to tend to pressing bodily functions, not even to perform the most basic of ablutions. I've watched her with Mary Leigh. No response whatever. I took the liberty of phoning Charter—"

"Wait a minute! Who said you could do that?"

"I'm her doctor, Ms. Sweet. Of record. Your sister is in deep denial, and even deeper depression. She needs very good help very badly. Lying upstairs in a morose state and a pungent nightgown is not remedial."

"Now you listen to me—" Benella started.

The good doctor stood. "I have made a decision. You can fight me, of course, but I see no point in it. I will prevail. Your sister needs help. Now. I intend to see she gets it."

"Who'll take care of Mary Leigh?" Benella said.

"Has Katelin no extended family?"

"Just me."

"Your parents?"

"Both dead."

"I'm sorry. Then I suppose the child's care falls to you. Or the state," he finished ominously.

Oh, God, thought Benella. *Not an orphanage. Never.*

"We'll take care of Mary Leigh, Doc," Connor said. "You just tend to Katelin."

Benella looked at him, startled.

"I dislike very much being referred to as 'Doc.' "

" 'Sawbones' suit you?"

"You needn't be unpleasant."

"And you needn't be insensitive. You come in here, dump all this in Bennie's lap, and expect us to be pleasant? Your bedside manner stinks."

"I have neither the time nor the inclination to hone my bedside manner, Mr. Gibbs. My concern, my *only* concern, is the welfare of my patients. What you think of me is immaterial. I have determined that psychiatric assistance is required, and I have made the arrangements. Katelin's insurer has agreed to those arrangements. Transportation will be here within the hour. It would be very helpful, Ms. Sweet, if you would pack a bag for your sister. She is obviously incapable. And I suggest that Mary Leigh not be present when her mother leaves. Or we may have two in need of treatment."

"An hour. All right," Benella reluctantly conceded.

"I said *within* the hour. For all I know, they could arrive any moment."

"Then they can wait," Connor said firmly. "Next time, give us some warning, Doc. A little preparation time."

Ignoring the barb, Sorenson said, "Katelin is not flying to Mars, Mr. Gibbs. You will be able to visit her at Charter."

And so it stood.

● ● ●

Connor took Mary Leigh for ice cream while a drawn Katelin Stuart was sponge-bathed, dressed, and mostly carried downstairs to a waiting conveyance. The attendants were gentle, courteous, and professional. Dr. Sorenson supervised, from a comfortable distance, because Benella was in a mood. No more hospitality for him, not in this house.

As the van pulled away, Benella stared after it, fighting back tears and wondering if she should wave. Would Katelin see? She lifted a vague hand as the vehicle turned a corner and drove out of sight, then went upstairs to collapse on the bed, disquieted and distraught.

When Connor brought Mary Leigh home, the little girl was full of mint chocolate chip and sound asleep. He carried her into the house and up to her room, placed her on her bed, covered her with the Barney blanket, and kissed her softly so as not to awaken. He watched her sleep for a bit, then went to check on Benella. She, too, was asleep, her face moist and salty. Connor brushed the hair back from her eyes, eased down beside her on the bed, and stroked her back lightly. She didn't stir, but was subliminally aware that he was present. And there he stayed, comforting, until she opened her eyes an hour later.

Then he quietly closed and locked the door and they made tender, life-affirming love.

Chapter 18

It was after nine o'clock the next morning, and the Gibbs contingent—both of them—were in much better spirits. Mary Leigh, too, in the den watching a Care Bears tape. So far, she hadn't asked about her mother.

"What's on your agenda for today?" Connor asked.

Benella looked up from her paper. "Don't you need to go to your office? Or to see Cameron?"

"I do."

"Then I suppose one of us has to look after Mary Leigh."

"I'll take her with me."

"You will?"

"She can putter around the office while I check a few things, make a couple calls. Then we'll go play with Cameron and Pop."

"You sure?"

"Absolutely."

"Okay, I'll work on a kata, maybe kick the bag. Get good and sweaty," Benella said.

"Enjoy," from Gibbs, who then cleaned up, mopped up,

put out some frozen pintos to thaw, diced a juicy tomato, and finished his tea, all in less than fifteen minutes.

"You sure are handy to have around," Benella observed.

"If you weren't in love with JoAnn, you could marry me. I'm great in the sack, too."

"For a man."

He came up behind her, bent over slightly, snaked his arms around her waist. "For either gender. Admit it," he teased.

"Not to your face."

"Then choose another body part." He drew her to him and cupped a breast.

"Connor, Mary Leigh might come in," she objected, but not strenuously.

He nipped her nape and made a deliciously lewd suggestion.

She dipped her chin and arched her neck for his freer access while reaching around, finding him.

He jumped.

"Well, hey, big fella," she breathed. Then: "Put up or shut up," as she turned to him.

He pressed into her palm with increased urgency.

She nibbled his lip.

He fondled her breasts.

Her fingers squeezed.

The phone rang.

"ARGH!" they expleted in unison.

She went to the phone.

He went to sit down.

"Hello," she said, a tad breathless.

It was McDermott Neese, a Triangle car dealer. Her new Solara had come in, and he was sending it to Mountain City Toyota for her to pick up.

"The driver will have all the paperwork. You just need to sign them," he said. "I'll mail your copies. The deal's done, so don't try to give anybody money."

"Thanks, Mac."

"Always a pleasure doing business with you and Connor," Neese responded, as personable as ever. Then his voice lowered. "How're things with you? I read the papers."

"Okay, I guess."

"Katelin?"

"Not so good," Benella replied, then nothing else.

Neese correctly interpreted the silence. "Well, if there's anything I can do, call me. I can be there in two hours," he said, meaning it.

"I appreciate it."

"And it's not just that you've bought a lot of cars from me."

"I know."

"Remember me to the behemoth."

"I will," she said, and rang off.

Mary Leigh walked in. "I'm hungry," she announced.

"How about some grapes?" from Gibbs.

"How about a Pop-Tart?"

"Grapes are better for you."

"Mommy lets me eat Pop-Tarts for a snack, and my tummy feels like a snack, not a grape," Mary Leigh countered, then brightened to offer a compromise. "*Winkie* can eat some grapes."

Connor accepted. "You want the Pop-Tart toasted?"

"You betcha."

So they toasted it together.

After Gibbs and Mary Leigh had left for his office, Benella called Tom Smithson, a local antique buff and one of her favorite customers. Tom opened the sally. "I need a kitchen cabinet, preferably a Sellers."

"I just found a twenty-four-inch Hoosier, in a barn under a tarp."

"A twenty-four? What kind of shape?"

"Best I've seen in a while, though not immaculate. It'll bring maybe twenty-eight hundred dollars."

"What'd you pay?"

She laughed. "I'm ashamed to tell you."

"Did you take advantage of some poor farmer?"

"No, but I left myself wriggle room."

"Five bills' worth?"

"More."

"Pirate."

"Brigand."

"By the way," said Tom, "tell me again about the McDougall you mentioned last time."

"Oak, forty-eight inches, original flour sifter, original meal bin, original spice jars and rack. And a salt dish."

"Pullout drawers?"

"Only Sellers cabinets have pullouts. What, are you testing me? By the way, a couple of glass coffee jars also came with the McDougall, but they're not original."

"What else have you run across lately?"

"A reverse gingerbread cookie jar, no name. A Metlox Pierre the Chef—"

"How much?" Smithson said excitedly.

"Two and a half?" probed Benella.

"That's all it'll bring to a customer. Leave me some room, for Pete's sake."

She paused for effect. "All right, I'll let you have the Metlox and a Hobart Kitchen Aid coffee grinder for two seventy-five."

"The Hobart in good shape?"

"I've been using it."

"I thought you liked that lap grinder Connor gave you for Christmas."

"I did, until Ted Janes offered me three bills for it."

"You sold a Christmas gift?"

"Yeah, then bought a European continental couch with the proceeds, walnut with web feet in back, only on its second upholstery. The original horsehair backing is in place. I figured Connor and I can both enjoy a couch. I didn't tell him what it's worth. If he knew, he'd never sit on it."

"I'll give you three grand. Today. Send Sturm to pick it up."

"Forget it."

"Now, Bennie . . ."

"Not for sale. So what have you recently stolen from some bereaved widower?"

"How about a primo pre–Civil War mahogany rosebud table, hmm? It was hanging from a rafter over in Reidsville, next to a slipper side chair with original silk covering, never reupholstered."

"Floral print?"

"You bet. I've got a walnut gateleg, circa 1900 or so. Oh, you told me you like Janet Greenleaf? I just bought one I'll let you have for eighty-five bucks. It's a vase of flowers, nothing special, but in a nice oak frame."

"Mostly earth tones?"

"I said it's a Greenleaf."

She considered. "How about I let you have the Metlox and the Hobart for two hundred and the painting?"

"Thief."

"Charlatan."

Having completed the obligatory haggling, they settled on one hundred eighty dollars, thus, in ten minutes Benella had cleared ninety dollars and gained a Greenleaf to boot. She planned to hang it in the den.

After showing her collection of Los Angeles Pottery and Franciscanware to a patron from Kentucky, Benella quickly showered, shaved her legs, applied such makeup as she wore (not much), slipped into jeans, and into the jeans slipped a Smith & Wesson .380 about the size of a bagel, but not as heavy. Since the day was reasonably warm, she eschewed a coat, opting instead for a bulky pullover sweater. It covered the gun nicely.

Then she went alone to get her new Toyota.

Well. Almost alone.

Chapter 19

"SHE'S ON THE MOVE!" BACHISON BARKED AT Bobb, and picked up the phone.

Bobb bobbed his head in agreement and snatched up the binoculars. "The Fibbie's got her. He's at the window with a cell phone in his ear," he said.

The dance had begun.

"Subject is getting into a blue Celica convertible," the dark aerobic FBI agent said to one of his superiors, which included nearly everybody. "Can't make the plate, the car's facing out."

"We have the number," said the superior. "Top up or down?"

The fed blinked at the question. He started to say *duh,* but suppressed it. "Er, it's fifty-one degrees. The top's *up.*"

"She's originally from the mountains, Tyles. Mountain folk don't view fifty-one degrees as being exactly gelid."

Gelid? Tyles thought. *What the hell does that mean?* What he said was, "I guess you're right. She didn't have a coat on." Web Tyles was from Miami; he got out earmuffs when it dipped below seventy.

"Which way is she headed," from the phone.

"South. And in a hurry."

No response for a minute, then: "Okay, we've got her. Good work."

"Putz," Tyles said into the telephone. When he was sure it was off.

"Which way's she headed?" Marvin Delaney asked.

"Which way? Left! I mean . . . where's the sun? East! No . . . south! I think," said Jim Bobb.

Bachison jerked back the phone. "South on Longview, ace."

"Remind me to shoot him later."

"He's doing his best."

"Then I hesitate to contemplate his worst. There she is . . . and there they are."

"The feds?"

"Right, in a Ryder rental. Gimme a break," Delaney said, and shifted into gear.

The Ryder followed too closely, and of course Benella spotted it. "Hi, boys," she mumbled to herself, and drove on. The Chrysler Concorde she did not spot. Unfortunately.

Not far from the exit to Route 42, Benella, tooling along next to the median, made an abrupt lane change that caught the Fibbie driver lollygagging. He missed the turn. She didn't.

She did wave good-bye, though.

But not to the Concorde. It was two cars back.

Benella, confident that she had eluded pursuit, made a few halfhearted switchbacks and detours, checking her mirrors all the while. Traffic was moderate but not nonexistent, so she couldn't remember every car. After five miles of two-stepping and doubling back, she gave it up. Surely no one back there was interested in her.

Except maybe the brown Chrysler.

When Benella turned in at the Toyota store, it kept going, U-turning down the block to park by a meter that still had time on it.

And there it sat, engine idling.

Like a vulture.

Benella's new ride was a black Solara V-6, a few-frills base car, no leather or sunroof or CD player or electric windows and locks, but featuring a twenty-four-valve, fuel-injected motor that yielded two hundred horses, a pretty good herd for a car not much over one and a half tons in curb weight. It was underpinned by an athletic chassis.

After signing the papers and taking delivery, Benella went immediately to a relatively deserted, relatively flat, very rural stretch of road and made a series of back-to-back zero-to-sixty runs: 7.4, 7.5, then an impressive 7.1 seconds once she'd learned the shift points and how to launch without bogging or producing excessive wheel spin. The muscular rocket squawked rubber as she hit second on each pass, which gave it high marks on her personal grin meter.

While Benella was doing all this, the Concorde sat athwart the entrance to a tote road a half mile away. Watching. Inside it, Marvin Delaney thought, *Why do I have this feeling that I should just shoot her and have it over with. Forget it. I'm going to run her off a mountain.* He slipped into his driving gloves.

Delighted with her new ride—just what she needed to lift flagging spirits—Benella headed for home with her rearview mirror empty . . .

. . . until she passed Baker's Road. There a brown '97 Chrysler Concorde appeared in it.

She glanced into her mirror. Away. Back again. Nothing there but Concorde.

"I think I've seen you before," she said aloud. "I remember the ugly color."

She downshifted to fourth, the dun-colored Chrysler close behind.

"Let's see what you got," she said, eschewing third for second and mashing the accelerator. Sixty passed quickly. Seventy. Eighty. The Concorde stuck like Velcro.

Twisties were coming up. Benella slowed through sixty, downshifted to third for compression braking, drifted through a thirty-five-mph curve at 50 (*Nice balance, easy to bring the tail out*), and punched it on exit. Ditto the Concorde. Only the driver was visible in the trailing car. Others might be hunkered down out of sight. But more likely it was just him and her and the challenging stretch of road . . . A hard right-hander next, at twenty over the posted limit, the Solara's tires protesting vehemently, then punch and aim (*Whoa, torque steer*), the tires were finding every rut at full throttle . . . a lefty now, tail going wide when she backed off too abruptly (*Remember this is front-wheel drive*), switchback looming (*Hope no one's coming*), the tires protesting as she entered a controlled slide to tackle the apex then squirted out the other end amid even more strident rubbery protestations . . . the Chrysler hard on her heels, its tail oscillating more than hers (differences in skill or suspension?) (*Whoops, GRAVEL! Watch the ditch! Ha, him, too!*).

And suddenly there was a CAR!

She sawed the wheel, darting left, the Concorde whipping right, nearly out of control . . .

Bessie O'Neal, seventy-one and feeling every day of it, came out of her reverie to discover the road in front of her full of cars. Both sides. That left no room for her.

So she chose the ditch. Or tried to, anyway.

Marvin Delaney and the Concorde went over the edge and down the mountain, having been nudged to that fate by a rusty Lincoln the size and heft of a coal barge. Fortunately, he was buckled up. Equally fortunately, his car didn't ignite. Not so fortunately, one foot somehow got twisted crosswise, which hurt like hell and temporarily hampered his clambering out of the ruined but valiant vehicle.

"I'd have *had* her in another second!" he groused to himself as he hobbled along, smelling of gasoline. Despite the odor, within ten minutes he'd hitched a ride in a milk truck routing back to Wendover.

"Are you all right, honey?" Bessie O'Neal asked Benella, whose spanking-new car had become intimate with a mountain laurel. Two, actually. The valiant Toyota was not in good shape.

"I'm fine, but how are *you*? I nearly ran you off the road."

"I thought I was gone, too, till that turd-colored car got in my way. Reckon he's hurt bad? I didn't hear no 'splosion."

"I'll call the highway patrol. They'll go down and check it out."

"All right. Want a Dew while we wait?"

"No, thank you," Benella said, and made the call.

Chapter 20

"WHAT DID YOU THINK YOU WERE DOING!" Connor Gibbs was very upset.

"Connor," said Benella soothingly.

"They could have been scraping *you* off that mountain instead of that schmuck's car!" He was pacing and gesticulating.

"Connor," she tried again.

"What were you thinking of!" Red-faced, short of breath, restive in the extreme.

"Connor." A model of patience.

"What!"

"I wrecked my brand-new car today. I'd rather not be yelled at."

"You deserve to be yelled at," obviously volunteering his services.

"Connor?"

"What!"

"What would you have had me do?"

"Call the cops on the cell phone!"

"Could they have gotten there in time to help? The guy was practically in my trunk."

"Well, you could have . . ."

"Yes?" She smiled in the face of his anger and concern, defusing, something she was very good at, with Connor, at least, and always had been.

He gave up and sat down, exasperation epitomized.

"Y'all finished now?" said Hank Yarborough from his chair by the hearth. The trio was at Connor's home. Mary Leigh was in the den watching *George of the Jungle* with Blister McGraw and Zepper, a Boykin spaniel. Ice cream was being consumed by all. Including Zepper.

"I suppose so," Benella said. Then: "You want the rest of this?" to Connor, indicating his unfinished pistachio.

Gibbs waved a hand. She picked up the bowl and began to spoon. She loved pistachio.

The sheriff began: "The car, of course, was stolen. Utah plate, stolen off another car. Credit card over the visor they used for gas."

"That stolen, too, I presume," from Benella, to hold up her end of the conversation.

Yarborough nodded. "We also found a pair of driving gloves he left behind."

"Were they stolen, too?" Connor said acidly.

"Who knows? My point is that there ain't likely to be prints."

"Gloves," Connor mused.

"And I doubt comfort was his main concern. Forensics checked the car for hair and found at least nine different types, including some from a ferret."

"Family car," Benella surmised.

"We think so, but the owners weren't home when we phoned."

"I hope they're okay," Gibbs said.

"This wasn't a carjacking. The Chrysler was boosted three days ago up in Danville."

"What now?" Connor asked.

"We wait, patrol the area, look for out-of-place vehicles,

bank-robberly-looking guys hiding amongst the azaleas," Hank said. "We're going from house to house in the neighborhood. If Bennie's feeling was correct—that he had been behind her for quite a while—then he probably picked her up not far from here. Since you can leave from here in any of three directions, they probably have your house under surveillance."

"That's great," from Connor. "So why aren't you banging on doors right now?"

"We are. You sit tight till you hear from me, Bennie. No more solo flights."

She nodded her acquiescence, then to Connor: "Why don't we just leave town like we talked about?"

"They might follow us," Gibbs explained. "Better the terrain you know."

"Right," said Hank. "Well, good night, folks. Sleep tight, don't let the bad guys bite."

Conner smiled in spite of himself.

After the sheriff left, Benella quietly admonished Connor. "That was embarrassing, especially in front of Hank."

"I'm sorry, I was just letting off steam. This whole situation is beginning to get to me. The cops can't seem to help, my normal, ah, legality-marginal channels aren't producing, and there are four well-trained paramilitaries out there laying for you."

She kissed his cheek. "I understand that, but let's wash our linen privately in the future."

He nodded assent. "Tomorrow I'll make it up to you."

Leaning into him, she whispered, "What you got in mind?"

"The Mimosa Grill."

She leaned away from him. "Double-cut pork chops, garlic mashed potatoes, Southern greens, Carolina tomato jam? Be still, my heart. Chocolate crunch cake for dessert?"

"Only if you clean your plate."

She leaned into him again, her head against his broad chest. "That'll sure knock a hole in a fifty-dollar bill. Are you willing to spend that kind of money on someone who's in love with another?"

"Well, sex is involved."

"I might have guessed," she breathed. "In advance, I presume."

"Not necessarily. Your credit's good." He tipped her chin up to look into her eyes. "Will the Mimosa make up for your car?"

"No," she said. "But it'll help."

"You *lost* her?" yelled C. Lewis Tattersall, over the phone.

"She made a tricky move. If I'd tried it, I'd have ended up in the weeds. Whose idea was that freaking monster truck, anyway?" complained Ib Blankenship.

After ten seconds of line hum, a frosty, "Mine."

"Uh . . ."

"Never mind, Blankenship. I'm sending Web Tyles over to relieve you for six hours. Get some sleep. I'll think about replacing the truck."

"Oh, and sir?"

"What?"

"Since she obviously knows we're watching, I think maybe we should—"

"I'm not interested in what you think. If Tyles can do his job right, I expect you to do yours even better. You've got five years seniority. *Step up,* Blankenship."

"Yes, sir."

"And lose some weight. You're an embarrassment, in more ways than one."

Blankenship reflexively sucked in his gut, not much of one. "Yes, sir," he said into the empty connection. Then he sat, tuned in a local FM station—National Public Radio, some soothing chamber music—and laid his head back. In three minutes, he was snoring.

"I got blindsided by a Lincoln, that's how!"

"But she's just—" Jim Bobb began.

"What?" from Delaney, fire in his eye.

"A . . . a girl."

Matt Bachison closed his eyes against the coming storm. K.K. Kapatchnik crossed his arms. Marvin Delaney gritted his teeth.

Jim Bobb was unperturbed over his lack of propriety. "We leaving now?" he said.

Delaney breathed deeply. In through the nostrils; out through the mouth. In . . . out . . . until the urge to maim had passed. Calmer, he answered, "Affirmative. The cops will guess that we have surveillance on the lady, so this house isn't safe anymore. It's why we came to get you guys. Pack your Twinkies and let's move."

"Any plans?" from Bachison.

"We'll talk about them at the motel."

"How about the body?" said Jim Bobb of the folded, spindled Purley Faber.

"What, you want it for a souvenir?" quipped Delaney.

Bachison snorted, then he and Bobb tossed into a bag their personal items and snacks and headed for the rear of the house.

Just as the front doorbell rang.

Chapter 21

ALSTON CHALMERS HAD COME TO THE SHER-
iff's department roughly three weeks earlier, fresh off a
stint in the navy. He was twenty-five, a former high-school
tennis star, of medium height and build, and had a birth-
mark on his left thigh and a tattoo of the Statue of Liberty on his right. (He'd acquired the tattoo in Wilmington,
where he'd served two years as a shore patrolman.) Alston
was fair, fit, and fanatical about law enforcement.

And his family. There were: his wife, Clare; twins
Thomas Lyle and David Blane, three; and baby Jasmine,
six months and still nursing. He was talking to Clare now,
on a mobile phone, while his partner was ringing the doorbell of a rambling clapboard house.

"When you coming home, sweetcheeks?" Clare said.

"This is the last house. We've checked ten already, and
everything was right as rain. This is about the dumbest
thing I've done since joining the force."

"A whole month ago. Well, not quite a month," she chided.

"Those guys are long since gone from Charlotte metro,"
Alston speculated to his spouse.

"I hope so."

"Hey, I wouldn't mind seeing a little action."

"After you come home tonight, studly, I'll give you all the action you can stand."

"Better stop, or I'll go tell Grunt I'm leaving right now. He can check the last house by his ownself."

"Talk, talk, talk." Clare giggled. "Here, Tommy wants to speak to his daddy."

Short pause. "Papa?"

"Yo, pumpkin."

"When you comin' home? I wanna rassle."

"You got a match, little dude. When I get there, we'll wrestle till dawn."

"You coming soon?"

"*Real* soon."

"Promise?"

"Promise," Alston told his son, and he'd always been a man of his word.

But not this time.

No response at the door, though Jefferson Granticelli—called "Grunt" since junior high—kept his finger on the button and could hear the buzzer jangling away inside. When Chalmers joined him on the porch, Grunt said, "Dunno where Purley could be. His old car's in the driveway and the doorbell's sure as hell working." He bent to peer into the hallway, but his view was obscured by chintz curtains, a lacy legacy from Purley's late wife. Grunt was six and a half feet high, weighed nineteen stone, and was predominately hairless. He'd been a cop in one organization or another for thirty-one years.

"I'll ease around back," suggested Alston Chalmers.

"We'll both go. I'll go around the west side, you take the east."

"Okay," Chalmers agreed. He looked up at the sky. "Moon rises in the east, right?"

But Grunt was already moving. "That frigging Purley," he grunted. "Probably passed out on sloe gin."

No, Purley wasn't.

He was in his closet decomposing.

"They're going around the side," Bachison whispered.

"Which side?" hissed Delaney.

"*Both* sides!" was Matt's susurrous reply.

"Shit!" sibilated Jim Bobb.

K.K. Kapatchnik, gently stropping his knife, said, "No noise, girls. The feds are practically in our pockets," and slipped out the back way.

Jim bobbed his head. "Dang right," he said, then withdrew his own tanto and followed K.K. into the tenebrious night.

Alston Chalmers had on a vest, a good one, Second Chance. It would stop a .357 magnum bullet, even a shotgun slug, and would turn some knives.

But not a tanto.

"*Messerschmitt!*" he bleated when a low branch caught him across one eye, initiating instant tearing. "Damn pine tree! Now I got pitch on my face."

He didn't, but he had other things to worry about anyway.

Grunt Granticelli had his flashlight on; he didn't give a rat's ass who saw him coming. Better if someone *did*, assuming someone was really in there. Then they could skedaddle out the front door, or climb out a window.

I don't like this, he thought. *We should've called for backup.*

He was right, of course.

K.K. Kapatchnik stepped into a shadowy corner where the added-on back porch jutted from the east-side exterior wall of the house. And there he waited, spectral, dressed all in black, as murkily sinister as Charon himself.

Even his knife blade failed to reflect light.

Jim Bobb spotted the flashlight first off, but had no real visual sense of what was behind it. The light was pretty high off the ground, though; if it was being held waist-high, this was one big son-of-a-bitch. He sheathed his knife and unholstered the K-9. There was no safety to click off, so the sounds he made were minimal.

This fucking mimosa ain't all that big, Jim thought, crouched behind it, head lowered now that the light was drawing near. *He'll spot me sure as an ostrich lays big eggs,* he thought, and when Anthony Jefferson "Grunt" Granticelli was still thirty feet distant, Jim Bobb made a major mistake.

Inside, nigh the front door, Matt Bachison had a SIG .45 in one hand, a Kahr 9mm in the other, and a wad of gum in his mouth the size of a golf ball. He was chewing and singing *sotto voce,* something by Smashing Pumpkins. Ready to rock-and-roll.

The Lollapalooza would be held early this year.

Marvin Delaney was in the den, kneeling by a window, observing one huge cop walking by, flashlight blaring. *Where the hell is Jim Bobb?* he thought.

In fifteen seconds, he would find out.

Ten more steps, cowboy, thought K.K. Kapatchnik as he watched Alston Chalmers approach. *Your picture will be on the station-house wall for all to see. "Killed in action," it'll say. "Old What's-his-face, valiant hero." Such crap! You're no hero, just a piece of meat about to be butchered.*

He turned the knife in his hand and fairly salivated.

Jim Bobb could stand it no longer. He jumped to his feet and emptied his Kahr in the direction of Deputy Granticelli's flashlight, now fifteen feet away.

His ears rang from the reports.

Only one bullet struck Granticelli, but that one splintered his patella, which hurt like *blazes.* So he sank to the ground to favor it.

The move saved his life.

•   •   •

Delaney saw Jim Bobb make his play as the huge cop's torch caught him in its illuminating spray. Saw Bobb's muzzle flashes and the big cop's flashlight blink out and the bastard stagger, obviously hit. Not all the way down, though, so Delaney opened up with the Benelli twelve-bore—seven shots, through the window, double-ought pellets singeing the night, thwacking into who knew what . . .

Now the big lug was down. "Hot *damn,* I'm good!" Delaney crowed.

Not especially.

All seven shots had missed.

Shots from Granticelli's side!

Alston Chalmers's hand closed on his gun just as K.K. Kapatchnik was about to bolt from hiding . . .

Twenty-three feet away.

Dead cop! thought K.K. Kapatchnik when he heard Jim Bobb open the ball. *And this one's made me!* thought K.K. Kapatchnik as he saw Chalmers's hand sweep toward his gun.

K.K. Kapatchnik was wrong on both counts.

After dumping his load, Jim Bobb turned on his heels to duck around the corner, where he ran head-on into Matt Bachison, coming to his aid. The collision was hard, painful, and propitious.

They both went flying.

"What the hell?" said aerobic Web Tyles when he heard shots and jumped to his feet, dropping the latest issue of *Guns & Ammo.* He kicked it in his haste to leave, tearing one of its pages.

No matter. He wouldn't get to read it anyway.

No sooner had Grunt Granticelli hit the turf than a shotgun opened up and the air where his head had been was filled with singing lead. He rolled toward the sheltering mimosa, clutching his ruined knee. Once there, he simply bled quietly, incurious as to what was going on elsewhere.

He had a pension to collect.

Alston Chalmers's gun was unsnapped and coming out when K.K. Kapatchnik burst from his hiding place . . . Chalmers's gun cleared leather as K.K. was taking two swift strides, closing the distance to fifteen feet . . . Chalmers's gun was coming level as Kapatchnik brought up his knife, going for the throat . . . the hole in Chalmers's barrel was pointed at K.K.'s aorta when the gun fired . . . once, twice, thrice . . . the first one slamming into K.K.'s sternum, the second into his neck as the gun climbed in recoil. The third—at a range of two feet—performed a messy lobotomy.

No more K.K.K.

Marvin Delaney was pounding through the house—boots thumping, blood pressure rising, adrenaline pumping—thinking, *Time to get out of Dodge. The feds will come a-running*.

Delaney was right. Running was exactly what Special Agent Webster Tyles was doing. He didn't want to miss anything.

Bounding onto the Faber front porch just in time to see a shadowy figure inside the house dart toward the rear, Tyles decided to cut him off. He headed around back via the west side—not seeing Granticelli in his haste—and arrived not long after Matt Bachison and Jim Bobb had disentangled themselves. Everybody saw everybody at the same time. Bachison had somehow lost his K-9, but he still had the SIG, which he immediately brought to bear. Tyles had a SIG of his own, a .40 caliber, and it was in his hand. At Quantico, Web's instructors had not stressed unaimed fire, so he unconsciously sought his sights. Bachison, on the other hand, was a well-read disciple of Colonel Rex Applegate and thus versed in the fine points of instinctive shooting, in fact had spent many hours practicing. He was very proficient. Instead of searching vainly for his pistol's sights in the dark, he simply pointed the gun as he would a finger and triggered eight shots in less than three seconds. Four of the eight found flesh—one of them plowing through a lung—and abruptly Web Tyles lost all interest in his sights, and pretty much anything else.

In less than ten minutes, he was dead.

The riddled but still-advancing body of K.K. Kapatchnik slammed into Deputy Chalmers with sufficient force to knock him backward onto the ground, Kapatchnik's now-impotent tanto clattering to the ground. So intent had Chalmers been on survival that he had not been aware of the fusillade of shotgun blasts on the far side of the house. At this moment, so delighted was he to be alive that he simply lay there a spell, with K.K.'s blood oozing over him.

Type O-Negative.

Marvin Delaney kicked through the screen back door just as Matt Bachison was popping the hapless Tyles; he watched the agent fall, shouting, "Great shooting!" to Bachison over the ringing of his ears. "Car's this way! Through the fence, next street over!"

They ran to it and drove away.

When silence had descended, Grunt Granticelli, in severe pain, hollered, "Chalmers! You okay?"

From underneath a thoroughly bled-out K.K. Kapatchnik, Alston Chalmers insisted that he was.

As sirens wailed.

Deputy Alston Chalmers did not get home as early as he'd promised his son.

But he did get home.

Chapter 22

"WELL SA'SPARILLA," SAID CONNOR, USING Mary Leigh's favorite swear word. "Lollipop Woods. Now I'm stuck till I draw a blue card." They were in the child's room, surrounded by stuffed animals of various sizes and shapes and textures.

"I get stuck like that all the time. Mommy hardly ever does." Mary Leigh drew a card, then moved her yellow plastic gingerbread man to the nearest green square. "Can we play Chinese checkerds next?" she said.

"Only if you let me win." Gibbs drew a card. Orange.

"Okay," she said lightly.

"I'm just kidding, sweetie."

"I'm not," she insisted, while he moved his piece and the doorbell rang.

Benella answered it, then yelled, *"Connor!"*

It took him maybe four seconds to make it down the stairs.

Outside what remained of the Faber residence, the new FBI agent-in-charge (Tattersall had been very hastily called back to Washington) was livid. He stalked circuitously, barking orders, tossing his maned head, giving a fillip to anyone near him, regardless of whether they needed it. Lights flashed, vehicles came and went, people milled.

Deputy Mike Everette observed from a distance, standing in the yard with Connor and Benella Mae, newly arrived on the scene. "An agent down tends to put the feds off their feed," he commented.

"That's callous," from Benella.

"You want callous? It was obvious to everyone who checked his pulse that Special Agent Tyles was beyond help, and equally obvious to all that Deputy Granticelli was *not,* and in severe pain besides. Nonetheless, this new hotshot AIC sent Tyles off in the first ambulance, not Granticelli." Mike bit off a chew of Red Man.

"What's the story?" Gibbs asked.

Everette told as much as he knew, some of which was pretty obvious.

"So one more of the bad guys bites the dust," Connor said when Everette finished.

"Chalmers shot him to dollrags."

"ID'd him yet?"

"No, but the sheriff had prints lifted then and there, despite the AIC raising hell over his shoulder, wanting to take over. But he had only five men on the scene."

"And Hank had twenty of the county's finest," Connor said.

"Thereabouts," Mike confirmed, and spat on the grass.

"There going to be a council of war?" Benella asked.

"I expect, as soon as this is all mopped up. There's the sheriff now. He wants us."

They all trooped into the Faber house.

Purley Faber was out of the closet at last. Still folded, though; rigor had set in. Yarborough watched as they carted him out. "Poor Purley," he said.

"What I wonder is where's Jerico?" said Wendy Rakestraw, the coroner.

"Wendy?" said the sheriff.

"Uh-huh?"

"Who cares?"

Wendy pinned him with her eyes. "I do, Hank Yarborough. I like cats."

"Two men died tonight. I don't give a bugle blast about Purley Faber's raggedy cat."

Wendy said, "That's one of your problems, Hank. No sensitivity. Want me to point out some others?"

Yarborough grinned. "Naw. My wife thinks that's her job."

Wendy's big face split in return. "See ya, Hank," she said, and whirled away.

Yarborough spoke to one of his minions: "There any coffee? My gallstones might start acting up."

"Irish crème decaf," answered the minion.

"Flavored decaf, wouldn't you know it? Well, fix me a cup, will you? Connor, Bennie?" They declined his offer, so he led them into the den for a confab.

"Look at that window," Benella said, settling into a rocker.

Yarborough nodded. "There was one helluva firefight in here, folks. Notice the spent shells, and all the glass blown outward? Somebody was sure making a twelve-gauge strut its stuff."

"Is that how Tyles bought it?" asked Connor.

"No, he got his around back. All this was directed at Grunt Granticelli. I have no idea why he isn't dead."

Just then the new AIC stomped in, glared at everyone, hiked his trouser legs, and plopped on the settee. "Well, screw me," he said earnestly, running long fingers through his thick head of hair.

"Excuse me, but there's a lady present," Gibbs pointed out.

The AIC, whose name was Havershaw, looked up. "Walk softly, pal. I'm in no mood."

"I don't care what kind of mood you're in, watch your mouth."

Havershaw jumped to his feet. Connor was still on his. Belatedly, the FBI man took note of Connor's size, and kept his distance.

"Oh, boys?" interjected Benella.

Havershaw looked at her.

"The testosterone's so thick in here you can cut it with a butter knife. Don't think I don't appreciate it. The sight of all balls and few brains thrills my heart no end, but could you just can it for now? Please."

Yarborough suppressed a smile as Havershaw sat down. Gibbs remained standing.

"Connor," she continued, "I've heard worse language and you know it. You don't need to shield me from this salty dog. Besides, maybe he feels the need to cuss. He lost a man tonight.

"And you, sir"—she addressed Havershaw—"need to realize that we're all on the same team here. Leggo the posturing."

Havershaw stared at her for maybe twenty seconds, then his face relaxed. "Fair enough."

And they talked for a very long time.

"Man, that was close!" said Jim Bobb, back at the motel.

Delaney punched on the television, surfed the local channels, flopped on the bed, and rubbed his bad ankle. Nothing so far, but it had been only thirty minutes; the anchors were probably still putting on their mascara.

Matt Bachison sat cross-legged on the floor, still suffering the effects of an adrenaline high from offing Web Tyles. "Half of us gone," he said, shaking his head. "We take three banks in one day without a snag, then some skirt blows one of us away and starts a rock slide." He popped some gum in his mouth and the room instantly took on the odor of Double Bubble.

"We'll get her," Delaney assured.

"Yeah?" from Bachison. "When? So far she's shot one

of us, run one of us off a mountain, and her little sister cut one of our throats with a tin-can lid. That's oh-for-three, boys. It's beginning to look like the smart money is on the lady."

The room fell abruptly silent. Marvin Delaney sat so still you couldn't see him breathe. "You want out, Matt?" he said quietly.

"Did I say so?" from Bachison, unimpressed by Delaney's menacing air.

"I'm asking. Because if you do, there's the door," Delaney said, pointing. Then, as if in afterthought: "But the money stays with me."

Silence again. Much more ominous this time. Bachison uncoiled slowly, face like granite. He said, "I'm sticking till this is over, Marv. But let me tell you one thing, you try to cut me out of my share and I'll kill you. No threat, no warning, no games. I'll . . . just . . . fucking . . . kill you."

Delaney shifted to the vertical as well. If he was frightened, he showed no sign of it. "Think you can handle me, do you?"

"Oh, yeah," said Matthew Bachison.

Chapter 23

MARY LEIGH WAS AT A NEIGHBOR'S, CONNOR was on the telephone, and Benella was in her office, at her keyboard, trying to think of something to write. To Seth. Who was eight. And ill. Terminally ill.

Benella had learned of the urgent need for pen pals from a friend who'd lost a son to cancer. The child, eleven when he died, had received letters regularly through a program specifically intended for terminal children. Benella's friend claimed that the correspondence kept her son alive nearly three years longer than doctors had predicted. She further said that she'd heard about the organization—called Love Letters—through the parents of another sick child.

Benella, touched by her friend's story, contacted Love Letters by phone to volunteer, and had since written many letters to children all across the country until the inevitable . . .

But, she'd learned, there were always more names and addresses.

She dawdled now, trying to think of something cheery to tell Seth. *Dear Seth, my brother-in-law was recently killed by a cretin, my sister cut a man's throat and is in a psychiatric ward, I wrecked my new car, and a band of really nasty men are after me, hope things are going well for you, too. Love Benella. This is tough, I'm in such a foul mood. But perhaps so is Seth, maybe just back from chemo, always a load of laughs, I'm sure. Stop feeling sorry for yourself, girlie, and just write the letter.*

So she wrote the letter.

It wasn't bad once she got going.

"Can you mail this for me?" Benella asked Connor as he started out the door.

He glanced at the envelope. "Seth?"

"Yep."

"How is he?"

"Holding on."

He nodded. "You sure you don't want to ride with me? I promised you the Grill, remember?"

"I'd be poor company."

He kissed her forehead. "Never. But I'll mail this for you, despite the fact that it appears to have no stamp."

She made a halfhearted attempt at a smile, failing miserably. He said, "A for effort," pulled her to him, hugged her tightly for a moment, then headed for the city.

Benella went to lie on the divan, depressed to the gills. And there she lay, remembering the night her father had last hugged her . . .

John Richard Sweet had been a fine cop, an honest cop, a caring cop. No matter what travesty he saw when working, he always hoped for better from his fellowman. Often he was disappointed, but sometimes not.

Danny Harper had grown up in the neighborhood, had played in the Sweet home many times, had sat at the table with the family to break bread. Big John had taken Danny and Benella fishing when they were tiny. Danny was from a good home, did well in school, was good to his ailing mother, was a Boy Scout, went regularly to church . . .

And began selling drugs at age eleven.

Mostly he peddled his wares outside the neighborhood, so Benella didn't know about it for years. Nor did Danny Harper's parents, nor his scoutmaster or pastor. But John Richard the cop did, and it vexed him. He'd taken Danny aside on numerous occasions to warn, threaten, cajole. No good; Danny liked the money, so kept it up, all the way into high school, without ever being busted. John tried hard to catch him selling, but was always a step behind.

Until one Christmas Eve . . .

Danny was on his way home, the trunk of his BMW full of gaily wrapped gifts for his mother, but he had a drop to make. No big sale, just a dime bag. But John, out buying last-minute presents of his own, saw it going down. He hesitated briefly—after all, it was Christmas Eve and he was off duty—but decided to throw a scare into Danny. Danny's customer spotted John Richard approaching and drew a gun, a tiny .25 automatic. Danny told the jerk to put the piece away, that it was just John Sweet approaching, a cop to be sure, but an old friend. The buyer, a two-time loser from upstate, didn't put away the piece. John noticed and drew his off-duty revolver, instructing the stranger to drop his gun, NOW!

Danny intervened. "Holster your piece, Mr. Sweet, and he'll put his away. Then we can all talk."

So Officer John Richard Sweet, knowing that Danny was good for his word, holstered his revolver. As soon as he had done so, the man from upstate shot him five times, then Danny Harper once. Both died.

The man from upstate was never caught, and Benella Mae Sweet and her younger sister, Katelin, were orphans.

Chapter 24

CONNOR PLAYED WITH MARY LEIGH ALL MORN-
ing while Benella was refinishing a footstool and con-
ducting a conference call with Lyn Jones, her manager at
the gym. Said gym, Benella's primary source of income,
catered to martial artists and aerobic fitness buffs. Since
Benella was staying away from the place, to avoid leading
trouble there, the day-to-day business concerns were handled by phone.

Sleep had finally overtaken Mary Leigh, so Gibbs had
a chance to catch up on his reading. He habitually devoured
four novels at a clip, going several chapters in one until
reaching a lull, then to another, and so forth. Currently, his
quartet included *The Maggody Militia* by Joan Hess; *The
Great Gatsby;* John J. Nance's *Medusa's Child;* and the
new Thomas Harris. He was finishing a stretch of *Gatsby*
(" . . . like that ashen, fantastic figure gliding toward him
through the amorphous trees") when Benella came in and
sat on his lap.

"Hi," she said.

"Don't bother me, I'm reading."

She took the book from his hands and tossed it onto the table. "Uh-uh," she demurred.

"I *was* reading," he corrected.

She snuggled close.

"Something I haven't had much time for lately."

She burrowed deeper.

"And which I love to do."

"Gripe, gripe, gripe," she said, her sultry voice muffled by his shirt.

It was two hours before he got back to *Gatsby.*

Connor answered the phone. "I'm reading."

Hank Yarborough said, "No, you're not. You're talking to me."

"I'm *trying* to read."

"Forget it. Havershaw wants to palaver."

"Where?"

"At Fibbie headquarters in Charlotte."

"Will they validate my parking?"

"I doubt it."

"Can I bring a book?"

"Which one?"

"Hannibal."

"How far into it are you?"

"Not far. The FBI is about to sacrifice Starling for gunning down Evelda Drumgo and her compeers."

"Compeers?"

"Companions, henchmen, buddies."

"Want me to tell you how the book comes out?"

"Oh, sure, then I won't have to bother reading it."

"Bring Bennie with you."

"Will there be refreshments?"

"No," Hank replied.

"Then I'm not coming," Connor said.

"Four o'clock, sharp," said Hank, and hung up.

•   •   •

The Federal Bureau of Investigation, the local sheriff's department, and the Gibbs contingent were playing show-and-share. The FBI first:

Amos Thorton and Jacoby Lennart had been traced as far back as Fort Jackson, South Carolina, where they'd met during basic training. From there to Fort Ord, California, then elsewhere, inseparable buddies. Their military records, while not spotless, were not especially enlightening. Both had combat experience in the Gulf; neither had distinguished himself; neither rose higher than specialist 4; neither had shown much initiative. After they mustered out at Fort Lewis—following a thirteen-month stint in Korea—the thread of commonality was lost.

No other close friends had been unearthed; in fact, the two seemed to avoid binding ties. They had lived and worked and fathered children while maintaining no demonstrable contact with each other for seven years. Neither had received so much as a parking ticket in all that time. While not exactly bastions of community spirit, the men were at least untroublesome.

End of story.

Sheriff Yarborough's turn:

His office had identified the dead men through their fingerprints, and had accumulated a paper trail courtesy of the authorities back home. Aside from an occasional credit problem the two were as clean as the tooth fairy.

End of story.

Connor and Benella, of course, didn't know anything at all, except what Hank had told them.

End of show-and-share.

"Why am I bothering with you people?" Special Agent Havershaw asked, after Conner had delivered his claim of ignorance.

"Because," said Hank Yarborough, scratching his chin, "it'll take you federal boys months to sneak around the back way on these guys, if you ever do. Remember, the others may have no prior connection to Lennart and Thorton. Hell, they could've met at Disneyland. Bennie here is our shortcut."

"Shortcut?" said Gibbs.

"He means bait," Benella said.

The sheriff: "It's quite likely that the only thing keeping them close by is the desire to clean her clock, if you'll pardon the expression."

"Then I want in," Havershaw said.

"In?" Connor shouted. "What, you guys plan to sit around waiting for the T-rex to come after the sacrificial goat?"

"Connor," said Yarborough. "The situation's gone critical. We'll cover Bennie like Saran Wrap, with the FBI's help, of course. She'll be safe as Tinker Bell, I guarantee."

But, as Connor knew all too well, in situations like this, there were no guarantees.

While in Charlotte, Connor made good on his promise to take Benella to the Mimosa Grill. Hank, too. The sheriff had Carolina mountain trout, from an iron skillet, and vino, from California. Bennie ate what she had told Gibbs she would, and Connor left with his cash supply seriously depleted.

But the smile on Benella's face was worth it.

Chapter 25

A FEW DAYS LATER, A MAN SAID TO BENELLA, over the phone: "Name, rank, and serial number, please."

And Benella said, "Beg pardon?"

And the man said, "Make, year, and model."

And Benella said, "Oh," and proffered the requested information.

"And the date of the accident?"

She gave that, too.

"Now, what happened, exactly?"

"I ran into a tree. Well . . . two trees."

"And how did you manage that?"

"Sir, as you know, this is a no-fault state. If you'll just send an adjuster over to—"

"Madam, we need to know if the damage was intentional."

"Intentional? I just bought the car. Why would I wreck it?"

"Indeed. Which naturally makes me curious as to exactly how the accident happened. Most people are exceptionally careful with a new car."

Sighing, "I ran off the road."

"Yes. And why exactly? Perhaps a celebratory libation? A tiny toddy?"

"It was barely *noon*."

"Ah, several beers, then, to wash down a hoagie."

"What's your name, slick?"

"Jarviston Greer."

"Well, Jarviston Greer, I don't normally *drink* beer with my hoagies, nor anything else alcoholic much before dark, and on those occasions when I *do* get falling-down drunk, I stick close to home so I can vomit in my own toilet. But I surely don't drive. Have we an understanding here?"

"You don't have to be insulting."

"Why should you be the only one? You've been subtly abusive since our conversation started. Now, I won't threaten to cancel my insurance, because one less customer to you is insignificant. So I'm going to make this negotiation personal. Petty pencil pushers like you give all insurance people a bad name, and I don't intend to suffer you gladly.

"So here's what you're going to do. You're going to send an adjuster to the body shop at Mountain City Toyota to speak with the shop manager, Terry Bledsoe. That adjuster will look at my car, okay the repairs, and dance a jig if Terry wants him to . . . or her, I don't mean to imply that all insurance weenies are male, though I suspect the bulk of them are. And then Mountain City will fix my car all up, like new—well, almost—and you will cut them a check. And if the scenario I just detailed does not happen *exactly* as I detailed it, I will personally come over to your office and do things to your body that will make my car look undamaged by comparison. Do you need to read that back to me?"

"Uh, no . . . I think I have it."

"You better!" she said, and hung up the phone, feeling much better.

The insurance weenie followed through on his end. It was a good thing, too.

• • •

"Who was that on the phone, hon?" queried Connor from the laundry room.

"Just some dweeb I was threatening."

"Good to keep in practice."

"Can I use one of your cars this morning?" she said, slipping into a slip.

"Which one?"

"The SVO."

"No. You'd wrap it around a tree. Two trees."

"Thanks, sugar pie."

"The keys are on the credenza."

"And how will you spend your day?"

"I was planning to take Mary Leigh and the boys to the library. There's a puppet show."

"You're taking eleven-year-old boys to a puppet show?"

Long pause. "How about some football in the park?"

"You want a little girl to play football in the park?"

Another pause. "A movie would be good."

"Right." Sweater next; the weather had turned cool.

"Then maybe the park after. Mary Leigh can swing, or slide, or run amok."

Skirt now. Then a strand of pearls, fuss with the hair, dab of perfume, eyes next, and some lipstick, gun in the waistband, check the mirror for a bulge. Ready. And in less than twenty minutes—discounting deciding what to wear, of course. You couldn't count that, not and be fair.

"Nineteen minutes, big guy," she said loudly.

"Does that include decision making?"

"You can't count *that*. That's not dressing, that's choosing."

"Ha," he said.

She went to the bathroom door. "Did you say 'ha'?"

"Ha," he said again.

" 'Ha' as in 'I told you so'?"

Silence.

"Connor?"

More silence.

"Connor Warren Gibbs!"

More silence yet.

She peered into the hall, checking the door to the laundry room. Closed. "Where are you?"

Nothing.

She tiptoed down the hall to the head of the stairs.

"Warren . . ."

"I told you never to call me that," he said, ambushing her from the spare-bedroom doorway and taking her to the carpet.

"Don't smudge the lipstick," she warned, wrapping around him her long legs.

He did anyway.

"So what's on your agenda after the puppets or the movie or the park or all of the above?" she queried, repairing the osculation damage.

Connor was desmudging his own lips in the mirror. "Eggs."

"Eggs?"

"Easter."

"The kind the bunny lays?"

"I knew he left them, I wasn't aware he lays them."

"Of course he does. Where did you think they came from?"

"I'll admit I was vague about that."

"Well, there you are." She finished lipsticking. "Is Mary Leigh involved with the eggs?"

"Why else would I be doing it?"

"Part-time job?"

"Go shop."

"I love it when you're forceful."

He tried to swat her rear, but she adroitly blocked the blow and skipped down the stairs.

"Where we heading, gal?" asked Mike Everette, waiting on Benella's stoop, hat in hand.

"Grocery store, beauty parlor, lingerie department at Belk, gun shop. You know. Woman stuff."

"Can I try on some lingerie?"

"No, your gun might tear the fabric."

"I'll take it off."

"And how will you protect me if bad guys are hiding in the dressing room?"

"Growl at them."

"Faithful Fido," she said as they headed for the car.

"Actually, that's redundant. The root word of 'fido' is *fidus,* Latin for 'faithful.'"

"What's Latin for 'cat'?" she asked.

"Disloyus."

"You made that up."

"Yeah, but it sounds reasonable."

"I like cats."

"You would."

And off they went to run errands.

"They're gonna have her covered now, you know that," Matt Bachison complained.

"So we're going to uncover her."

"How?" questioned Matt.

"Simple. You're going to take out a cop. Or maybe the big bastard. With the Ruger," said Delaney.

"Why not just take *her* out?"

"She's destined for other things. Slower things. Go get the red case, Jim Bobb."

Bobb removed the red case from the trunk of a car, carried it in, and set it on a bed. Inside it: a scoped Ruger heavy-barreled semiautomatic rifle, caliber .22 Long Rifle, with silencer and military sling; a Bushnell rangefinder, accurate within one percent out to three hundred meters; two boxes of Eley subsonic match-grade ammunition. At a hundred steps, with top-flight ammo, the rimfire rifle would group five shots on an orange, or a lemon without the silencer in place.

Good enough.

● ● ●

Barry Snipes and his wife, Gladys, lived across the street from Benella Mae Sweet. The pair owned and managed a pancake restaurant and went to work each morning at four o'clock. In their front yard, among other trees, stood a stately magnolia, well foliated, heavy-limbed, and thirty-two feet tall. It was precisely thirty-one yards from that magnolia to the curb in front of Benella's home, where Deputy Roy Greeson say in his squad car listening to Dr. Laura.

At two in the afternoon, Matt Bachison—wearing a beard and a brown UPS uniform—walked up the sidewalk to the Snipes front door. In his hand was a package for delivery, or so it would appear to anyone watching. Bachison deposited the package on the porch, turned, and began to retrace his steps. He did take a slight detour, stopping beside a tall magnolia tree to raise an odd-looking device to his face, bring it down, then quickly regain the sidewalk to hoof it up the street.

No one noticed him, not even Deputy Roy Greeson, who should have, as he sat in his car a short distance away with Rush Limbaugh in his ear.

Inside the Sweet home, Connor was saying to Mary Leigh: "No, hon, we won't boil the eggs, we'll hard-cook them. Boiling is an improper term. Now, my mother had a very complicated way to hard-cook eggs. For her, it was almost a ritual."

"What's 'ritual' mean?"

"It's a way of doing something the same way every time, kind of like a ceremony."

"Like decorating the tree at Christmas?"

"Right."

"So how did your mom boil . . . I mean hard-cook eggs?"

"She pricked the eggshell with a needle, covered it with cold water, brought the water to a boil, left the egg standing in hot water for exactly seventeen minutes, dropped it into ice water, then brought the original water back to a boil for ten seconds, and finally placed the egg back into ice water."

"No wonder it's called hard-cooked."

Gibbs smiled at that.

"So how hard are we gonna cook 'em?" asked Mary Leigh.

"We'll use a method I learned from a cookbook. First, we'll use eggs that are at least a week old. Fresh eggs are hard to peel." He went to the fridge. "See here? I turned the carton over last night, to center the yolks."

"That's the yellow stuff."

"Right." Connor put a dozen eggs into a shallow pan, covered them with a couple inches of tap water, and added a tablespoon of salt to the water.

"Why did you put sugar in?" Mary Leigh wanted to know.

"That was salt. It'll help seal any tiny cracks in the shells." He partially covered the eggs with the pan lid, brought the water to a roiling boil, then completely covered the pan and reduced the heat to low, letting the eggs simmer for thirty seconds. Then he removed the pan from the heating element and let it stand for fifteen minutes, still covered, then drained off the hot water and placed the eggs under the faucet, running cold water over them for about five minutes, to cool them completely.

Mary Leigh watched every move. As the eggs were cooling under the cascading stream, she asked, "Is this gonna be our ritual?"

"If you want it to be."

"Can I do the next batch?"

"If you'll let me help. The stove gets really hot. The water, too."

"Okay, you can help."

And he did.

•   •   •

Benella, newly redecorated with a rinse and a perm, was currently examining apples at an open market. "What's your favorite?" she asked Mike Everette, there beside her.

"Braeburn, hands down. Especially for baking. They hold their shape."

She stared at him. "They don't have Braeburns."

"What do you want the apples for, to bake in a pie?"

"Just munching."

"Esopus Spitzenburg, then. Very sweet and spicy."

Everette's daddy owned apple orchards in four states, and he'd started picking for extra money at an early age.

"Gimme a break," said Benella. "This is just a local market."

"Okay." He smiled. "Try some of those Jonagolds. They've got yellow flesh and a balanced sweet-tart flavor."

Benella instructed the attendant, who said, "Want those in a paper poke, ma'am?"

"Plastic's fine." She received her apples and the two headed for the tea section; when Connor was deprived of Emperor's Choice for long, he tended to grouch.

"That stuff's dear," Everette observed.

"Connor will pay me back," she said as, two aisles away, someone watched them closely.

"How far?" Delaney asked.

"Thirty-one yards to the patrol car," Matt Bachison informed him. "Seventy-six to the lady's front door."

"There a streetlight?"

"Right beside the car."

"Then you can do it after dark."

"Depends. It's colder at night. The cop's window has to be down for the .22."

"True." Delaney thought a minute. "If you climb that tree after dark, can you get down and away in daylight without being spotted?"

"Don't see why not, unless someone notices the cop sitting there with a hole in his head. The shot won't make any noise."

"Hey, Jim?" called Delaney.

"Yo," from the bathroom, where Bobb was plucking his eyebrows, which tended to grow together.

"Come in here."

Bobb came in. "Yeah?"

"Change of plan. You'll be down the street, in a boosted car. If you don't see Matt come down out of the tree and make it away, or if anyone spots him, or if anyone spots the dead cop, it falls to you to create a diversion."

"What kind of diversion?"

"Just fart, that'd do it," Bachison quipped.

"Funny," Bobb rejoined.

"I'm sure you'll come up with a plan," said Delaney. "Run over a dog or something."

Jim said, "How will I know when Matt pops the guy?"

They considered that.

"Maybe you could drop something to the ground," Delaney suggested to Bachison.

"Better yet, how about I just set off firecrackers?" Bachison said sarcastically. Then, seriously: "Here's what I'll do. Jim Bobb, you park down the street to my left, facing me. After I shoot the cop, I'll take out your outside passenger mirror to get your attention. After you see me climb down, you just leave, assuming I don't attract a following, of course."

"Voilà," said Marvin Delaney.

And they adjourned the meeting.

"Tea! I was all out," said Connor, unloading the bags.

"Aren't I sweet?" Benella said.

"And not in name only, snookems."

"I think I'm gonna be sick," from Everette, now seated at the counter.

"You want lunch or not?" Gibbs replied.

"What a cute couple you two make," Everette amended.

"That's better. Mary Leigh!" Connor called.

"Threatening to withhold food from a law enforcement officer. Isn't that illegal, Bennie?"

"It certainly should be," Benella agreed, digging out the flatware.

"What?" came a distant tiny voice.

"Lunch, sweetheart!"

"Can I bring Winkie?"

"Sure!"

"And Pooh?"

"Of course!" Connor continued to speak loudly.

"And Barney?"

"You bet!"

So she brought down all three, and while they ate lunch, she told Mike and Aunt Bennie how to hard-cook eggs.

While outside, down the block, someone watched.

That very same someone was still watching at eleven-forty that night when Matthew Bachison went up his tree with the cased Ruger and a thermos of very hot cocoa. And two doughnuts.

Odd, someone thought, and stepped back into the shadows to remain unobserved, there to wait all night, watching.

Chapter 26

JIM BOBB PULLED UP TO THE CURB JUST AFTER daybreak, seventy yards from the magnolia. The cop hadn't shown yet, so he eased down in his seat, turned on the radio, and went to sleep with the motor running, because it was freezing out.

Matt was cold and stiff and his fingers felt like they'd been lubricated with pine rosin. He flexed them repeatedly. A squirrel hopped on the ground, rooting for nuts. Somewhere off to the north, a dog barked. A kid bicycled the street, tossing newspapers. The air smelled of wood smoke and bacon grease and, faintly, a cigarette. Low clouds scudded overhead as a woodpecker droned.

What kind of wood would a woodpecker peck if a woodpecker could peck wood? Stupid song. What brought that on?

The squirrel abandoned the yard for better pickings elsewhere. And not far down the street, someone watched; someone equally cold, equally stiff.

Equally patient.

•   •   •

Roy Greeson, on the last morning of his life, was in no special hurry. *Hell, Everette's inside the house. What they need me for?* But he hadn't said that to the sheriff when Yarborough had been explaining his assignment. Pulling into Biscuitville, Roy waved to Sally Peeler, just going to work. Wasn't she a vixen, though? Maybe tonight, after he got off, he'd call her up for a date, give her a thrill.

Maybe, he thought.

Then again, maybe not.

Comings and goings on the street, now. People heading to work, or school, or to Mars for all Matt Bachison knew. He felt as exposed as a flasher up a flagpole. Whose damn-fool idea was this, anyhow?

His.

What in the hell is he still up there for? someone thought. *I'm freezing to* death. *So is he, I'll bet. Well, I can take it if he can.*

Full of biscuits and bonhomie, Roy Greeson left a tip, grabbed his hat, and strutted to his car.

He tilted his hat rakishly in case anyone was watching.

No one was.

Jim Bobb was awake and quaffing lukewarm java from a cardboard cup with LINDY'S DINER on its side as down the street and up his perch Matt Bachison thought: *Here he comes, and it's about damn time. If his window's up, I'm going through the glass before I fall out of this stupid tree.*

But he knew he couldn't.

Three blocks away, teens Greg Brandt and Larry Larkin were climbing into Greg's new BMW. "Betcha can't hit sixty between here and the stop sign," Larry dared.

"My old man'd kill me if he hears me squeal off," from

Greg as he backed into the street. "Besides, the engine's still cold."

"Pussy," taunted Larry.

And off they went.

"*Man,* it's cold," twelve-year-old Charley Finnigan said to himself as he tossed his last paper. "I need some hot, hot oatmeal," he said, pedaling hard and thinking fondly of an impending breakfast. So caught up was he in those preprandial thoughts that he squirted out between two parked cars without looking . . .

Directly into the path of a speeding BMW.

"LOOK OUT!" screamed Larry Larkin.

Too late.

Deputy Roy Taggart Greeson didn't see the kid on the bike; he was too intent on the idiot in the Bimmer. "What the—?" he said aloud.

His final words.

Greg Brandt wrenched the wheel just in time to miss the kid on the bike but not the patrol car, which he hit head-on at sixty-seven miles an hour. Since the deputy's vehicle was doing thirty, the impact was more than sufficient to send an unbelted Roy Greeson through the windshield.

Oh shit, thought Greg Brandt, his left leg *on fire* as he sat pinned in his car in front of Benella Mae Sweet's house.

Oh shit! thought Jim Bobb, in his car down the street.

Oh shit! thought someone who had been watching closely.

Oh shit! thought Matt Bachison, from his aerie.

Dadburn it! thought Charley Finnigan, unhurt but on his rump in the street.

Then all of them quickly left the scene, except for Greg Brandt and Larry Larkin.

They were in a bad way.

•   •   •

Connor was in the kitchen when he heard the crash. Benella was upstairs giving Mary Leigh a bath when Mike Everette hollered up the stairwell, "EVERYBODY STAY INSIDE!" Benella ignored him. Pounding down the stairs as Connor came running down the hall, she yelled, "Connor, stay with Mary Leigh!"

Then out the door she flashed.

Greg Brandt was conscious and hurting badly when Mike Everette reached him, but he stayed fairly still as the big deputy attended to him.

Larry Larkin stayed completely still as Benella lifted an eyelid, listened to his chest, then rapidly unbuckled his seat belt and gently laid him on the cold ground to perform CPR. She undoubtedly saved his life.

His parents never let him ride in a car with Greg Brandt again.

Chapter 27

THE LARKINS HAD JUST LEFT, GRIM AND TEARY-eyed, but profuse with thanks to Benella for saving their son's life. Benella, in the wake of such outpouring, was a bit damp herself. Mary Leigh was upstairs napping, Connor was nursing a cup of black tea, Hank Yarborough was darkly somber, and AIC Havershaw was in a funk. "What a fiasco," Havershaw was saying as he circumnavigated the room. "This burg has more crap going on than Chicago in the thirties."

"Two kids speeding is hardly catastrophic," Connor commented. "Unfortunate, stupid, and deadly, but not pertinent to our problem."

"We've been camped nearby for two days. These guys can't wait forever. For all we know, they were planning a move for this morning and this debacle scared them off," grumped the AIC.

Yarborough spoke for the first time. "Havershaw?"

"What?"

"I've got a man in the morgue, the third in not much

more than a week. This department hasn't lost three men in its history. Show some respect."

Havershaw sat down. "I'm sorry, Sheriff. About your men, about Ms. Sweet, being put in this position, about losing one of my best agents. But being sorry doesn't help."

"I'll just have to reassign someone, pull a man from somewhere else. But my resources are limited. I was stretched pretty thin as it was, and now this," Hank Yarborough said as the doorbell sounded.

Connor answered it, with Everette right beside him, just in case. "Yes?"

Someone tall and lean and pale and cold and disheveled, even in jeans and a plaid wool coat and navy watch cap, said, "Can I join the meeting?"

Everette said, "What meeting?"

"You, Mr. Gibbs here, and Ms. Sweet, Sheriff Yarborough, the FBI's top dog from Charlotte. That meeting."

"How in the—" Everette began, but Connor said, "Come in."

"Thanks. I will."

Seated with decaf in a blue mug, relieved of outer garments, brown hair in disarray from all night under a cap, curious eyes taking in everyone and everything, the center of attention: "My name is J.P. Foster. I'm an investigative reporter."

"For whom?" asked Havershaw.

Foster waved a hand. "It's not important."

"No interviews," Connor said sharply.

Shake of the tousled head. "I'm not here for an interview."

"Then why are you here, J.P.? You don't mind if I call you J.P.?" said the sheriff.

"Of course not, Hank."

Benella hid her smile behind a hand.

"In a moment, I'll tell you why I'm here," said the newcomer. "First, a negotiation."

"What's to negotiate?" replied Havershaw. Yarborough just squinted and stared and stroked his chin.

"Immunity."

Havershaw's suspicious nose smelled a rat. "From what?"

"Anything at all."

Yarborough worried his stubbled chin some more. "Been in town long?"

"Couple days," the reporter admitted.

"Been asking around, not just drinking coffee at the hotel waiting for something to happen?"

A nod and a sip of coffee, concurrent. "Waiting's not my style, watching is. I observe."

"So what have you observed?" said Yarborough.

"We have a deal?"

"I don't deal with reporters," snapped Havershaw.

"Let's not be hasty," cautioned Hank. "If J.P. here hadn't observed something pretty important, there'd be no concern about immunity." He paused, then asked, "Did you break any laws?"

"None that I know of," said Foster.

"Okay," Hank agreed.

"Okay what?" from Havershaw.

"I'll grant immunity. I wanta hear this."

"That's up to a prosecutor," Havershaw protested.

"Not if what I say stays in this room," Foster insisted. "Or at least the fact that the information came from me."

Havershaw still hesitated.

"Come on," Benella prompted. "Let's hear this."

Havershaw relented. "It'd better be good."

"I'll let you decide," said J.P. "You know that big magnolia tree across the way?"

"In the Snipeses' yard?" Connor specified.

"If that's the yard directly across the street." Foster took a sip for dramatic effect. "Last night a man climbed that very magnolia. With a rifle. He was still up there this morning."

•   •   •

Connor was practically vibrating, and couldn't believe that no one else seemed to be as upset as he was. The guy in the tree had obviously been waiting to shoot Benella, and knowing that Foster had still lurked all night, watching instead of coming to warn them, incensed him! Bennie could well be *dead*, and he said as much.

"If I had seen Ms. Sweet come out, I'd have yelled," J.P. insisted. "Besides, Everette usually precedes, and the gunman wasn't after him."

"As far as you know?" Hank Yarborough remarked casually.

That silenced everyone.

"Why would they want to shoot me?" Mike asked after a long moment.

"Who knows? Listen, these guys should have been long gone by now. The longer they linger, the better their chances of being nabbed, yet they don't seem to care. Obviously, we don't spook 'em. And if we don't scare 'em, then why *not* shoot a cop? Or maybe Connor. They might figure that would spook *us*."

"Connor?" from a suddenly worried Benella. "Why shoot him?"

"Again, who knows? I can't figure these guys. They're bold—they had to be to knock over three banks simultaneously. Then they kill Purley Faber right down the street from us, and move into his house, then drop an FBI man and a deputy when we start closing in. Now they stick a sniper in a tree right under our noses. These fellas scare the hell out of me."

Everyone was quiet again, until Everette broke the silence: "So what's next?"

"We have forensics go over the tree. Maybe the sniper left something behind," Havershaw said.

"I'll be around," Foster said, standing, then making for the door.

Everette scrutinized that hip-swinging exit carefully, then whispered to Gibbs, "Nice boobs."

"Gorgeous eyes, too," Connor observed.

"Blue as blue can be," from Mike, obviously smitten. "I'll keep a peeled eye on J.P. Foster."

Benella, overhearing the exchange, mumbled, "It's a gonad thing," and smiled to herself.

Chapter 28

THE ROOM WAS STARTING TO STINK. THREE GUYS too often missing the toilet, neglecting to brush their teeth, subsisting on greasy provender, bowels roiled by nocturnal spates of flatulence as they slept on sweaty sheets.

No maid service, either.

At the moment, Jim Bobb was scratching an oily armpit and saying, "No shit? Right through the windshield?"

"Hit the pavement so hard I'd swear my tree jumped. You should've heard his head go"—Matt paused in his narrative to make an onomatopoeic *pop* with his lips—"when he landed, like smacking a melon with a bung starter."

Bobb delighted in the image. Delaney, however, was annoyed. "But now we've got to start all over, and after all the trouble we went to."

"Not to mention me freezing my fundament all night. Shuck that noise," was Bachison's assessment.

"I've been thinking," Delaney went on. "Maybe there's a better way."

And he laid it out.

•   •   •

Anderson and Brenda Zane had dated since junior high school and were perfectly suited to one another. And, surprise, surprise, were still deeply in love. They'd been married nine years (to the day) when they closed on their first new home (a brick ranch). She ran a shoe store and he was a barber, and they had lived all their married lives in a ramshackle old house that had been in Brenda's family since World War I. Finally, after much scraping and saving and scrimping and buying bargain brands, they had accumulated enough scratch for a down payment on their dream home. They celebrated with champagne (domestic) and sizzling tenderloin (eight-ounce) and chocolate cheesecake (spare no expense), then made familiar, comfortable whoopee until long past midnight. Next morning, Anderson drove a "For Rent" sign into the ground in front of the old home place.

Cradling the classified section (real estate) between his chest and the steering wheel, Jim Bobb found the house. Big sucker. Lots of rooms. Old, though. "Hope they got indoor toilets," he said aloud, and snorted at his wit. Parking in the driveway, he went up the walk to knock.

A tall, spare twenty-something man let him in, introduced himself as Anderson Somebody, and when his wife came in (a juicy specimen), allowed as how she was Brenda. They chatted amiably for a while, then Anderson turned away for an instant and Jim Bobb cracked him a good one on the side of the head. Down went Anderson. Brenda started to scream, so Jim Bobb backhanded her across the kitchen table, then stuck a knife under her nose. That quieted her right down. He duct-taped her to a kitchen chair, got out his ice pick, and knelt beside her prostrate husband.

"If you watch this, you and I will get along. You don't and you're next," he promised.

Then he performed his magic trick, using Anderson's ear as a prop and the ice pick as a swizzle stick. Despite deep unconsciousness, Anderson's body jerked spasmodically and continuously, because Jim Bobb didn't go in very deep at first. Eventually, the body ceased all movement.

Brenda watched through a veil of tears and despair.

Chapter 29

MARY LEIGH WAS PLAYING HOPSCOTCH IN THE Stuart backyard. Connor, too. He was doing pretty well, his big feet usually planting themselves pretty much where intended.

"You're very good at this," commented Mary Leigh diplomatically.

"Thanks."

She took his hand, little face earnest. "Are you as good as me?"

He scooped her up, nestling her into the crook of his thick left arm. "Never that good. What's next?"

"Get Corny Kind," she said, pointing. "Corny Kind" was Mary Leigh's favorite Beanie Baby, in the shape of a piece of candy corn but with arms and legs.

Gibbs picked it up from its resting place against a croquet wicket. "Got him."

"Her," she corrected.

"Her."

"When can I go see Mommy?"

"Soon."

"Damorrow?"

"Maybe not that soon. We'll see. I talked to her doctor on the phone. She's doing better, but she's not well yet."

"Yesternight?"

"I'm sorry?"

"Did you talk to the doctor yesternight?"

"Oh . . . No, this morning."

They were going in the back, the screen door slamming shut behind them. "Do I have ballet today?"

"At three."

"Goody," she said.

He smiled in response.

"Can we play horsey now?"

"My knees are numb," Connor protested.

"Pleeeze?"

"All right," he said, feigning pique.

But she saw right through him.

Twelve-oh-nine. Lunch. Mary Leigh at the kitchen table with six bows in her hair, all colors. And two hair bands. She'd put them there herself that morning, but Aunt Bennie had taken most of them out before she'd left. Mary Leigh immediately put them back. Currently, she was examining a bowl Connor had placed before her. "I hate collards," she intoned.

"How about with ketchup?"

"How 'bout I don't eat 'em."

"They're good for you."

"How about *you* eat 'em."

He did, a mouthful. "Yum," he said.

Ineffective. She picked up his sandwich and took a small bite, then made a face. "What is *this*?"

"Refried-beans-and-tomato sandwich, with onions and garlic and crumbled cotija cheese."

"Yuck. What kinda cheese?"

"Cotija."

"Mommy likes Colby."

He ate some of his sandwich. "Me, too."

"I don't like Colby."

"That's okay. I don't like rutabagas."

"What's rutabagas?"

"Something you should never put in your mouth."

She giggled. "Can I have some more samwich?"

"Thought you didn't like it."

"I didn't say so."

"You said 'yuck.' "

"That doesn't mean I don't want more," she reasoned, and they spent a pleasant lunchtime together.

"Is it time for ballet yet?"

Mary Leigh had appeared soundlessly at the bottom of the stairs dressed all in white—tights, leotard, skirt, and shoes. And a white bow in her curls. Just one this time.

"Not quite, sweetheart," Gibbs said, putting down the newspaper. "Another twenty minutes."

"Do I gotta take a nap? It'll smush my ribbon."

"How about a little piano practice?"

And she did, playing "Waltz Time" and "Popcorn" and "A Super Sorta Special Song" with a verve and panache beyond her years.

Connor moved his foot along with the music.

Chapter 30

ARCHDALE HOWARD HAD LONG MAINTAINED that he was directly related to the Howards of Stooge fame. And although he did indeed look very much like a benignant Moe, most folks discounted his claim. After all, they reasoned, any true Stooge relative should be well-to-do, and old Arch had never shown signs of money.

As if to underscore the point, there he sat at the diner, on his customary stool, at his afternoon break, slurping coffee from a saucer without so much as a vanilla wafer to soak it up, the tightwad.

"More coffee, Arch?" proffered Fat Gerty, who used to be, but was now down to 112 pounds on account of having her stomach stapled. Though fat she no longer was, pretty she would never manage; excess skin hung off her in folds, she had a wart on the side of her nose, and her hair grew in tufts from her ears. Still, she was affable.

"No thanks, Gert," Archdale declined. "Time's a-wastin'." He stood, brushed imaginary lint from his uniform, hitched his trousers, and headed for his car, a ten-year-old Chevy that he'd been delivering mail out of despite rain, gloom, and—sometimes—snow. He squinted in the afternoon sun; some nebbish in a van had parked so close that Arch would barely be able to get his door open. He tried anyway, but didn't make it.

Because the sliding door of the van opened and rough hands jerked him inside.

Deputy Alston Chalmers glanced up from *People* when he heard a vehicle approach his squad car. In his rearview he saw Archdale Howard's old Chevy pull into the Stuart driveway. Chalmers waved, then went back to his magazine as the Chevy disappeared behind tall bushes.

The mailman, tall and besuited and whistling a gay tune, strode jauntily up the walk toward Mary Leigh, who was sweeping grit out the front door with her toy broom with Winkie under one arm. The mailman had a package in hand, and he grinned and said, "Hi, Mary Leigh. Where's Mr. Gibbs?"

"In the basement," said the girl.

"And Ms. Sweet?"

"In the shower."

"How about Deputy Everette?"

"In the kitchen eating Jell-O."

"Well, I have this box for Mr. Gibbs, and a larger one in my car. Can you help me carry it? I'm too old to carry it all by myself."

He didn't look all that old to Mary Leigh, but he was smiling real big and seemed nice enough, so she said, "Sure I will," and the two of them went out to his car.

It was just that easy.

Benella was toweling off when Connor stuck his head in the bathroom door. "Have you seen Mary Leigh?"

"She was downstairs pretending to sweep just before I climbed into the shower."

"I'll go check with Mike," he said, and closed the door.

Twelve minutes later, the FBI was on the scene.

· · ·

"I saw Archdale Howard's Chevy pull in about fifteen minutes ago," said Deputy Chalmers.

"Who's Archdale Howard?" asked Havershaw.

"The mailman," from Connor, sitting on the couch with Benella, massaging her neck. She was distraught.

"Funny thing is, nobody's got their mail yet. Not on this street. I checked," Chalmers said.

Hank Yarborough said, "Phone Gerty. See if Arch stopped by for his cup of joe."

"Right," said Chalmers, and went to make the call.

"I can't believe we let them take her," Benella moaned. "I simply cannot *believe* it."

"There was no reason to think they'd go after her," Connor tried to soothe.

"The hell there wasn't. They wanted me. What better way than through her?" She lowered her head, rotated her neck to ease accumulated tension. Ineffective.

"They'll call, Bennie. Then we'll see what's up," Yarborough said . . . as the phone rang.

Everyone sprang into action. tracing devices were activated, headsets were shoved hurriedly into place, blood pressures jumped twenty points. On cue, Benella picked up the phone, said hello, listened for five seconds, then held it out toward Yarborough. "For you."

The sheriff snapped it up. "Yeah?"

"Yeah," he said again.

"When did you first notice one missing?" he queried.

"Yeah," he said for the last time.

"We're on the way. No, don't do anything, Jack! Just lock your door and keep an eye out." He punched off the phone. "Let's go. I'll tell you about it in the car."

After calling for every available man, and giving Havershaw time to do the same, Yarborough explained their hurry: The man on the phone had been Jack Murphy, day clerk at a motel just off the interstate. Ten days ago, three men had rented double rooms, all at different times but on the same day, one man per room, none of them together. In fact, there had been no indication at all that they knew one another. Nonetheless Jack, watching them come and go, noticed that they began to fraternize. He also noticed that a pair of other men had joined them. Though he never saw a rig, he figured them all for truckers. Then he didn't see one of them for a while, and figured that the man had lit out. A couple days ago, one of the others disappeared, or at least Jack hadn't seen him around. Which started him thinking. He reread an article in the paper—about a shooting at some Faber guy's house—and the description of the man killed by police seemed to tally with the guy who'd recently disappeared.

So he called Yarborough.

And that was why they were speeding to the motel with the roof lit but no siren . . .

"Anybody inside?" the sheriff asked Murphy.

"Ain't seen nobody, but oftentimes I don't. They stay inside for long spells, or come and go when I'm in the back, or off duty. That I ain't seen 'em don't mean nothing," Jack hypothesized.

"Got an unoccupied room?"

"Lots."

"One out of their range of vision, should they be looking?"

"One-oh-four, right around the corner."

"Show me."

The Sheriff and three of his men—and Havershaw—went to room 104. Hank examined the door, both inside and out. "All the doors like this one?" he asked Murphy.

"You bet. One good kick right . . . there"—he pointed—"and you're in."

"Unless the chain's on," Havershaw warned.

"Then it'd take two good kicks, right quick like," Jack instructed unnecessarily.

"What if the little girl's near the door?" Everette asked.

"Then we'll have to be very fast and very good," said Yarborough.

"Or very lucky," from Havershaw.

No more conversation.

"How long's he been gone?" Jim Bobb said.

"About two hours. Look, he wanted to go alone, so fine, he went alone. Chances are he can handle the task. If not, I'll come up with something else," assured Delaney as he watched on television a full-figured woman—unfettered by clothing or modesty—wrestle a similarly endowed lady, both in a bed of slaw. At the moment, it was difficult to tell who was winning.

Bobb looked at his watch, then pointed at a table and said, "You want them fries?"

"No. They're cold."

Jim snatched them up.

After having gained close proximity to the proper room—two men to one side of the doorway, two on the other, ten nearby with drawn guns—the sheriff whispered, "Now!" and Mike Everette kicked in the door.

When the door burst open, Delaney came up with his gun and Jim Bobb nearly fell off the sofa. Matt Bachison stood in the doorway, grinning possumlike. "Kinda jumpy, aren't you boys?"

"One day that twisted sense of humor's going to get you shot," said Delaney, holstering his Colt. "How'd it go?"

"Piece of cake, like I told you it'd be."

"So where's the kid?"

"In the van, asleep. Chloroform takes a while to wear off."

"Go get her," Delaney ordered. Matt did.

"Shit!" said Mike Everette.

"My sentiments exactly," from the sheriff.

"Get a team in here, right now!" Havershaw barked to an underling.

The underling went to summon a team.

"No question these were the ones," Yarborough stated, looking around.

Benella was over by one of the beds, staring into space. Gibbs was going over the room inch by inch.

"Connor?" said the sheriff. "We don't want to muck up the scene." Belaboring the obvious.

Gibbs, unoffended, nodded. "I won't touch anything."

Yarborough nodded in return and left.

Benella looked at Gibbs. "It's my fault."

"No. It's *their* fault."

"Because of me Mary Leigh is gone, Katelin is a mental case, and an FBI man is dead, not to mention Roy Greeson. It all comes back to me. If I'd just—"

"What? Stepped out into the street and yelled, 'Here I am. Come get me?'"

"More or less."

"Then *you'd* be dead."

"But the others wouldn't. And Mary Leigh . . ."

Connor went over and pulled her to him. "Don't blame yourself. This is *not* your doing."

Benella placed her forehead against Connor's broad chest and breathed deeply. She was coming to a decision.

Inside the Zanes' downstairs bathroom, Mary Leigh was kicking and screaming and raising a ruckus, and Matthew Bachison said to his cronies, "Listen to that. Didn't I tell you guys a house would be better than where we were? Aren't you glad we moved?"

Marvin Delaney said, "Tickled pink. Now somebody shut her mouth."

Jim Bobb jumped up. "I'll do it."

Matt Bachison said, hand against Bobb's chest, "No, I will."

And he did, while Jim Bobb sat and sulked.

•   •   •

Matt Bachison stuck his head around the door and asked: "What's the matter, sugar?"

A bar of soap narrowly missed his head, then bounced off the wall. "I don't like being locked up in this old *bath-room*!" Mary Leigh exclaimed.

"Sorry, little one, but you have to be locked up. There are windows in the other rooms, and you've been making a lot of noise. At least you have a TV in here. Rabbit ears are better than nothing. By the way, are you hungry?"

She put down the deodorant she'd been about to throw. "Rabbit ears?"

"Those long rods on top of the TV." He asked again, "Are you hungry?"

She thought about it. "What can I have?"

"What do you want?"

"Choc'lit pudding," she announced. "And a samwich."

"What kind of sandwich?"

Her little brow knit, searching. "Fried beets and damatos, with cheese."

His stomach rolled involuntarily. "Not a pizza?"

"Wellll . . . Okay, but no mushrooms."

"No mushrooms. I'll go get it right now."

"And pudding," she reminded.

"You got it." He closed and locked the door.

Before going to the grocery store, Bachison drew Marvin Delaney aside. "You have nothing to say to that little girl, right?"

Delaney was surprised. "What would I have to say to her?"

"Right. Keep it that way. I stole her, she's mine."

"Sure, Matt, she's yours. After we use her for trading purposes, do whatever you want with her." Delaney couldn't understand the point of this conversation.

"Right," Bachison said, then: "Hey, Jim!"

"Yo," from the den.

"Come here a minute."

"Yo," Bobb said, appearing from around the corner.

"I'm making a food run. Want anything?"

"Some Apple Jacks and a Hershey bar, almonds. And salsa, we're almost out. And an A&W root beer. Big bottle."

"That all?"

"I reckon. For now, anyway."

"Okay." Matt turned to go, and then, as if in afterthought: "Oh, and Jim?"

"Huh?"

"You so much as go near that little girl, for any reason at all, and I'll chloroform *you*, then cut all your fingers off, clear up to the knuckles. Understand?"

Jim bobbed his head.

"Tell me."

"I understand," he said. And he did. But he didn't like it.

And Jim Bobb was strong, and tough, and mean, and he could hold a grudge.

One hour after dark, Archdale Howard climbed naked out of a Dumpster beside State Road 4156, four miles north of the Wendover city limit. Suffering mildly from exposure and the aftereffects of chloroform, he flagged down a car driven by Miss Agatha Spey (a spinster from Southport), who, upon seeing a pale, unclothed apparition suddenly appear in her headlights, skidded into a full three-sixty, and, once stopped, promptly fainted. "Sorry lady," Arch said as he shoved Agatha aside to slip beneath the steering wheel, "but if I stay out there, I'll catch my death." He drove straight to the sheriff's department, bare buttocks clinging to the vinyl seat. Miss Agatha woke during the jolting journey, noticed her uninvited chauffeur's peaked body right *next* to her, and once again sought refuge in syncope. She was soon revived and wanted tea.

Chapter 31

They crowded around him as he gulped his soup.

"What happened, Arch?" said the front-desk deputy.

"Who knows?" Archdale's teeth chattered against his cup, so he pulled the blanket tighter around himself. "I had my coffee, same's I always do. Went out to my car, same's I always do. Some *bulvon* in a white van had parked too close by half. When I was trying to squeeze in my door, somebody grabbed me from behind, slammed me back, and stuck a foul-smelling cloth up my nose. That's all I remember."

"Did you see anything inside the van?" a friend asked.

Archdale gave him such a look. "Yeah. The inside of my eyelids."

And that pretty much ended the debriefing.

Forensics went over the motel room, and the rooms rented earlier by the other men, plus the Dumpster on S.R. 4156. Nada; at least nothing that helped. A few empty cartridge cases, a ten-dollar bill, some trash, a comb, a partial bottle of root beer, two pennies and a nickel under the bed, trash, some bank wrappers from Knoxville, a shower cap, trash, a broken bootlace, a Virginia map, a quantity of what appeared to be eyebrow hair in the sink, a *TV Guide,* and some trash. The place was filthy.

The lab boys were happy, though; there were prints galore. "It's almost as if these fellows couldn't care less if we know who they are," one technician observed.

"That's what worries me," said another. "When that's the case, they're hard to take down. And they generally don't give up, you have to cut them off at the knees."

The first tech said, low-voiced, "We tried that already. It didn't go as planned."

"Just shut up and do your job," said the supervisor. "Let the grown-ups worry about taking these scalawags out."

One tech mouthed, "Scalawags?" when the supervisor turned away, but they went on with their jobs and shut up.

At the Gibbs home, Yarborough was saying, "It's just a matter of time, Bennie. They don't want Mary Leigh, except as a lever." He placed a consoling hand on her arm.

"I know," she responded. "But why are they waiting?"

"Letting you stew in your own juice, is my guess."

"Well, it's working. I'm going up to lie down."

"Do that. If anything breaks, you'll be the first to know," Hank promised.

So upstairs Benella trudged, light of head and heavy of heart, to lie down and rest. She hoped.

"Bennie." A gentle hand was pulling her up, up, up, and out of a deep sleep.

"Hmm?" She smacked her lips, which tasted pretty bad.

Connor said, "It's Katelin's doctor," and held out the cordless.

"Hello?" Benella said into it, then listened groggily for a half minute.

"No," she said, then "no" again, and finally an insistent "No, Doctor, I *can't*," and punched off the instrument.

"What is it?" asked Gibbs.

Benella had buried her face in the pillow. She said something, her voice so muffled Connor couldn't make it out.

"I can't hear you, babe."

She jerked her head up. "Katelin is much better!" she snapped.

"Great."

"No, it isn't. She wants to see me. Tonight."

"So go see her. It'll keep your mind off—"

"Are you crazy?"

He was taken aback by her vehemence.

"I *can't* go see her!" she said harshly. "What am I going to say? 'Hi, Katey, sorry about your husband being killed, and you having to cut that guy's throat and all, and by the way, *your daughter's been kidnapped*!'" She threw herself back into the pillow.

Good point, thought Connor. Then: "Want me to go instead?"

Benella looked up. "What'll you tell her?"

"That the strain has gotten to you. That you're too tired to—"

"About *Mary Leigh*." Benella's patience was paper-thin.

"That she's fine, eating well, missing her mommy."

"You don't know any of that's true."

"I don't know it's not, either. I'll assume it's true until proven otherwise. Like Hank said, those guys are after you. Why should they hurt Mary Leigh?"

"Because they're animals."

"Maybe, but we have to think positive."

"*You* think positive. I'm going to lie here envisioning those creeps being given lethal injections."

"And I'll go see Katelin."

"Give her my love." Benella sank back into the pillow.

Gibbs kissed her between the shoulder blades and left.

Chapter 32

MATTHEW BACHISON WAS SITTING ON THE BATH-
room floor, legs extended, barefoot, eating a bowl of Chee-
rios. Mary Leigh sat next to him, mimicking his position,
munching on Sugar Pops. Milk dribbled down her chin.
Bachison said, "Here, peaches," and dabbed with a napkin.

"Thank you, Mister Matt."

"You don't have to call me Mister Matt. Matt'll do."

"Mommy won't let me call strangers by their real names."

"I'm not a stranger, cupcake," he said, and shoveled a
spoonful into his mouth.

"Not anymore," she agreed. She put a trusting hand on
his knee, just for a second, then they ate in silence.

After rinsing the bowls in the sink, he said, "Got a surprise for you."

Mary Leigh steepled her fingers beneath her chin and
looked at him, wide-eyed, guileless. "What is it?"

He held up a finger. "One minute. Close your eyes till
I come back."

"Okaaay . . ." And she did so, fairly dancing from excitement.

Bachison ducked out the door, then came right back with something in his hand. "You can look now."

"Winkie!" she squealed, pouncing.

"I found him in the van," he said, and the two of them played for a while.

The sheriff woke Benella this time, beckoning her downstairs. "Nothing urgent, but at least now we know who they are."

She jumped off the bed, ran to the bathroom for a quick look at her face, which she gave a lick and a promise. Havershaw and Yarborough were at the kitchen table when she walked in, examining documents and looking at photographs.

"Meet our boys," Hank said.

"I'm worried about Matt," Jim Bobb said.

"Yeah?" from Delaney, looking up from a copy of *Shooting Times*.

"He spends way too much time with that little brat, and he leaves that stupid Buster in there with her. For her to have company, he says, like this is some sorta nursery."

"Why don't you tell him what you think?"

"Never mind."

"Uh-huh," said Delaney, dismissing the subject. Then: "This guy who writes about handguns"—he indicated the magazine—"is an idiot. Reckon he ever actually fired one?"

"What'd he say?"

They sat and argued the merits of the Forty-shorty versus the 9mm Parabellum for half an hour.

Havershaw was saying, ". . . Kapatchnik, a pretty salty character, but obviously not salty enough since he's currently on a slab being reduced to his basic parts. In the military, he hung around with a man we'll get to in a minute. First let's examine one of the living-and-still-at-large, James Quincy Bobb, not the smartest guy in the world, but strong as an ox. And mean, though he usually stays out of trouble. His mom's an ex-wrestler, and—"

"A what?" Benella interrupted.

"Ex-wrestler. She owns a gym in Anaheim, California, Jessie's Dreamworks, not much of a place is the word I get. She hasn't seen him in eight years, claims to have no idea where he is. The father's dead.

"Bobb's been sparking Ellen Clancey, a dental technician in Omaha. She hasn't seen him for a month, but would love to hear from him. His last job was loading trucks for a furniture company, but he failed to show up for work one day last month and they're holding his check. Said if we see him . . ." He looked up to grin wolfishly.

"Oh, we'll see him," Benella said.

"Bobb was trained to shoot a rifle," Havershaw continued, "toss a grenade, sharpen a bayonet—all by Uncle Sam—then sent off to Fort Knox for APC school."

"What's APC?" from Benella Mae.

"Armored Personnel Carrier," Havershaw said.

"Oh, good. I was afraid it might be Anti-Police Co-insurgency or something," Benella said.

Nobody laughed.

"If I may go on," said Havershaw. "Bobb then went to the Gulf, and was mentored by"—he paused to push a photo in front of Benella—"this man, Sergeant First Class Matthew Abraham Bachison, RA 12 980 4353, one tough hombre. Three tours in 'Nam, Silver Star, multiple Purple Hearts, hand-to-hand instructor, trained as an armorer, qualified 'expert' with eight different weapons. He's not Special Forces, but he's no wimp, either."

"Lovely," Benella murmured.

"And Bachison scored one thirty-four on the GT. He's no dummy."

"That makes me feel lots better," Benella said. "What challenge would there be if he were stupid?"

"But the brains of the outfit"—another pregnant photo pause—"is probably this man, Marvin Salter Delaney. Lives in Roanoke, Virginia, married, father of three, vice-president of a pet-supply chain, eleven stores in Virginia and North Carolina. The guy is loaded."

"So why'd he rob a bank? Correction . . . banks." Yarborough joined the discussion.

"Our guess is excitement," said Havershaw.

"Excitement?" from Benella.

"The wife, a pleasant lady named Melissa, says old Marvin has been disenchanted of late, 'disenchanted and intractable,' her words. Claims he lost interest in work, the kids, and sex. Note that she didn't say 'in me,' she said 'in sex,' perhaps a hint that daddy bear visited other dens."

"Did she ask you to deliver a message for her, too?" Benella asked.

"Yeah. She said tell him to get a good divorce lawyer," Havershaw concluded.

"That's not the only kind he'll need."

Yarborough said, "We've got the word out on the street. If any of our snitches spots one of these guys, we'll hear."

"What if they hole up?" Benella said.

"Then we wait," said the sheriff.

So they waited.

Gibbs drove to Greensboro in less than two hours, and spent four with Katelin, who had improved markedly. They spoke of Mary Leigh, Bennie, progress in the case (almost none), the weather (cloudy, cool), the movie *Grosse Pointe Blank,* hospital food, that Katelin might be getting out soon. The talk was for Katelin quite therapeutic. For Connor, not so much, though he was careful not to show it.

But something was bothering him.

"Make the call," Matt Bachison said.

"Don't tell me what to do, *Mister* Matt." Delaney said the name falsetto, mimicking Mary Leigh. "I'll call when I'm good and ready."

"We can't risk staying here forever. Someone might come by."

"So? We kill them."

"Make the call, Marvin."

There was something in Bachison's tone that gave Delaney second thoughts about being a smart-ass. He said, "All right, all right. Where's Jim?"

"Where do you think?"

"In with our landlady again? The man lives by his prick."

"If he doesn't let up, she'll go insane. He keeps that ice pick right under her nose, as a reminder. She does whatever he asks, like a zombie."

"Who cares?" Delaney said.

"I didn't sign on for crap like this. Robbing banks is one thing . . ."

"Yeah?"

"Just make the call."

Delaney punched in the numbers."

Benella caught the phone on its fourth ring. "Cellular," whispered Havershaw to the room at large.

"Hello," said Benella, tension plucking at her spine.

"This is a friend," came an unknown voice.

"Where is she?"

"Go to the pay phone on the corner of Elm and Standish. If anyone follows, anyone at all, including that big pussy-boy friend of yours, I'll turn Jim Bobb loose with his ice pick, like on that Faber character."

Benella tried to swallow but couldn't; her mouth was slate dry. She nodded instead.

"I didn't hear you."

"I understand," she breathed. "And if you hurt her—"

"Don't bluff when you got no cards. Agree?"

"Yes," she hissed through her teeth.

"Say it."

She was nearly hyperventilating.

"I said say it!"

"I'VE GOT NO CARDS!" Benella screamed into the phone.

"Right," he said, and hung up.

It took her five minutes to regain her composure.

• • •

"Charter Hospital, how may I help you?"

"This is Benella Sweet, Katelin Stuart's sister."

"Hello, Ms. Sweet. How nice to speak with—"

"Is Connor Gibbs still there?"

"No, I'm sorry, he signed out not five minutes . . . Ms. Sweet?"

"Connor's cell phone must not be working!" exclaimed a distraught Benella Mae Sweet.

"Maybe his battery's down," Yarborough suggested.

"Oh, God!" She pounded the arms of the couch.

"You can *not* do that!" Havershaw wanted to pound something himself, maybe Benella, to knock some sense into her. "We can't cover you if you won't—"

"I'm going alone, Havershaw," Benella insisted. "Live with it."

"At least wear a wire," Hank suggested.

"No wire. Just me and my .380."

"You're not a cop, young lady," from Havershaw. "You can't carry a gun."

Benella just looked at him. "Watch me."

"She's got a permit, Havershaw," Yarborough said. "I issued it myself."

"Oh, great."

"Nobody follows me." She looked at the FBI agent. "You understand? Nobody. And Havershaw, if your people screw this up and something happens to Mary Leigh, they won't need a body bag for your remains. A sandwich bag will do."

She seemed quite serious.

The pay phone was ringing when Benella got out of the car. She received directions from Delaney, then hung up and followed them explicitly . . .

. . . as Connor Gibbs was racing home, still more than an hour away.

Chapter 33

Marvin Delaney DIDN'T LOOK AT ALL LIKE Benella had expected, although on later reflection she couldn't imagine why; he was, after all, a VP in a fairly large, prosperous firm. His wavy hair was clipped fashionably short, though not *too* short, and not a hint of male-pattern baldness was in evidence. His figure was lean, the face as well, and square-jawed, with a mildly aquiline nose. Clad in a colorfully patterned Cutter & Buck, Dockers slacks, and slip-ons, with a lizard belt and tasteful gold bracelet as garnish, he strode confidently through the mall, turning heads.

"You are incredibly bold for a loser," she greeted when he stopped in front of her.

"I've never lost at anything in my life," he countered, flashing expensive teeth at her. "In fact, that's my problem."

"What is?"

"I win too readily and too often. Life has ceased to be much of a challenge."

"Maybe I can change that."

Again the teeth. "I knew you were not only beautiful, not only Calamity Jane, but bright as well. How in the world did you end up with that eunuch for a paramour?"

He's baiting me, she thought, and replied, "Tell him that to his face."

"I may have the chance."

"Where's Mary Leigh?"

"In due time, sexy lady."

"We may not have due time. The feds know who you are."

A slight glimmer of unease, just a flicker, there and gone. He flashed his whites to cover the minor glitch in his facade. "Then haste may indeed be in order," he said, "so listen carefully. By the way, if we are interrupted in our conversation, one of my compadres will beep the other, who is at this very moment comforting the little girl."

"Sure. Now, what do you want from me?"

"Go home, pack, and pick a pristine, rural spot. Really secluded. Then go there. Bring a gun. You'll be followed, of course, but not by one of us. I've hired a private eye. He, or she, or one of their associates, will follow you. If they're stopped by the police, well . . . they'll know very little and will have broken no law. Bear in mind that I'll be in constant contact with them. Any interference, and the kid dies. If the location you choose doesn't suit me, the kid dies. If the feds or that county lawman find us, the kid dies. Understand?"

Benella nodded.

"After you arrive at your destination, a member of my private investigator's team will contact you. You'll give them a phone number, then wait until you hear from me. When I'm satisfied that you've played the game properly, I'll release the child unharmed. In fact, she'll not only be alive but cheerful."

"Game?"

"Oh yes, luscious. This is indeed a game, and I expect a worthy opponent. Bring your big beau if you like." He raised an admonitory finger. "But no one else. If you cheat in this game of ours, but still fail to get us all, I guarantee the little girl will die. Tomorrow, next week, Christmas Eve, who knows? But she *will* die. I never leave loose ends. However"—he smiled again—"if you play fair, do your best, and manage to nail at least two of us, you win by default. The sole survivor will disappear, never to imperil you again. Those are the rules, you have my word."

"What's that worth?"

He leaned close, garlicky breath warm against her ear. "In all the time you've known me, have I ever lied to you?"

"I suppose not," Benella admitted.

But he just had.

Benella made it to her car without stumbling, though she did feel weak in the knees out of trepidation. If this didn't go right, soon she and Katelin might be sharing a room . . .

Ah, levity. A good sign.

No, she would not let this thing beat her . . . this *man* beat her . . . not while she breathed.

Dee-fense, her coach had always prompted.

Defense it would be.

Now, where was Connor?

Chapter 34

Benella was taking quite a chance, walking alone here in the botanical garden. She was taking a chance being alone *anywhere,* for that matter, but she needed to think, to stroll, to be outdoors. Besides, she had the .380 automatic—its slight weight against her hip reassuring—and she had taken chances before. (Just being Connor's friend was taking a chance!) She stopped in view of a slope that was irradiated by the declining sun; obviously too much rainfall was as destructive as too little. New trees would need to be planted there, and shrubs. In her weald, she paused to kneel amid the corpses of last year's foliage, uncovering the barrel-shaped bud of a wild ginger. She tilted the detritus for a moment to admire the plant, then replaced it carefully (ginger avoids sunlight) and moved on. A maundering creek appeared, its crest higher than usual from rainy excess, and opaque with silt. A crayfish seemed impervious to the reddish runoff as she wandered deeper into the tenebrious glen, overhead a leafy canopy of white oak, tulip poplar, and shaggy hickory. Far away and unseen a red-bellied woodpecker sought nourishment, a tympanic rend in the stillness. Directly overhead a cedar waxwing voiced a shrill counterpoint; there was just sufficient light for her to make out the red spots on its wings . . .

What to do? Delaney had insisted that she go home, toss some rags in a suitcase, depart sooner than soon. He'd said they'd be watching. But were they, and how closely? And where was Connor? Halfway to Wendover, or had he stopped for supper and a chapter or three? Probably. Not his fault, though; how could he know of her current urgency? The answer was that he couldn't. So she must decide alone where to go, and how to inform him where she'd gone without alerting Hank and Havershaw. After five minutes of appreciation for a patch of yellow trout lilies, she had it . . .

The woodpecker watched quietly her leaving, then resumed his rackety foraging.

Chapter 35

"FLYING LOW, WEREN'T YOU, SIR?"

Connor Gibbs handed the officer his license and registration. "I had a reason," Gibbs replied lamely, knowing that he was unlikely to be cut any slack.

"Eighty-one in a fifty-five zone. I could take your license, right now. Impound the car. Put you in the pokey." He was a tall man, hair clipped military style under the Smokey bear hat, and not very old—late twenties, Connor guessed, with the swaggering my-excreta-don't-offend attitude typical of the North Carolina Highway Patrol. If Connor wanted to see Bennie tonight, he would need to step lightly.

"Would you be willing to call Sheriff Hank Yarborough? He'll be glad to vouch for me, and tell you why I'm in such a hurry."

The HP looked carefully at the license, flashing his light in Connor's face for comparison with the photo. He said, "Had an officer gunned down near Monroe a few weeks ago. Routine traffic stop on Route 74. Car turned out to be stolen. Our man radioed for help, but the driver aced him with a shotgun, then killed the backup when he arrived. The first patrolman wasn't quite dead, just lying there bleeding by the side of one of the busiest highways in the county, and did anyone stop to help?" He paused in his narrative, for dramatic effect, then continued: "So the perp took the officer's own pistol and"—again a pause, to make a motion with his thumb and forefinger, like firing a gun— "finished him off."

"I read about it," Connor said. "A bad thing."

"A bad thing is right. Made me mad when I heard about it. I went down to Monroe for the funeral. Really sad, he had a big family and all."

Gibbs nodded commiseratively.

"I was upset for a week after."

"Anyone would be."

"Then here I am—in a good mood, just had my supper—and along you come doing eighty-one miles an hour in a fifty-five-miles-per-hour zone, like you own the road. So I pull you, a routine traffic stop like that one in Monroe, with you smiling all friendly, and I'm starting to feel sort of benevolent. Then you toss a name at me, of some shit-kicking sheriff, just as if *he's* the one got you by the scruff of the neck and not me."

"I just meant—"

"Well, bub," said the HP, "I think I'll run you in, let you cool your heels for a while, see what your sheriff buddy thinks about that."

"But—"

"Step out of the car, please . . ."

On the way home from the park, Benella used her DCS phone to make a call to McDermott Neese in Cedar City. It was five after eight and she was scared to death the dealership would be closed, but Neese himself answered the second ring.

"Mac, this is Benella. Thank God you're still there. I need a big favor."

"Anything at all."

"I need a car, any car, so long as it's reliable. And I need it tonight, say in two hours. I'll buy one if I have to, but I'd rather borrow it, though I know that's stretching our friendship pretty far."

"Not at all," McDermott insisted. "You can have my Avalon. I'll take a used car home."

"Thank you, thank you, thank you. This is a bona fide emergency. One day soon I'll tell you all about it."

"No trouble. Keep the car as long as you need it."

"Oh, and Mac?"

"Yeah?"

"Don't tell anyone about this until I have come and gone. Not anyone."

"Mum's the word. I'll have the car washed and gassed and waiting for you. I'll stay myself."

Thank goodness for friends.

Where's Connor? Benella thought as she packed, with Havershaw shouting in one ear and the sheriff in the other. Everette was keeping score.

"This is insane!" said an irate Havershaw. "You can't do this!"

"Really?" Benella said.

"I'll hold you as a material witness!" he yelled.

"To what?" Benella replied, tossing in a box of ammo and a new tube of toothpaste. "I witnessed none of the bank robberies, nor the shoot-out when your agent was killed, nor yet Mary Leigh's kidnapping."

"You met with one of the kidnappers!"

"You don't know that. I might have run out of gas on the way, or maybe he didn't show. You have nothing to hold me for, Havershaw, so it would be an unlawful arrest." She straightened from her packing to acquire his eye, then spoke with carefully measured words. "In this state, a citizen can resist an unlawful arrest *with all necessary force*. Catch my drift?"

"You forgot obstruction of justice, Bennie," said Hank Yarborough. "He can hold you on that. Me, too."

"Damn right!" shouted Havershaw.

Benella passed him on the way to the door, suitcase in hand, stopping briefly to lean down and kiss his cheek. "But you won't, will you, Hank?"

"Okefenokee," Yarborough expleted under his breath.

"That's great," from the head Fibbie. "She pecks you on the puss and you let her drive off into the sunset. Well, not *me!*"

"Want me to kiss you, too?" Benella tossed over her shoulder as she went down the stairs.

Havershaw threw up his arms and stomped along in her wake.

Downstairs, Havershaw said *sotto voce* to one of his men, "Put a tracking device on the sheriff's car, and right now."

"The sheriff's car?"

"Unless Gibbs gets back, that's the car she'll drive. Or so I assume. It's the one she took to meet the kidnapper. Put one on Everette's car, too. She may pull a switch just to be cute. That stupid Yarborough won't care, she has him eating out of her hand. Hell, the two of them probably . . ."

"Probably what?"

"Nothing. Go, go!"

"Can I still use your car, Hank?" asked Benella Mae.

"Better take Everette's. The feds may stick a bug up your tailpipe. They may not think of Everette's car, but don't count on it, Havershaw's no sap. A jerk, maybe, but no sap."

She kissed him again, ran upstairs to leave something for Gibbs on the dresser, then hurried back. As she pulled out of the driveway, in the house the phone was ringing . . .

Connor, wanting out of jail.

The trip to Cedar City was quick and uneventful, probably because she was in an official car. Benella passed two highway-patrol cars enroute, and they simply bobbed their heads in greeting.

One of them had recently arrested Connor W. Gibbs.

True to his word, McDermott Neese had his Avalon gassed, clean, and ready to go. He handed Benella the keys, wished her well, waved good-bye.

Two hours later, she was in the mountains west of Cedar City.

Chapter 36

Henry Ritter had been a close friend of Connor's dad, Walter, for many years. The two had met while in their first year of college, in Fayetteville, with Henry primarily dodging conscription and Walter Gibbs working two jobs to support his wife and brand-new baby, with Uncle Sam being the least of his worries. The young men had four things in common: a passion for deer hunting; an abiding interest in and remarkable aptitude for hearts (the card game); a twisted, barbed sense of humor; irreverence bordering on disdain for conventionality.

Walter Gibbs had gone on to other things, and another town, but Henry had hung around. After finishing school, he drew such a lofty draft number that Henry Kissinger would have been called before him. So he sold off some family land in Mississippi and Georgia, bought some in western and coastal North Carolina, and settled in to raise pigs, soybeans, cotton, two children—a boy and a girl— and Boykin spaniels. He kept up with his deer hunting, and developed not only a widely heralded skill at locating "the big ones," but a talent for placing other hunters in the right

spot at the right time. Henry had slain a number of bucks
with, as he put it, "right nice antly-rackers," and displayed
his mounts each year at the Dixie Deer Classic in Raleigh.
Even Tyler Vance—a nationally known outdoor writer from
the central part of the state—proclaimed Henry a master
hunter.

But there was something about Henry Ritter that few
people knew; in fact, only three—his wife, Jackie, the afore-
mentioned Vance, and Walter Gibbs. Henry had never slain
a trophy whitetail buck except under extraordinary circumstances. For instance, the 237-pounder he watched
come staggering through the woods one opening day, on
three legs, a rear one having been broken, most likely by
a car. A pack of wild dogs was on the old buck's trail, and
the deer was failing fast. He wouldn't be able to fight them
off once they caught him, since he couldn't rise up on hind
legs to flail with sharp hooves, nor did he have the leverage necessary to deliver powerful charges and thrusts with
his antlers. The aging mossyhorn was doomed.

Ritter—in full camo and covered with leaves—sat at the
base of a sweet gum and watched woodland reality, not
Bambi cavorting with Thumper. The slavering dogs arrived
en masse, and one of them immediately sank its teeth into
the deer's sagging flank. Another went for the throat. The
valiant buck managed to shake loose the rearmost animal
and neatly skewer the foremost with a surprise twist of his
thick neck, tossing the surprised mutt bleeding into the
weeds. But death was merely postponed; here came two
more, canines bared, malicious intent obvious and inevitable . . .

Until Henry's shot rang out—fleeting, merciful, final.
The buck scored 203 and a fraction Boone & Crockett,
dried and checked by three official scorers, but Henry never
entered it; that wasn't his thing. Communing with nature
was, and when he did kill the occasional deer, he ate what
he killed, made useful items out of the skin and antlers,
and passed up far more animals than he took.

Ritter was a consummate woodsman; he could track a

snail in a glue factory. Approaching his dotage (he was all of fifty-eight), he sold most of his soybean interests, his chicken interests, his timber interests, and some AT&T stock, and retired. Now all he did was spend time in the woods, play hearts whenever he could get up a game, and fish for bass, though he seldom kept one, most often kissing them good-bye (not on the lips) and releasing. Tall, whipsaw thin, flinty-eyed, gray-bearded, with a thick shock of hair under his hat, Henry spent his fall months divided between a Hyde County hideaway and a similar log cabin in the northwestern North Carolina mountains. It overlooked an apple orchard where cider grew, or so he told the occasional family that stopped by, usually seeking directions. He always filled their pockets with juicy fruit before they left . . .

"Well, hey, Bennie girl," he said from his perch on the porch as Benella pulled into the yard.

She had DCS-phoned to announce her coming. "Don't 'hey' me, you reprobate. I want a hug, and I'm too tired to come up there to get it."

So Henry shifted long, lanky limbs and went to greet her, there on the stone steps that he'd set in place himself, with the moon scudding overhead amongst the thickening clouds. Away up the hollow an owl hooted.

"See?" he commented. "Even Brer Owl, he say 'hey.'"

She looked up into the twinkling, patient eyes. "I love you, Henry Ritter. How's Jackie?"

"Still mean as a snake."

"She down in Fayetteville?"

"Um-hmm."

"Henry Junior?"

"Flying helicopters."

"And Jenny?"

"Near as mean as her momma, but with more stamina. She's in nursing school. Loves those needles. Prays every day for a typhoid scare."

Benella couldn't help but laugh. She hugged him again.

"Careful, now. Girls've been know to get pregnant hugging me twice."

They climbed to the porch, sat, and she unloaded her problem on him.

Afterward, he simply said, "My God," and went to fetch coffee. Then they watched the moon for a spell, like Henry had done many times with Walter Gibbs.

"Connor on the way?" Henry asked.

"I hope so."

For a long time, Ritter said nothing. Then quietly: "Me, too, honey."

Chapter 37

"I'M SORRY, HE'S NOT HOME. ARE YOU AWARE that it's almost one in the morning?" said Carolyn Neese.

Squawking sounds came rushing out of the receiver.

"No, I don't know where he is. There are three children in this house, the phone might have—"

More sounds, strident.

"I told you—"

Squawk!

"Sir?"

Squawk, squawk!

"I *beg* your pardon."

The squawker was even more insistent.

"He *has* no phone in his car, nor on his boat."

Angry squawking.

"Why, either freshwater or oceangoing, depending on—"

Angry interruption.

She was becoming equally angry. "I have no idea. None, zip, zero. Does that give you a clue?"

Screech!

"Well, same to you, moron!" She hung up and went back to bed while across town at a pancake restaurant, her husband McDermott was eating a waffle.

Lite syrup.

"She went to Cedar City, sir," was the report. "Dropped the squad car off at a Toyota store and left in a white Avalon." The private detective, a portly person in her forties, gave the tag number.

"Where are you now?" asked Marvin Delaney.

"Not far from North Wilkesboro."

"Good work."

"It's why I get the big bucks, sir," she said, and punched "off." Then she kicked the cruise up a notch—to sixty-three—and settled back with Steppenwolf slamming through the speakers:

> "Why don't you come with me, little girl?
> On a magic carpet ride . . ."

Right on, she thought, tapping time on the steering wheel.

"You let her go?" Unhappy was Connor Gibbs.

"I sure as hell didn't want to be the one to try and stop her," declared Hank Yarborough.

"Besides," Special Agent Havershaw cautioned, "it's probably better this way. She has no idea she's being tracked. She can check behind her till her eyes burn and there'll be nobody there. She'll lead us right to them."

Connor looked at him in disgust. "You don't know Bennie. She probably already found your tracking device and stuck it on an eighteen-wheeler bound for Cleveland."

Havershaw disagreed. "Too hard to find. It takes sophisticated electronic gear unless you know where to look, and she wouldn't."

The phone interrupted. Havershaw barked into it, listened, assumed his Cheshire-cat grin, and hung up. "Cedar City," he said smugly.

"Where in Cedar City?" queried Gibbs.

"Forrest Avenue, at a restaurant near the intersection. The car hasn't moved for fifteen minutes."

Connor smiled and shook his head and told Hank Yarborough that he could send for his squad car now. "She switched."

Connor found on the dresser a piece of typing paper. On it was the following:

He immediately began to pack a suitcase.

"You saw the note, didn't you?" Hank said from the doorway.

Gibbs nodded as he withdrew shirts from Benella's closet. (He kept a dozen there, and slacks.)

"Told you right where to go, didn't it?"

Gibbs shrugged as he took socks and briefs from a drawer.

"Don't forget pants."

"Thanks," Connor said. And a belt, a hat, a heavy coat.

"Don't forget a gun."

Connor looked at him. "I don't have one with me."

Hank offered his, butt first. "Take mine. If you and Bennie are gonna play this solo, you need a gun."

"She has one."

"Yeah, a powder-puff .380."

Connor closed the suitcase with a *snap!* "It'll do."

And downstairs they went.

•   •   •

Got my car bugged, too?" Connor asked.

Havershaw said nothing.

"Don't follow me," Connor instructed.

Havershaw shrugged.

"You either, Hank," Connor warned.

Yarborough raised his hands. "Not me. You're on your own."

So Connor got into his car and drove away.

It was bugged.

"The queen of spades and a *balloon*. What the hell is that supposed to mean?" bitched Havershaw.

"Don't forget 'I love you,'" prompted Everette.

"Stuff it, Deputy."

"Sorry, Havershaw, but only the sheriff can tell me to stuff it."

"If I do, will you?" from Yarborough.

"I know when I'm extraneous," sniffed Everette, and went to seek cookies.

"Must be a common experience," was Havershaw's aftershot. Then, to Yarborough: "Don't worry. We'll figure this out."

But they never did.

Someone else did, though.

"Hello," said young Cullen Vance, at his home in Greensboro.

"Cullen Vance, I presume," said Connor Gibbs, at his home in Wendover.

"Yes, sir."

"May I speak to your dad?"

"Can I tell him who's calling?"

"Connor Gibbs."

"Are you that great huge man I met some time ago? At the sports store?"

"I am."

"Are you in trouble again?"

Gibbs chuckled. "Seems like I always am."

"Do you need my daddy's help?"

"Only his advice."

The boy sounded relieved. "Good. I'll get him. Please hang on, Mr. Gibbs." Connor heard the handset being laid down.

In less than ten seconds: "Connor, how the hell are you?"

"Your son is the politest kid on the planet."

"He better be, or I'll have to beat him."

Gibbs chuckled again. "You beat him regular, do you?"

"Well, not regular. He's getting too big, and too good at tae kwon do."

"Thought he was into aikido."

"Both. Dave Michaels has been instructing him."

"Not you?" Tyler Vance was the best martial artist Gibbs had ever seen, and in more than one discipline.

"I teach him aikido, and coach him in baseball and basketball. He gets enough of me telling him what to do."

Pleasantries exchanged, Gibbs told Vance his problem.

"Your little Ruger 9mm carbine will do, if you stick to the woods. But if any really long shots are offered, you'd be as well off throwing pinecones."

"I'll have my .45, too. Unless Bennie carries it."

Vance thought a minute. "And you need something immediately?"

"Sooner."

"Do you know a man named Braxton Chiles?"

"He's an acquaintance, yes."

"How close?"

"Who can tell with Braxton?"

"True. Well, he has a Model 700 Sendero in .300 Win Mag, with a Leupold 3.5x10 on deck. He hand-feeds it 150-grain Nosler Ballistic Tips. He might lend it to you."

"You'll have to come carry it for me."

"Guy big as you could tote it *and* me. Up a mountain."

"Stop the crap and I'll call Braxton."

"You want help on this one?"

"Cullen wouldn't like it. Besides, if something happened to you, Odie'd have to raise him."

"I'll tell Pop you said that."
And they said their good-byes.

"Mr. Gibbs. What's doin', my man?" Braxton Chiles said into his end of the phone.

Gibbs told him what was doing, and what he needed.

"What you really need is for me to go with you," Chiles opined.

"Bennie and I'll have help, at least one that I know of. But thanks for offering."

"You can pick up the rifle anytime, or I can run it over."

"Is it sighted in?"

"What a question. I'll send forty rounds of primo hand-loads. Polycarbonate tips. They peel back like bananas."

And it was arranged.

Chapter 38

POLLY PETERSEN LEANED ON THE DOORBELL. A foghorn sounded inside the cabin. *How nautical,* she thought. The door opened under the hand of the tall, attractive lady she'd shadowed for seven solitary hours. "You got some information for me?" Polly said.

Benella Mae Sweet handed her a slip of paper. Polly looked at it. "This top number the one here at the house?"

Benella nodded.

"A landline, right?"

Nod.

"He said to tell you he'll call you on that one, from a pay phone. When he does, you'll immediately turn on your digital phone, then hang up the house phone. He'll call you back on the DCS and you'll chat."

"Be still my heart."

"You needn't get flip with me, cutes. I'm just doing my job. Some of us ain't got all the looks in the world. We got to work for a living," Polly quipped.

"Some sleazy job, peeping in keyholes, following people around."

"Pays my Visa bill, which is the size of the Mexican national debt." She cackled like a crone.

"Anything else?"

"Yeah, got a Mountain Dew?" Perky Polly tittered all the way back to her car. When she roared out of the gravel parking area, Rod Stewart was vibrating her headliner: "Maggie May."

> ". . . or steal my daddy's cue,
> and make a living outta playin' pool . . ."

"Was that the PI?" Ritter asked when Benella walked back into the kitchen.

"Or a corpulent coworker," said Benella.

"You give her this number?"

She nodded.

"Then I best skedaddle. Soon they may be watching the place, if they ain't already. Want an alligator pear?" He held out the viridian fruit he'd been slicing.

"What's an alligator pear?"

"That's what grandpaw used to call 'em. You hoity-toities might prefer the term 'avocado.' "

"I'll pass on the fruit, but thanks for all your help, Henry."

"Can't let anything happen to my best buddy's son's main squeeze. He'd come whup me."

In three minutes, he'd gathered his plunder and gone.

Connor Gibbs stood on a rise high behind Henry's cabin, eyes glued to a pair of binoculars. He watched—and heard—portly Polly come and go. Then, not long after, Henry drove off in his battered Cherokee.

So he climbed down the mountain.

"Hello the house!" he yelled thirty minutes later, after a circuitous—and cautious—descent that convinced him no one was around except Bennie.

The screen door slammed open and all of a sudden his arms were full of woman. Much kissing and hugging and weeping took place, and one thing led to another. An hour later, sweaty and serene, they lay entangled in Henry Ritters' sheets. Benella chuckled and said, "Viagra's some pill, huh?"

"That was Viagra?" he said, shifting his position slightly. "I thought they were the new blue M&M's."

"Put your hand right back where it was, I'm a very tactile person. For nonintellectuals like you, that's a euphemism for 'touchy-feely.'"

They continued to cuddle like teenagers while she brought him up-to-date on the situation, and he brought her up-to-date on Katelin and the hospitality of the highway patrol.

"You shouldn't have been speeding," she chided.

"As if you never do. At least I didn't run some poor bastard off a cliff."

"As far as you know."

They giggled and nipped and sighed and encouraged and tugged, and set the old bed in motion, enjoying themselves immensely. Much later, finally sated, they fixed supper and allied themselves martially. A plan was conceived: cunning, daring, deceptive.

It might even work.

But it didn't.

Polly Petersen passed along the phone numbers as instructed, then headed for Statesville with a Diet Pepsi and Linda Ronstadt wailing:

> ". . . 'Please don't hurt me, Mama!'
> Poor, poor, pitiful me . . ."

. . . with the syn-drummer carrying the heavy load.

Jim Bobb was wiping the ice pick on a towel when Delaney came to get him. On the bed beside Jim, the "landlady" lay prostrate and spread-eagled, arms and legs tied tight to the bedposts, her mouth full of semen and one ear full of blood. The eyes stared at nothing. She had obviously struggled mightily.

Delaney shook his head. "Jim Bobb, you're a sick son-of-a-bitch."

Jim just grinned. "Don't like loose ends," he said.

"I was only recently claiming that about you."

And they piled into the van, including Buster to entertain Mary Leigh. Not Bobb, though. He drove a Mazda fresh from a Kmart parking lot; its plate came off an Olds at the Piggly Wiggly.

Benella's phone rang just before dark. "It's me," Delaney said. "Hang up and turn on your DCS phone."

She did, and in ten seconds it buzzed. "Where's Mary Leigh?" she spoke into it.

"In Dallas. Where the hell do you think? She's with us."

"Bring her. Right now."

"You aren't giving the orders, cuddly-cheeks, I am."

"Listen, *Marvin*. If you or one of your brain-dead lackeys doesn't bring her to me pronto, I'm going to write her off and call the federal marshals' office about witness protection." She held her breath for a reaction.

Slow in coming.

Finally: "You're bluffing, but no matter. We're watching the house, from three directions of course. One of us will bring the girl, cut your landline, and leave. I'll call you back a few minutes later—giving you time for what I'm sure will be a tearful reunion—and we'll discuss the rules."

"So bring her," she said.

But he'd hung up.

Benella and Connor stepped into the gloaming. "There's Brer Owl," she said, upon hearing a hoot.

"You handled that fine, babe. You had to push him a little."

"But what if he—"

"No second guesses. Let's wait and see what happens."

"It's the waiting that's hard."

"I know," he agreed.

"Was it like this for you, in the CIA, when—"

"I don't want to talk about it."

"You never do. Except right after one of your dreams."

"Those years were the hardest of my life. Not because I was scared of dying, but because I had to . . ."

When he paused, she took his hand.

"Because I had to kill. There was no other choice, except be killed. I evaded, used every trick I could devise or had been taught, or ever heard about from other guys who'd been through it. Mostly it was enough."

"Not always."

"No," he said.

She squeezed his hand encouragingly, but he didn't continue. Something had caught his attention.

Headlights.

Not Delaney—a heavier man, nearly as tall, not nearly so dapper. He carried Mary Leigh in his arms carefully, and handed her to Benella. "She's asleep," he said. "Okay, though. Been eating good, and . . ." He reached into a back pocket: "Here's Winkie." In another pocket some Golden Graham Treats and a Baggie of carrots, bite-sized. "She might wake up hungry, and she loves these grahams." He looked away.

Bewildered, Benella said, "Thank you."

"No problem." Bachison looked over at Gibbs. "You the guy makes the fried-beet-and-tomato-sandwiches?"

"*Bean* and tomato," Connor corrected.

"Oh, *bean* . . . that's not so bad." Matt reached out a hand and gently brushed the hair back from Mary Leigh's upturned face, his eyes soft.

Benella, only slightly less bewildered, said, "Do you have kids?"

Bachison stared off into space. "Far away. I never see them." Then abruptly: "I have to cut your phone line."

And he did, then drove off into the night.

Mary Leigh was out like a light; Benella took the opportunity to examine every inch of her. No bruises, contusions, swellings; she seemed fine physically. After an hour, she woke, and was at first delighted to see them, but then, glancing around, she said, "Where's Mister Matt?"

"He's gone, honey," Connor assured. "He'll never bother you again."

"He didn't bother me, he was my friend."

"Did anyone else bother you, sweetheart?" Benella tip-toed lightly.

"I didn't see nobody else, not until we left. Then there was just this Marvin man. He was *not* nice."

"What did he do, sweetie?"

"Just yelled at me a lot, and told me to shut up and stuff. And he said the F-word. But Mister Matt was there to pro-tect me, so I wasn't scared."

"Honey," Benella said. "Mister Matt is not really a very nice man, and—"

"Don't you say that about my friend! He took care of me, and gave me stuff, and we ate and played a lot! I like him better'n *you!*" Mary Leigh shouted, and fled the room.

"Now I've done it," Benella said.

"Don't worry about it, or her attachment. She didn't have her mother or father to protect her, nor us, so naturally she bonded with Bachison. Fortunately, he seems to have taken good care of her."

"Not to mention bonding with her."

"Which is good. He saw to it she came through the or-deal okay."

"But he's a—"

"Bank robber? Lowlife? Murderer? Doesn't mean he can't like kids."

"How can you defend him?"

"I'm not defending him, I'm pointing out that because someone is subhuman in some areas doesn't mean they are in all."

Brooking no further exculpatory remarks, Benella, too, stormed from the room.

And then the phone rang.

•　　•　　•

Benella had the DCS phone with her in the bedroom.

"What?" she barked into it.

"Wow, are you in a mood. Listen carefully. None of you is to leave," Delaney instructed. "You'll be under surveillance around the clock, from at least one point on the compass. Maybe multiple points. When we're ready, we'll come for you."

"For me?"

"To kill you, baby. Maybe have a bit of fun first, if we work it right, but rest assured that you won't survive the week."

"Let Connor take Mary Leigh out," Benella said.

"Not a chance. If he even tries, we'll kill them both. Jim Bobb already sneaked in to plant explosives under both hoods. Anyone goes near a car and their pieces will rain down on Asheville. Remember, we're watching all the time. If boyfriend tries to go shank's mare and we catch him, we'll kill the girl. Capeesh?"

"Yes."

"So her best chance is with you, in the shack. Hey, you light my wick, maybe I'll let her go before we kill you."

"That a promise?"

"That's a *maybe,* are you deaf? Oh, by the way, while Jim Bobb was low-crawling around, he set a charge under the cabin. He said there was an amazing amount of crawl space, but don't let us catch any of you on hands and knees under there. All three of us have radio-controlled detonators. And if outside help shows up, things will go *boom* right quick. We have nightscopes and goggles, so if you feel like creeping around, you better be invisible, whether it's dark out or not. Bear in mind that if we simply wanted you dead, we'd blow the cabin. What we want is a challenge, sweet buns."

"Then come get me, girly man!"

She rang off without saying good-bye.

But it didn't make Delaney mad.

He was in too good a mood.

Chapter 39

Deep within the harried halls of an FBI think tank, the following exchange was taking place:

"This is nuts. How the hell does he think we can figure this out with nothing else to go on?" said decipherer Number One, a graduate of MIT. "I need my G-man decoder ring."

"Look upon it as a challenge," countered Number Two, his cohort out of Stanford.

"There's no pattern."

"Sure there is, you simply have to determine it. If you can't, make one up."

"You computer geeks are all alike."

"So are you 'there must be a pattern' wonks."

"Are not."

"Are, too."

And so went the highly technical discussion.

Clayton wanted sweetened tea but the cafeteria was out. So he settled for unsweetened and poured in six packs of sugar, stirring robustly. "Have you ever noticed that you can't sweeten cold tea? Not unless you use enough sugar to sink the *Monitor*."

"I believe it sank already," quipped Terri Joyce. "Shuffle the cards."

"Promise to pass me the bitch if I deal you a good hand?"

"Like I really want you playing behind me with the queen in your hand."

Clayton dealt as they gibed, two longtime friends. "I won't give it to you, I swear. Stanfield's the one we have to nail. He's been at minus eight for three hands."

Stanfield just smiled confidently and arranged his cards.

"So give it to him," Terri said.

Clayton sighed in mock exasperation. "I've been *trying*."

He finished shuffling the cards, offered Stanfield the cut, then dealt, placed the final card to one side, and picked up his hand. There she was: the queen of spades, along with five backers and a singleton diamond, which he immediately lay facedown on the table for passing to Stanfield. True bliss was having the bitch in your hand, a bevy of spades to support her, and a void in diamonds—though Terri would probably send one his way; she was a deadly and portentous passer.

For a *female*.

Benella had brought Mary Leigh a change of clothes and the child was dressed in those while Gibbs worked on the ones she'd been wearing when kidnapped. Using a can of brown spray paint found in Henry's workshop, Connor was changing their look substantially. Her blue jeans were now the color of mud; so was a yellow-T-shirt. Mary Leigh watched the transformation while Connor was instructing her: "Now remember, honey, you won't be completely invisible. If you have time, cover yourself with sticks and leaves, or anything else you can find. But try not to disturb the forest floor. It might draw attention to you. A hollow log or tree is a great place. It hides you from most directions. And if you do get into a hollow tree, try to pull your legs up inside. Then you really will be invisible.

"A blowdown makes good cover, too. That's when a tree has been blown over by the wind. If there're two trees lying together, slip in among the branches." He paused to interlace his fingers, illustrating what he meant. "Then if someone spots you, you can scoot out the other side from them and they'll have to slow way down to climb over the blowdown, or go way around to chase you."

As Mary Leigh nodded her understanding, Benella was amazed; the child didn't appear to be frightened in the least.

But Benella was. For Mary Leigh.

Connor continued: "Aunt Bennie is sewing bits and pieces of brown, gray, and green cloth onto a dark green baseball cap. If you have to lie down, try to cover yourself with leaves, and make sure you lie on your stomach or your face might show. And be sure to keep your head down, between your arms, with your hat on. You will be very hard to see that way. And whatever you do, don't look up. In fact, try your very, very best not to move at all, not even a teeny bit. Movement is what predators watch for."

"What's a predator?" Mary Leigh asked.

"Those men," Benella mumbled.

"A predator is an animal that hunts for a living," Connor explained. "Its eyes are in the front of its head, for binocular vision. That helps it catch its prey. The important thing to remember about a predator is that it sees movement first. So don't move."

"How will I know if someone's near?"

"That's a very smart question. Use your ears, like a deer does, or a squirrel."

"Or a bunny?"

"Yes."

"But my ears aren't that big."

Connor smiled at the logic. "That's right, sweetheart, so you'll have to listen really hard. An animal also can smell much better than you, and from farther away. But your advantage—and it's a big one—is your ability to reason, to think things through, and figure them out. To plan and prepare."

"Like you're doing now, painting my pants?"

"Right. Now remember, whenever you feel that it's safe to move, keep heading *away* from the sun. Eventually, you'll come to a river. When you do, follow it to your right, which is roughly south. After a while you'll come to a high bridge. The river runs under it. Climb up the river-bank at the bridge and you'll see a paved road. Stand right beside it and wave down any car you see. They'll likely stop for a pretty girl like you. Ask them to take you to the police, then give the police this note Aunt Bennie wrote." He put the note in Mary Leigh's back pocket.

"Which hand is my right?"

"See your pinkie ring?"

Mary Leigh looked down at the ring. "Yes."

"Your right hand is your *other* one."

"Then I'll move the ring to my real right hand." She did, then was quiet for a minute. "Do I really have to go by myself?"

"We talked about that, hon. It's the only way. Aunt Ben-nie and I will be dealing with the bad guys so that they won't catch you."

"Are you going to hurt Mister Matt?"

"Not unless he makes me."

"You promise?"

"I promise," Connor said.

He lived up to that promise, through no fault of his own.

Stanfield lost. Clayton did, too. The *female* won. She was on her way back to her cubicle when she passed the decoding room. From an overhead was being projected an enlarged rendition of Benella's "note" to Connor. Terri spot-ted the depiction, stopped, said, "What's with the bitch, boys?"

The decoding section was all male. They looked around at her. "Bitch?" one of them said, eyebrows elevated.

Terri pointed to the display. "The queen of spades."

Several chairs were turned over in frantic haste.

"What did I say?" Terri said.

She subsequently received a raise, a promotion, and a transfer to a warmer clime.

"So what about the balloon?" said Number One, the MIT alumnus.

"*Moolah* me," said Number Two, who had served in Seoul after Stanford.

Havershaw said, "Draw up a list of all the Gibbs acquaintances, then send as many agents as it takes. Find out how many play hearts. Do it now."

Both Numbers jumped.

"Be circumspect with her. She hasn't been told about her daughter, and she has no idea that you have no idea where her sister is," warned the psychiatrist.

"I'm not a fool, Doctor," Havershaw alleged.

"Really? I've seen no evidence of that."

"No, don't get up. My name is Havershaw, I'm with the FBI." He flashed an ID. "Now, Mrs.—"

"Please, call me Katelin."

"Okay, Katelin. Your sister and Connor Gibbs have gone to Myrtle Beach, and—"

"That's odd, Bennie hates the beach."

"Uh, well, Gibbs felt they deserved a rest, and—"

"Now, Mary Leigh *loves* the beach. Wonder if it's still too cool for swimming."

"I don't know. My problem is that they gave us no number where to reach them, and one of Gibb's friends left a message on their machine, which we've been monitoring just in case."

"In case of what?"

"The bank robbers are caught, maybe in another state. Gibbs said they'd like to hear if they were, but—"

Katelin sat up straight. "Have the robbers been caught?"

"No, they haven't, but a person did call to say that they wanted to get up a game of hearts, and we thought—"

"Hearts?"

"Yes, the card game, and—"

"I didn't think Bennie even knew how to play hearts."

"Maybe Gibbs, then."

"I don't know about that."

"So none of your friends, or those of your sister, or Gibbs, play hearts?"

"No, I'm sorry."

Not as sorry as I am. Havershaw thought. But he said: "Can I get you anything? A Whitman's Sampler, some magazines?"

"No, thank you, though it's kind of you to ask. I can't understand why Connor seems to dislike you so much."

It's reciprocal, he thought, but smiled disarmingly. "Well, good-bye, Katelin. I hope you'll be home very soon."

"Thanks, I mean to be."

Havershaw turned to go.

"You know," she said, half to herself. "I believe that Connor's daddy is a nut about hearts."

Havershaw turned back to her impatiently. "Walter Gibbs plays hearts?"

"*Plays?* He *lives* for those semiannual games in the mountains with his old school pals. I heard they play all night, sleep a few hours, fix a ripsnortin' breakfast, and have at it again. Marathon sessions of omnibus hearts." She shook her head. "Can you imagine?"

"You said he goes to the mountains. The rural mountains, or near Ashville?"

"Henry's place is rural in the extreme, I understand. Miles and miles from the nearest feed store or Stop & Shop."

"Who is Henry?"

"Henry Ritter."

"What town does he live near?"

She told him, and the phone number. Havershaw dutifully wrote them down, supposing it might be worth checking out. He said good-bye (again) and turned to go. She didn't seem to notice: "The only way I could ever remember Henry's name was because of that cartoon character. I always thought Henry Ritter looked just like him."

Havershaw paused (again) and turned (again) and said, with as much politeness as he could muster, "Cartoon character?"

"Remember the little bald-headed kid, always wore shorts, had a little turned-up nose, and pulled a wagon? He had this balloon on a string? He was *so* funny . . . Mr. Havershaw?"

But all she saw was his coattail whisking out the door.

Chapter 40

Henry Ritter had a plan; now, if he only had sufficient time to implement it. He was camouflaged from head to toe, covered on one end by a soft shapeless hat, on the other by deerskin moccasins he'd fashioned himself. In his hand he carried his compound Hoyt, which though shiny black when he'd purchased it was now as unseeable as the rest of him. The compact bow had a thirty-one-inch draw, and to it Henry had affixed five sighting pins (for ten-, twenty-, thirty-, forty-, and fifty-yard shots) and Cat Whiskers, to silence the *twang* of release. His arrows were Wasp triple-bladed broadheads, razor sharp, and tuned to the flight characteristics of each arrow shaft. With the foregoing equipment, Ritter could reliably hit a soccer ball out to fifty yards. Unreliably a bit farther.

Henry's plan was simple: ease through the woods like a wraith; find his targets one by one; render them inoperable. Since there were only so many points from which the cabin could be viewed, his choices were not infinite. So here he went, searching for sign, quiet as a newt's whistle, trying to spot without being spotted.

He was successful.

For a while.

Benella Mae Sweet and Connor Gibbs also had a plan: don't get shot. They even had a vague idea as to how to implement that plan, and were discussing it, two hours from dusk, in the kitchen over cocoa.

"I still think Mary Leigh should go out with you," he said, and took a sip.

"You're better equipped to protect her," argued Benella. "Especially if you take Henry's shotgun. He left it here for us."

"No thanks." Connor took another scalding sip. "Too range-limited. I'm going to carry that cannon of Braxton's."

"But if what they said is true—that they'll blow the house if we try to leave—then getting clear is going to be our immediate problem. The shotgun is handier."

"Only marginally."

She grinned. "Not when you're also carrying thirty-five pounds of four-year-old."

Mary Leigh came in, her paint-stiffened jeans swishing as she walked, to climb onto Connor's lap. She squeezed his neck and said, "This's really gonna work. I'm not scared a whole, whole lot, either. Just a little."

He squeezed back. "Me, too, babe. Me, too. Let's have a snack for good luck."

They did. Nabs, with orange juice for a chaser. Afterward, with Mary Leigh in the bathroom washing her face and hands, Benella sighed and said, "Well, you ready?" She had her little .380 in a holster on her belt, Henry's larger 9mm high-capacity pistol in a shoulder rig, an extra magazine for each in her coat pockets, and Henry's pump twelve-gauge (an ancient Ithaca 37, bottom eject) from which most of the bluing was gone.

Connor pointed at the table beside her. "Only six shells of double-ought?"

"Henry's primarily a dove hunter," she explained, "at

least as far as his scattergunning is concerned. So his ammo supply is not fraught with large-size shot."

Gibbs nodded ruefully, slipped into his jacket, scooped up a freshly scrubbed Mary Leigh, and took one more mouthful of tepid cocoa.

His mood was positive. And premature. Because he had a date with an ice pick.

"Operator says there's trouble on the line," said Ib Blankenship.

"I knew it!" from a strung-out Havershaw. "Let's go!"

"We can call in the locals, get them right out there."

"No! We broke that imbecilic code ourselves, so this thing is all ours. The cops around *here* are incompetent, why do you think the ones way back in the boonies will be any better? Besides, I *want* this one. For Tyles."

You mean for the glory, for the promotion, for the media attention. Meanwhile, some pretty nice folks might die, including a little girl, Blankenship thought, but didn't say it.

"The Fibbies are on the move," Polly Petersen said into her DCS phone, to Sheriff Hank Yarborough on the receiving end.

"Can you keep up with them?" was Yarborough's response.

"Does a possum have a pointy prick?"

"I have no idea."

"I'll get back to you," she said, shifting into second with the Bee Gees in the background doing "Stayin' Alive." She ratcheted up the sound:

> . . . "You know it's all right, it's okay,
> I'll live to see another day . . ."

and as they hit Albacore Street, she was singing along:

> ". . . ah-ah-ah-ah, stayin' aliiiiive . . ."

while picturing John Travolta's rolling buns.

Chapter 41

BENELLA MAE LEANED THE SHOTGUN AGAINST the jamb of the front door and hugged and bussed her niece, then her best friend. "Connor . . ." she began.

"Don't get maudlin, this'll all be over soon. In an hour, we'll be sitting here with Henry, quaffing brews and dandling Mary Leigh on our collective knees."

No they wouldn't, and somehow Benella knew it, but she said, "Good luck," and laid a hand softly against Connor's face. He tried for a smile, standing there with the little girl in his arms, but it didn't take.

So Benella leaned over to pick up the throw rug, took a deep breath, and stepped through the door onto the front porch. Once there, she began to shake the rug vigorously, making dust and grit fly. *Just a little housekeeping chore, Delaney,* she thought. *Really it is.*

Gibbs went out right behind her, holding tightly to Mary Leigh.

And ran for all he was worth.

"God help us," Benella breathed, dropping the rug to grab the shotgun, all the while watching from the tail of one eye as Connor and Mary Leigh disappeared around the corner of the house . . .

. . . *no explosion* . . .

. . . and Benella hit the ground running, her runner's legs churning, work-hardened, surefooted, adrenaline-spurred . . .

. . . *no explosion* . . .

. . . the tree line on her side of the house sixty yards away, with almost no cover between . . .

. . . *no explosion* . . .

. . . she could almost *feel* a bullet, see in her mind's eye a rifle scope tracking her, the intersection of its cross wires leading her speeding torso to allow for forward movement as the marksman took up slack on the trigger . . .

. . . *still no explosion* . . .

. . . *two seconds, please God,* the trees were there, right *there,* and suddenly she was in their sheltering embrace and there had been no shot, no searing, tearing, disabling bullet . . .

AND NO EXPLOSION!

She looked back. The cabin was still there, still intact, still a haven. Delaney had screwed up, or something had gone wrong, or a detonator had failed, or . . .

. . . Delaney had lied.

Were there never any explosives, either under the house or in the cars? Had he simply manipulated things, forcing this type of game because a sturdy log cabin would have been highly defensible against only three men, assuming that no explosives were in the mix?

Yes, Delaney snookered us, she thought.

And then she heard the shots.

Marvin Delaney grinned to himself as he watched his prey scatter exactly according to plan. He waved an arm at Jim Bobb, over on the low ridge, who would go after the big muther and the little girl, and heaven help whoever got in his way. Meanwhile Delaney would intersect the woman, while Bachison, the designated hitter, lurked in the spruce thicket with a scoped AR-15—

POW! POW! POW! POW! POW!
Why, there he was now.

Ten seconds after the woman took to the trees, Bachi-son took out the cars—five carefully spaced shots into each engine compartment. He could have taken out the woman just as easily; she'd been only a hundred yards or so away. Running or not, it would have been pretty much a sure thing . . .

Oh, well. Marvin wanted her for himself. All Matt Bachi-son wanted was to get this over and to get his money.

Time to move.

I wish there were more downed trees in these woods, thought Henry Ritter as he listened to Bachison perforat-ing the automobiles. *Sure would help for hide-and-seek. But El Niño had to put the kibosh on the hurricane sea-son. Well, no use griping when you should be hunting.*

So he went hunting.

For the man with the AR-15 who had a grudge against cars.

Jim Bobb watched as Gibbs and Mary Leigh came hus-tling his way. "First I'll gut the man with my tanto. Then the baby," he said to himself.

And moved.

The feds were closing fast, and would have been clos-ing faster if they knew exactly where the hell they were going.

But, being elite members of the Federal Bureau of In-vestigation, they did not.

Polly pulled in behind a Peterbilt to avoid detection. Odd, the direction the Fibbies were heading. Just yesterday she had followed that tall, tense, sarcastic woman this way, the one whose nice husband (or at least the man had seemed nice on the phone, and he sure did pay well) suspected her of romping beneath the sheets with someone other than himself.

But did he lie to ol' Polly? It would appear so, especially if the direction of the posse up ahead didn't soon change. In a minute, she was going to have to get on the horn to Hank Yarborough and take a wild guess. No need getting her nipple in a crack, she figured, tapping her non-driving foot in time with Boz Scaggs:

"Lido missed the boat that day he left the shack . . ."

Paused at the base of a forty-foot pine, Gibbs was telling Mary Leigh: "Sweetheart, I may be able to stay with you the whole time, but we can't count on it. So if I tell you to run, you run. Don't hesitate, don't look back, and don't try to hide unless you hear someone right behind you. You can't outrun a grown-up, so don't even try. Go for sneaking and hiding. Move only when you know danger has passed you by. If everything works out, I'll come to you. When I do, I'll call you by your mother's name, not your own. That way you'll know it's me."

"Can I come out if I see Mister Matt?"

"Better not. He's with the bad guys on this one, honey, though I know he used to be your friend. Okay?"

Mary Leigh nodded her agreement.

But she didn't mean it.

Poor skunk, Henry thought, looking down at the fetid carcass. *Prob'ly rabies.* Great; now he'd have to watch out for real animals, not just human ones. He moved very quietly, although the forest was carpeted with leaves. Crackly ones. Absolute silence was thus impossible, unless you stayed absolutely still. And since he didn't know where anyone was (not even the car-shooting demon), he knew he'd have to keep on the move, crunchy leaves or not . . .

In the end, it wasn't leaves that gave him away.

• • •

Matthew Bachison had moved immediately after rendering the cars just inert sheet metal. He was directly behind the house now, climbing a treacherous talus slope while trying not to break his neck or give his position away. Not easy. Jim Bobb was to the southeast—or so Matt thought—trying to waylay the big man and the child. Just thinking what would happen when Bobb caught up with them made his head hurt, but there was no help for it.

Unless . . .

He stopped abruptly.

Maybe there was. If he could take Jim Bobb's gun away—so as to avoid any noise—then he could just kick the lug's thick skull in.

Bingo.

So Matt Bachison went to help Mary Leigh, his only real friend. He had no idea of how tough Jim Bobb really was.

Bobb couldn't see his prey, but he could hear them talking. Were they stupid or what . . . ?

Maybe eighty yards due north, on the other side of a saddle. He examined the terrain; not too thickly wooded, but leafy.

I'll injun up on them, he thought.

But he was no Indian.

"Honey, please don't talk anymore. I gave you instructions when we entered the woods because at that time they knew where we were. But we've come a long way since then, and we have to be very quiet now, and hope that they won't find us," Connor admonished.

"But I have to pee!" Mary Leigh whispered urgently, legs crossed.

"Okay, go over there, behind that tree. But hurry."

"No peeking."

"Okay," he said, and turned his back to her.

A mistake.

•   •   •

Though Henry Ritter's hearing wasn't what it used to be, he was certain that he'd heard sibilant voices, and maybe the murmur of shifted foliage.

So he homed in on the sounds.

When Jim Bobb peered around the granite outcropping, the little girl was thirty yards away, just pulling up her pants (Painted *brown*?). He couldn't see the man. Did the jerk have a gun? Surely. So it might be prudent to circle, see what was what. He had them placed now, he wouldn't lose them.

Henry Ritter was coming in from the north when he spotted a big ugly head peeping around a hunk of granite. It sure wasn't Connor Gibbs, unless the man had changed a *lot* since Henry had last seen him. Ritter drew an arrow from the quiver attached to his bow, shifted slightly, trying to see what the ugly mug was peering at. Henry had heard voices, and unless this creep had been talking to himself, someone else was near. And if it was one of the ugly guy's buddies, why weren't they still talking?

No, it had to be Connor or Benella.

And the stocky guy had them flat-footed.

Henry moved without caution.

From behind a rock a man stood. Connor saw him instantly and hissed to Mary Leigh, "Run!"

But the girl said, "Mister Matt!" and ran toward the man.

From behind a different rock appeared another man. Mary Leigh spotted him, too. This one was *not* Mister Matt, but the one who looked like a troll. She hit the brakes when the troll-man hollered, "Hold up!" but when Mister Matt yelled, "Run, cupcake!" she took off again, though not as quickly as she might have.

"Go!" encouraged Bachison, seeing Jim Bobb's pistol coming up, so he fired his AR-15 from the hip and narrowly missed, showering Bobb with rock shards and causing him to duck back behind his redoubt as Mary Leigh was finally pounding out of sight and Connor Gibbs was charging Bobb's position like a fool. . . .

Thing can't get worse, thought Matt Bachison.

He was wrong.

On the far side of the basin, Marvin Delaney heard a shot and said to himself, "That was Matt's AR." He chuckled and continued upslope.

Benella Mae, who was not as far from Delaney as would have been healthy, also heard the shot, and sat leaning against an oak to wait. A chipmunk climbed onto a nearby stump to stare at her. She stared back. The chipmunk lost its nerve and flitted away. *At least I can intimidate a chipmunk,* she thought, and shifted the shotgun to her lap for quicker access.

Ritter had just come upon the scene when Bachison took his potshot at Jim Bobb. Ritter, mildly startled, was anything but indecisive. He knelt, nocked, and sought his target . . .

. . . the rugged man with the AR-15.

Sixty-five yards, give or take a smidgen . . .

. . . *too* damn far.

But Connor was probably nearby. And Mary Leigh . . .

So Henry let fly.

"What the hell you shootin' at me for?" a thoroughly pissed Jim Bobb shouted at Matt Bachison.

But Bachison didn't answer . . .

. . . because a razor-sharp arrow had just zipped clean through a lung and out the front of his shirt. His rifle clattered to the ground and his legs buckled.

Jim Bobb, noting all this, decided that elsewhere was better than here. *Any* elsewhere. Making surprisingly little noise for a heavy man, he quit the battlefield without firing a shot.

Too bad about Matt, he thought. *Now, where's that little girl?*

Matt Bachison was embarrassed. Not only had he let someone sneak up behind him, but he'd fallen over after being strafed by a freaking *arrow,* would you believe it. He tried to get back to his feet, but his legs weren't working well. He decided to rest a minute, then get up . . . until he heard a twig break twenty yards to his left and upped his SIG .45 to toss eight rounds into a laurel thicket. All the noise made his chest hurt afresh, so he lay back down for a spell.

Stupid twig! Henry thought as soon as he knelt on it. He hadn't been careful enough, had been in too much of a hurry. Now it looked like—
. . . eight bullets came his way in less than three seconds. The laurels didn't deflect them all.

"Did I hit you?" yelled Bachison, sitting up now, and hollering because his ears rang from the reports of his .45. The shouting made his chest hurt much worse.

"You think I'm over here napping? Hell yes, you hit me," replied an annoyed Henry Ritter as he applied a tourniquet to his leg, twisting the stick tighter, tighter.

"Hey, you shot me first. By the way, how far were you?"

"Sixty, sixty-five yards," Ritter replied.

"You got pins?"

"Hell, yes, you think I'm Robin Hood?"

"What's your lowest pin set for?" The wound in Bachison's chest was bubbling froth.

"Fifty yards."

"Then that was some shot."

"Yours wasn't too bad either."

"You're lots closer than sixty-five yards, and I fired a whole magazine."

"But you were shooting blind, and with a hole in your chest."

"Yeah. I'm, a whiz," Matt mumbled to himself.

Henry was trying out his leg. Not bad. "If you promise not to shoot me, I'll come have a look at your chest."

"I won't shoot you, but I can't speak for my pal."

"He's long gone. Skedaddled right after you took the hit. Loyal, ain't he?"

Bachison chuckled, then coughed up blood. "Brave, too. But at least he's ugly and not very smart."

"I'm coming," Henry allowed. "You shoot me again and I'll take it hard." And there he came, hobbling and grimacing. He sat down next to Bachison and took a look. "Your chest appears to be leaking. The name's Henry Ritter, by the way, as if you were interested. Want a smoke?"

"I'm Matt, and no thanks. Quit years ago."

"Wish I could," Henry mused, taking a long drag.

"On second thought . . ." Bachison held out his hand for the cigarette. Ritter handed over the butt and lit another.

They sat side by side for a while, bleeding, in pain, but enjoying the smokes and the wooded tableau and the coming dusk. Two squirrels chased each other around the trunk of a tree. Somewhere close a grouse took wing.

"I reckon I won't have to sweat lung cancer after all," Bachison said finally, grinding out his stub on a rock.

"No? Why not?"

"Because I'm not gonna make it."

And he didn't. In ten minutes, he was dead.

Ritter left him there, gently laying him over, and went to do what he could for the living. He had to walk very slowly or his tourniquet would loosen, so despite good intentions, in the end all he managed to do was kill Matthew Bachison, Mary Leigh's friend.

Chapter 42

JIM BOBB WENT SCURRYING DOWN THE SADDLE with that damned crazy Gibbs guy in hot pursuit, his heart pounding, blood racing, rocks rolling underfoot. He fell on his keister twice, and whacked his conk on a low-hanging limb, until suddenly it dawned on him that *he'd been looking for this guy*. He skidded to a halt, spun on his heels, and whipped out his gun.

"Come get it, bozo," he shouted.

Things had been looking up for Connor, what with Quasimodo running from him and both of them getting farther and farther from Mary Leigh, until his quarry had seemed suddenly to remember his *gun*.

Gibbs was too close and rushing too headlong to go for his own pistol, so he shifted from a head-on attack to a zigzag approach, like a broken-field runner, as he pounded on, the forest floor seemingly live under his feet, sticks rolling where he stepped, and there were rocks and depressions ready to sprain an ankle . . .

Close now, and the Neanderthal was shooting—not too

accurately—the bullets thwacking into trees all around, so instead of continuing his suicidal frontal assault, Gibbs dove into a convenient declivity and disappeared.

Delaney heard shots, lots of them, and smiled to himself. "Sounds right lively over there on the mountain," he said to the sky.

He was sitting with his back to a boulder and his binoculars to his eyes, watching a shallow bowl a few hundred feet below his position. He had no idea where the gorgeous bimbo might be headed, but if it was west it would probably involve that grassy bowl, unless she wanted to tackle one of the dense, virtually impenetrable laurel thickets. Or retrace her route.

Of course, if she was good in the woods . . .

A woman? Nah, not in his experience. A mall, maybe, but not the forest . . .

So he stuck with the glassing, patient and intent.

Let's see, thought Benella. *That first barrage was eight shots, and the second was seven, and from a smaller caliber. Henry carried no handgun, and Connor wouldn't waste shots like that, so that was probably two of our bad boys, unless it was just one of them but with two guns.*

She'd come to the edge of a broad, clear, bowl-shaped park, grassy and boulder-strewn and extremely exposed.

Right, I know I'm going to cross that and get my cellulite-free and aerobically rounded fanny shot off. It is to laugh.

She began searching for a better way. She did not find one. To the north was a laurel thicket Brer Rabbit would eschew; to the south ran a steep, rocky crevice. If she got caught down there—assuming she didn't break a leg climbing *into* it—she'd be a sitting duck taking fire from above.

Not much point in that.

Well, it would be dark soon. Assuming that Delaney had indeed lied about the explosives, maybe he'd lied as well about having nightscopes . . .

She'd take a chance, and cross the bowl after dark.

• • •

Mary Leigh had run and run. But now her little legs were tired. And the woods were dark. And getting darker. And she was scared. She started to cry, but in mid-sniffle she heard a sound. Not a squirrelly sound, a *big* sound . . .

An intruder.

Drawing on good sense, and courage derived from the genetic link to her mother (who had summoned sufficient resolve to cut a man's throat when necessary) and her father (who had died heroically trying to shield her with his body), Mary Leigh did not panic.

Instead she looked for a hiding place.

She found one just in time for the intruder—a whitetail doe—not to spot her. The deer, however, smelled the child and melted away. Mary Leigh never saw the deer, or heard it leave, so, true to Connor's instructions, she stayed right where she was, and fell asleep with the stars twinkling down upon her leafy canopy.

"If we go in now and Delaney and his crew are there and have control, then everyone is dead. Since there's only one access road, and we own it, I think we should wait until daylight, then go in and see what's shaking," counseled Ib Blankenship, junior G-man.

Havershaw, the senior G-man, reluctantly agreed, and went to a motel several miles away while his subordinates weathered the cold.

To keep warm, they said mean things about him.

Usually, Polly Petersen packed a parka to ward off cold. She put it on now, topped her thatch with a wool cap, pulled on some gloves, and slipped into the woods by the roadside, with a clear view of the feds. Everything was comfy but her tootsies, but the Petersen clan had long been noted for cold feet.

Literally speaking, of course.

After a time, she dozed.

• • •

Jim Bobb had never seen anything like it. The son of a bitch had *evaporated*! He'd seen the bastard take a dive, and figured he'd popped him a good one after all with the 9mm, but when he'd gone looking for blood, or a body, or *some fucking thing,* all he'd found was air. So he'd thrown the Kahr-9 against a tree in frustration, then spent half an hour on hands and knees in the dark finding it. Afterward, he'd sat on a stump to eat a whole bag of Hershey Kisses, which only made him hungry.

Damn, it was cold.

After a while, despite feet like blocks of ice and an upper lip smeared with nasal sludge, Jim nodded off.

Connor, having retrieved the long, heavy rifle he had hidden in the leaves, was easing carefully along, stopping to listen and whisper, "Katelin, honey," at regular intervals like he'd promised, so Mary Leigh could be certain it was him.

No response so far.

Quite frankly, he expected to find the girl rigid with fear, crying her little heart out, and he didn't blame her one bit. He'd be scared, too, if it were he out there, alone and four.

But Mary Leigh, made of stern stuff, was snoozing, thank you very much, inside a hollow log just her size.

Henry Ritter's leg was killing him. *Killing* him. Every time he loosened the tourniquet, he nearly cried out in pain. But he didn't; it would probably just get him shot again. By everyone. Who the hell knew where anyone was, good guys or bad guys, with it so dark? He looked up: *Where's the moon?*

So he sat beneath a persimmon tree with his wife, Jackie, on his mind, having a smoke like they always did, afterward . . .

Uncharacteristically sentimental, Henry said to the night, "Yep, Jackie Ritter's a fine gal. Way too good for the likes of me."

And he was right.

But she loved him anyway.

• • •

Delaney watched and watched, then rubbed his eyes and watched some more, alternating between his rifle scope (he wished he *did* have a nightscope!), his binoculars, and his naked eyes, which felt like they had sand in them . . .

"Mr. Sandman, bring me a dream . . ."

Where did that come from? I hate *that song. Ah, but how dear old mom used to love it . . .*

His mind was wandering. He wanted to light up, but with his luck, the sharpshooting Amazon would see it and shoot his nose off . . . Now, wouldn't that look funny? *No, ma'am, I didn't lose it in the war, I* sneezed *it off. Damn, I'm giddy. Can't kill folks on three hours' sleep.* Which reminded him of that time in Kuwait . . . night training with those, watcha call them . . . in . . . *around* those APCs . . . Thorton driving one . . . but his daddy wouldn't take him to the circus, and . . .

The AK-47 slipped from his grasp and he was asleep.

And while he napped, far below, Benella Mae Sweet was finishing her snack.

Benella buried the orange peels so as to provide no clue for anybody following, and gathered her manavelins. Time to go; soon such moon as would be, would be.

And as she slipped silently across the shallow bowl-shaped pockmark on the mountain's face, Marvin Delaney slept.

"That was Havershaw on the phone. He says we go in at first light. Not first gray, he says, but first real light. Otherwise we'll be shooting each other," Ib Blankenship reported to his peers, gathered round. " 'Shooting each other,' that's a direct quote. Who does he think we are, the CIA?"

His fellow agents laughed, to humor him, though two of them used to be CIA. Then most of them went to their cars to catch some sleep, though one stayed up, writing poetry on a yellow legal pad far into the night. Occasionally, the insomniac looked up to check the access road, just in case of attempted egress by the suspects, but by three o'clock she, too, was asleep.

The skunk was not feeling up to par. It had been eating poorly of late, due to having been bitten on its muzzle by a fellow skunk, one exceedingly ill-tempered. The wound had bled profusely, then festered, hampering normal food intake.

And aside from an empty belly, the animal was cold. So it sought shelter.

Inside a hollow log.

Mary Leigh sensed movement rather than heard it. It roused her slowly, for she had been deep in REM sleep. The moon, far and fractional and wan, cast its angled glow into the far end of the log. And there, filling the space where only space should be, was . . .

. . . what?

It was close, *very* close, scarcely more than arm's length, small and fuzzy and mostly black.

What kind of woodland critters were mostly black? She couldn't think of any, except a penguin, and this probably wasn't one of those. They lived in Aunt Article.

Should she risk a peek, a quick flick of her little flashlight? Or would that startle the creature? Maybe make it angry?

She decided to take the chance.

There was something there . . . smelly and unfrightened. But benign? The skunk didn't know. It did know that it was chilly, and that while it was quite willing to share the log, it was not willing to relinquish it. Unless evicted, of course.

So it stood its ground.

Until blinded by the light.

•   •   •

On went the flash, illuminating a pair of beady eyes, a pointy snout with a festered fistula, and a familiar two-toned face.

"Flower!" Mary Leigh said delightedly.

But the skunk would have none of it.

It hissed and she screamed.

Gibbs heard Mary Leigh's scream—quite near—and heedless of the noisy consequences, he ran to aid.

Benella heard Mary Leigh's scream, wafted on the wind from an uncertain direction. It made her blood run cold.

Delaney slept through the child's scream, dreaming as he was of demons and pearls.

Henry Ritter was separated by too many rocky corners from Mary Leigh to hear her scream. Besides, he was about to pass out from pain and blood loss.

Jim Bobb woke from a bad dream, at first unsure of what had awakened him. He sat very still and listened to the night. Voices nearby. He went to them.

"Katelin, where are you?" shouted Gibbs, in response to Mary Leigh's second scream.

"Connor!" Mary Leigh answered, scrambling backward out of a hollow log.

Gibbs spotted her, yelled, "Over here, honey," and leaned his rifle against a tree.

Mary Leigh jumped into his arms, hugging him tight, tight, *tight*.

"Are you okay?" he said quickly.

"I think so." Still suffering the cobwebs of sleep.

"Why'd you scream, hon?"

"'Cause he hissed at me!"

"Who?"

"Flower."

"What?"

"You know, Flower. Like in *Bambi*."

"A skunk?" His stomach flip-flopped.

"Yes."

"Did it bite you?"

"No, but he sure hissed a lot."

Quite obviously the skunk hadn't sprayed, either, so, cognizant of the more immediate danger created by their commotion, Connor turned to leave.

Too late.

Chapter 43

"WELL, LOOKEE HERE," SAID JIM BOBB, breathing hard from his sprint and standing triumphantly in the night, legs spread, feet planted, arms akimbo, the apotheosis of malicious menace.

Connor Gibbs sighed. "There goes the neighborhood."

Mary Leigh's eyes were as big as saucers.

"Run!" Connor hissed out of the side of his mouth.

"No," she whispered.

"I said *run!*"

"No!" Pleading.

"Hold it, sister," from Jim Bobb, lifting his sweater to show the pistol in his belt, barely visible in the pale wash of moon.

She ran.

Connor did, too.

Straight at Jim Bobb.

The distance was maybe twenty-five feet, and though Jim Bobb was no quick thinker, he did have good reflexes. Once his stegosaurus-sized brain finally processed the threat and decided that he did in fact need to *shoot this son of a bitch,* he went for his gun.

Too slow; Gibbs was upon him. When Jim jerked free the gun, Connor slapped it from his hand, knocking it skittering into the leafy darkness.

"Unkh," said Jim Bobb at the loss of his gun, right before Gibbs whipped a left hook to his mouth, then a follow-up right that connected with the side of Bobb's jaw. The blow staggered the burly man, who said, "Unkh," again and threw up his own fists in defense.

Connor Gibbs enjoyed an eight-inch height advantage over his opponent, superior boxing skills, and he was fighting for survival—his and Mary Leigh's. Bobb, though shorter, had orangutanlike arms, a low center of gravity, and he was gut-wrenchingly mean. Plus his mom had taught him how to wrestle. Reflexively, Jim went after Connor's legs, so Gibbs parried by socking him behind the ear with the heel of his hand, which dropped Bobb to his knees but otherwise failed to discourage him. The shorter man kept scrambling, grabbed Connor's ankle, then reached up with his other arm to clutch a handful of Gibbs's britches and pull. Gibbs, overbalanced, stumbled forward, but when Bobb strove to shift his body higher—closer to Connor's chest—he briefly exposed his granite chin. Gibbs hit him there, another sharp left, but without the full power of his hips and legs behind it. Nonetheless, it rattled Jim's cage and he missed his hold. Gibbs danced sideways and broke free. When Jim Bobb bounced up to charge back in, Connor hit him with a combination—left jab, right hook, left hook—twisting his hips for power and driving off his legs. Bobb grunted at each impact ("unkh-unkh-unkh"), the blood spurting from his ruined nose and coursing from a split lip, but showed no signs of flagging. Since Bobb was too close for a kick, Gibbs tried the left hook again since it had proven effective before, but Bobb saw this one coming and swung his arm in a clockwise circle—up and around the incoming fist to trap Connor's wrist—then reached over, grasped Gibbs's left shoulder tightly, grabbed his own grasping arm with his trapping hand, and simply arched both wrists, putting tremendous stress on Connor's already hyperextended elbow. Levered high on his toes, Connor realized that he was virtually at Jim Bobb's mercy. But Bobb had his own problem—what to do next. He could go ahead and break the big man's elbow, which would be balm for his split lip, or he could simply spin Gibbs around and smash him into . . .

. . . that tree.

So Jim took a giant step sideways—with Gibbs and his elbow going along with him—and, spinning his massive torso, swung the taller, heavier man into the tree trunk, which split Connor's scalp but also loosened Bobb's grip on his elbow. Gibbs felt the loosening and took immediate advantage by jerking his arm free and hitting Jim Bobb the hardest right cross he'd ever thrown. It cracked into Bobb's jaw like a rifle shot. The tenacious lout stumbled backward, windmilling his arms for balance before hitting the ground hard, where he lay still.

Good news to Connor, who was seeing double from his bout with the tree; his knees suddenly buckled and down he went. Bobb, on the other hand, was getting back up. Connor realized it and staggered to his feet, but Jim Bobb slipped aft, knelt as Gibbs was rising, and snaked both arms under, up, and around the back of the taller man's neck, to lace his fingers in a dreaded full nelson. All Bobb had to do now was use his tremendous forearm strength to force Gibbs's head forward. He tried to do so. Gibbs kicked and squirmed and bucked and twisted, easily lifting Bobb clear off the ground, but couldn't break the hold. Bobb, enjoying the histrionics, only regretted that he didn't seem to be hurting Gibbs much. So he switched his grip, unlacing his fingers and shifting his hands to Connor's subclavian area, where he grabbed the collarbone. The pain to Gibbs was immediate and excruciating. The battle intensified, with much pawing and kicking and grunting, until Gibbs finally broke loose—due primarily to the increased leverage afforded by his height advantage. Unfortunately, Connor's collarbone snapped as he burst free, removing the effective use of his left arm, so he decided to apply a low side kick. As Jim Bobb waded in to deliver more punishment, a broad grin on his subereous face, Gibbs shifted his left foot forward, brought his supporting right leg up across his body for balance, and kicked out with all his strength and desperation. The edge of Connor's hiking boot caught Jim Bobb's onrushing knee on the inside (its most vulnerable point) with tremendous force; the sickening *snap* of ruined cartilage was sharply audible. Jim emitted his final *"UNKH!"* and went to ground clutching the ruined knee, his face a contorted mask, as Gibbs returned his leg to the chambered position and lashed out with it once more, this time aiming for the nose. Bobb saw it coming. At the last second he lifted his head to avoid, thus stopping the boot with his mouth instead of his snout. He hit the dirt faceup and swallowed three teeth. Connor sat in a heap at what he thought was a safe distance.

It wasn't.

As Gibbs sat breathing heavily, Jim Bobb, prone and in agony, snaked his left hand toward his boot—deliberately bypassing the tanto knife at his belt—then came up off the ground on his good leg, managed to get a foot solidly planted, then made a final precipitate lunge, ice pick in hand . . .

The pick entered Connor's stomach dead center, two inches below the point of his sternum, and penetrated to the handle. Instinctively, he grabbed Bobb's hand to prevent him from withdrawing and plunging again, but in so doing ignored Jim Bobb's swinging right elbow, which found the side of his neck directly over the carotid artery . . .

All consciousness receded.

Chapter 44

AFTER CROSSING THE BOWL-SHAPED DEPRESSION, Benella settled in for the night. She ate an apple and a handful of Raisinettes, took several swigs from her canteen, and lay down on a carpet of soft, dank leaves, covering herself with a Space Blanket and using her cap as a rest for her head. Far off, Brer Owl hooted, a comforting sound, and she could catch a glimpse of the moon now, over in the east. Her mind drifted, through this and that . . . then, as it often did, back to the "suicide" . . .

Benella was fresh out of college and working with disadvantaged kids from the inner city in Atlanta, trying to help them sort out their lives like she so painfully had. She and a partner, a twelve-year police veteran, were first on the scene at an eight-story apartment building—not in the high-rent district—and a cluster of people had already gathered in the street, hoping for a jump. In a top-story window—feet dangling over the sill with nothing between his soles and the pavement except the sultry summer night— sat a small figure. Benella and her partner, Bobo Kersey, went right into the building, then up the stairs to the eighth floor (the elevator was inoperable), trying to hold their noses against the noisome mixture of stale vomit, chronic incontinency, and the ghosts of sexual liaisons.

The living-room door was ajar; inside, a shambles: SnackWell's devil's food cookies and Rold Gold pretzel sticks strewn about; human waste smeared on the walls; tin cans and empty McDonald's bags helter-skelter; the odor of cats and mice and despair.

And death . . .

The feet of someone could be seen, toes up and protruding from a filthy bathroom. The cop's gun came out of its holster very fast. Benella took a closer look: an elderly woman, long dead, her remains nidorous and cloying. There was a bullet hole in her throat, and much blood—dried mostly—pooled beneath her.

"You don't need to be here, B.M.," said Bobo.

"I can handle it. Besides, I may know this kid."

"If you get whacked, it's my fat ass," Bobo insisted.

"I agree with half that statement," Benella said.

"Okay. It's your casket."

A closed door led off the living area; on the other side of that door was a room with an open window that had a person perched in it. Had that person slain the old lady? Or maybe come upon the scene and retreated into a lofty despondency? Perhaps he was merely enjoying the view.

"Let's wait for the experts," suggested Kersey.

"What if he jumps before they get here?"

Bobo shrugged. "We go home, he goes to the morgue."

"Not acceptable," Benella said, and knocked on the door. "Hello in there!"

No reply.

"Hello? Are you okay?"

Still nothing.

"Sir ? May I come in?"

"No," came a faint response.

"Why not, sir?"

"I don' care to see nobody jus' now."

"Sir? Maybe I can help you."

"Can't nobody help me."

"Maybe not, but I'd sure like to try. Please let me come in and talk to you. I'll just stand near the doorway."

No reply.

She took that as a yes, and entered the room.

The boy was eleven, not a day older, with scars on his skinny back. Old scars. New scars. Lots of scars.

Burn scars.

He was looking out at the night; not down, just out.

"Sir, will you tell me your name?"

No response.

"Sir?"

"What?"

"How'd you get those burns?"

No reply.

"Sir? Can you tell about the burns?"

He looked back over his shoulder. Tears there, on a thin handsome face. "She give 'em to me."

"Who is 'she'?"

"Her in the bafroom."

"And who is she, sir?"

"My grammy."

"Is she responsible for you?"

"What?"

"Where's your mother?"

He turned his head away. "She dead."

"She died? When?"

"Long time ago. Jump out this same window. Grammy made her crazy."

"Do you know where your father is?"

"In the ground."

"He's dead, too?"

The boy nodded. "Po-leece beat him to deaf. I won't even born yet."

"Will you tell me your name?"

"Don' matter."

"It does to me."

He looked back at her. *"Why?"*

"I want to be able to call you by your name. Mine is Benella."

His brow knit. *"I know a Benella. At my school."*

"What grade are you in?"

"Third."

"So, will you tell me your name?"

"Samson."

"Samson, what a magnificent name. Strong."

"Mama say my daddy strong. Could lif' a horse." He smiled slightly. *"Could eat like one, too, I reckon. Mama say he a real big man."*

"Someday you'll be big like your father."

"No."

"Why not?"

"Ain't gonna be here."

"And why is that?"

" 'Cause I'm gonna jump out this window."

"Hold off on that a minute. How'd you get the burns, Samson?"

He looked out at the night again. *"Grammy done it,"* he finally said. *"Wif a cigarette."* Benella could hear sirens in the distance. The boy could, too. He looked down.

"Why did she do that?"

" 'Cause I slow."

"Slow in what way?"

"I don' learn stuff fas' enough. My grades wasn't so goot. She burnt me to teach me a lesson."

"She seems to have burned you a lot, Samson."

He nodded.

Bobo Kersey joined them in the room. Samson eyed him suspiciously. *"I didn' say you could come in."*

Benella said, *"How about waiting outside while Samson and I talk?"*

Bobo shook his head. *"Come on in, kid. You don't want to jump. You'll just make a mess."*

Samson stared at them. *"I ain't goin' to no jailhouse."*

"You're a juvenile," Benella said. *"They won't put—"*

"Come on in," Bobo interrupted. *"We'll treat you right. Better'n you treated grandma,"* and he stepped forward.

The boy brought his right hand into view. There was a gun in it, a Saturday night special, one of those pot-metal wonders that more often than not don't shoot when you pull the trigger. He didn't aim the gun at anyone, just brandished it for effect, but Bobo Kersey leveled his own piece and blew the boy off the windowsill.

It turned out that the gun hadn't even been loaded. The child had obviously found it beside his grandmother, who had used her only cartridge on herself.

Benella had given up social work that night.

She began to shiver violently—more from the horrible memory than the cold . . .

. . . remembering how she'd quit under a cloud because she had slammed Bobo Kersey's head with a ceramic lamp, and later threatened to testify against him if the case ever went to trial.

It didn't, of course. So she moved to Wendover, where her sister lived, and opened a gym, and began trading in antiques on the side. She earned a good living, and told herself every day that she was doing fine, just fine . . .

But Samson would haunt her until the day she died.

Maybe after.

Chapter 45

THE DELANEYS WERE STRONG SNORERS, ALWAYS had been. Marvin's daddy had driven his mother to distraction, and then to the guest room when in their early forties. If not, she'd never have slept. Still, whenever the house was uncommonly quiet she could hear him all the way from the guest room, so she took to wearing earplugs or leaving her radio on all night.

And Marvin took after his daddy.

The raccoon was in the "furious" stage—resulting from increased excitation of its central nervous system—and not long from death. Afflicted with fever and hyperesthesia, the animal was a walking (more correctly, staggering) mine-field. It snapped at anything that moved, and many things that didn't.

Oddly, it sought solace, but from what or from whom it had no idea.

Its keen sense of smell—enhanced by the disease—told it Man was near.

And he was.

•   •   •

Delaney was cavorting on a sun-swept beach with a bevy of bare-breasted beauties until a fiery comet lit on his neck.

Man was there, as foul smelling as ever—no, *worse*, given the animal's heightened olfactory—but as still and quiet as a half-eaten mole. The raccoon, beginning to froth, was about to go on its way when Man let out a frightful *SNORT!*, and moved his head.

The enraged raccoon attacked.

"WHAT THE FUCK!" yelled Marvin Delaney, abruptly wide-awake to find his *neck* under attack from a FURY with razor-sharp teeth and maniacal tenacity. Grabbing a handful of furry appendage, Delaney cast from himself the snarling apparition, then tried to stomp it into oblivion, a mistake discovered and regretted at once when the monster struck again, through the pants legs and into soft calf skin, then deeper, into muscle, and Marvin abetted his blunder by reaching toward the slavering maw. He promptly received a bite on the hand as his reward. In desperation, he drop-kicked the benighted creature thirty feet into the wood, where it scampered off in search of another foe, though it would be dead by morning.

And Delaney sat to curse his wounds.

Benella Mae Sweet heard Delaney's cries, and came for him in the night.

Chapter 46

He could see a light coming through the woods, flickering periodically as it went behind trees or was aimed in another direction. It had to be the little girl; no adult would walk around with a flashlight on, not with killers on the prowl.

His leg hurt like hell, but he managed to get up on his good one. He wouldn't have to go far. She was coming right at him.

Connor awoke shivering, not only due to the cold but to loss of blood. A serious loss. His head throbbed where Jim Bobb had slammed it into the tree, his broken collarbone was painful and annoying, and his stomach . . . well. What had the guy used, an ice pick? Where could anyone get an ice pick these days? He hadn't seen one in years. Just his luck, the first one he sees is sticking out of his abdomen. Wouldn't Bennie find that a hoot. But he was too woozy for joking around, so he tried to stand instead.

And promptly fainted.

•   •   •

Mary Leigh was finally calming down. A little. She had been afraid to call out to Connor 'cause that mean ol' troll-man might get her. But where was Mister Matt? And Aunt Bennie?

She was very frightened, but so far crying had only succeeded in making her face cold. So she munched on a granola bar from a jacket pocket and walked slowly and carefully, training her flashlight on the ground before her. Occasionally, she would shine it around her in a circle, to check for critters like that unfriendly Flower.

Connor had told her to walk away from the sun, but the sun was gone. So she'd been heading away from the moon . . .

And going the wrong way.

Another twenty yards and I've got her, he thought. *Don't change course; don't change course.*

And she didn't.

When a hand suddenly clamped across her mouth and a strong arm slid around her shoulders, Mary Leigh tried to scream, but couldn't. So she kicked.

His ruined leg.

It hurt so badly he let her go.

She tried to run, but he caught her coat and pulled her back.

And now she did scream.

"Shh, Mary Leigh, it's Mister Henry!"

Mary Leigh stopped screaming. "Who?"

"You know, Mister Henry." *Damn,* his leg hurt; she'd kicked him right on his wound.

"Mister Henry that owns the cabin?"

"That's right, honey."

"Who always calls me his 'cutie pie'?"

Henry laughed in spite of the pain. "That's right."

"Mister Henry!" she yelped, and grabbed him around the arm.

"WATCH THE LEG, WATCH THE LEG!"

"Oh, did I hurt you?"

"Yeah, but don't worry about it. You didn't know who I was. I grabbed you like that to keep you from yelling and giving away our position."

"It didn't work, Mister Henry."

"I noticed that. So we better move, though I'm not in much shape to."

"You can lean on me."

"Why, thank you, cutie pie. I will."

But he didn't; he only pretended to.

Jim Bobb heard Mary Leigh's scream through a veneer of pain, horrible pain, mostly from his ruined knee. His other wounds, although extensive, were nothing by comparison. He hurt so badly, in fact, that he'd forgotten to stir that big son of a bitch's brains. Oh well, he reckoned that poke in the belly took care of him . . .

But it hadn't.

Yet.

Mary Leigh and Henry hobbled along (with him doing the hobbling, her doing the "helping") for about an hour, taking them well away from Jim Bobb and his ice pick.

But closer to Marvin Delaney.

Delaney was soaking his multiple wounds with water when he heard the scream. He was so jumpy from his recent ordeal with the raccoon that it made him wet his pants. "Shit!" he expleted, then kept on mopping blood from rips and puncture wounds as urine spread its sticky warmth down his leg. "That'll turn cold directly," he observed of his soiled trousers.

Benella Mae heard Mary Leigh, too, but couldn't determine the direction. She had to trust Connor to handle his end, so kept moving toward where she figured Delaney was hiding. And she was right, but by the time she got there, Delaney was gone. All that was left was a bloody handkerchief. How could she know he'd left it there deliberately, as bait, and was looking at her now, from nearly two hundred yards away . . .

. . . through a rifle scope.

Gibbs groaned and rolled over and pushed himself up on all fours, then to his knees, then upright. Sort of. Hunched over involuntarily, unable to straighten, he put one leg shakily in front of the other. Then again. And again . . .

And discovered that he could walk.

He aimed for the river, and hopefully, Mary Leigh.

"Where were you heading, honey?" Henry asked as he hobbled.

"Connor told me to go to the river, turn toward the hand with the ring on it, and find a road with a bridge under it. Then wave to cars."

Henry said, "That's a gem dandy plan."

"Was I going right?"

"Pretty close."

"Will you help me find the river?"

"You bet."

The child started to skip in delight. "I wonder where Mister Matt is," she wondered aloud, ducking under a low limb.

Mister Matt? Oh . . . "Back there a ways," Henry replied somberly.

"Is he a bad man, like Connor says?"

How to answer? "Well, honey, there are bad men and then there are good men who make bad choices. Maybe he was one of those."

She accepted that. "I hope he isn't feeling real cold right now," she said.

"I'm pretty sure he's not," assured Henry.

Well, it was true.

Matt Bachison wasn't feeling anything.

●   ●   ●

The river, that's where the girl will go. Then she can find the road if she knows which way to turn, Jim Bobb reasoned with himself while fashioning a crutch out of a dead branch.

He started for the river.

The 7.62/39 rifle cartridge is not a powerhouse as rifle cartridges go; nor is the AK-47 an especially accurate rifle. Sturdy, reliable, and cheap—but not accurate. So it should come as no surprise that instead of hitting Benella smack in the spine where Delaney had intended, the rather anemic .30-caliber bullet missed its mark. In fact, it was off to starboard by nearly five inches, entering her latissimus dorsi just aft and below her armpit, where it impacted and followed along a rib to exit her left side, directly under her arm, then went on to clip the front edge of her biceps muscle. Not much flesh was penetrated, and the range was long, so the bullet's speed—not much to begin with—had dropped off precipitously. Therefore there was no significant expansion of the bullet's lead nose, and little energy transfer.

In other words, the wound hurt like the blazes but was neither lethal nor disabling.

The blow took her breath away all *awhoosh!* Benella staggered, reaching out for a tree to keep from falling, but missed, which was a very good thing since Delaney had recovered from the minimal recoil of his heavy, tricked-out AK and was essaying another shot. She didn't give him one. Once on the ground, she had the presence of mind to stay there, and to shift her body behind a protective rock. She had no idea where Delaney was (if it *was* Delaney—after all the time she'd spent in these woods, it could have been *anybody*) because she hadn't heard the shot, only felt its result. Speaking of which, she was bleeding all over herself. Better go somewhere and try to fix that, what she could reach, anyway. The problem was in the going somewhere. Although it was fairly bright now that the moon was at its zenith, she suspected that Delaney had not lied about having a nightscope. Ergo, she couldn't safely move around very much. Conversely, if she lay here with her thumb in her ear, he could be running a sneak. Then he wouldn't *need* a nightscope; a slingshot would do.

Dee-fense, she thought, and skulked away.

Delaney's neck was bleeding again; he could feel it trickling down his neck. *"Mother of pearl!"* he quoted W.C., and dabbed with his last hanky.

He'd seen the bimbo fall, thus knew he'd hit her. Problem was, he'd also seen her slither away. She could be lying close, waiting for him to come administer a coup de grâce.

Not Mrs. Delaney's little boy, Marvin, he thought, and stayed where he was.

After an hour, he decided that she was either dead or gone, so he went to see.

Gone.

His wounds were still leaking, but he tried to ignore that as he examined her spoor. She'd left plenty. Blood everywhere at first; then a drop here, a drop there. He cupped his flashlight and held it close to the ground. After twenty minutes of that, he said to hell with it, it was too risky if she was laying an ambush.

He looked ahead, in the direction she was moving.

The river, he thought. *Smart. That's where I'd head, too.* So he did.

"Mister Henry, I'm tired."

"Me, too, cutie pie, but we're almost there. Can't you hear it?"

Mary Leigh listened. "Nope," she allowed.

"I can. Just a little bit more and we can take a nice long rest on the riverbank. Okay?"

"Okay," unenthusiastically.

And within ten minutes, they were there.

•   •   •

The arm, she fixed. The side, she fixed. The back . . .
. . . she couldn't reach

What had Henry taught her? That a wounded deer goes
to water, or at least to very soggy mud, which not only
soothed but usually stopped the bleeding.

Where was there enough water for that?

The river.

Connor had fallen many times, but each time he laboriously climbed back to his feet and continued on. Step after
step, yard after yard, fall after fall, half-unconscious, using
the moon as his guide without being aware of it, mind
numbed by pain but unwilling to quit, even to rest, because
Mary Leigh needed him, because Benella was counting on
him, and because he was no quitter. It seemed to take all
night but finally he sank to his knees and submerged his
aching head in river water, shockingly cold. He didn't know
it, but he was less than a quarter mile upstream from Benella.

The icy water took Benella's breath away and caused
her heart to skip. Within four minutes, she was numb; within
eight, hypothermia was a real possibility; within nine, all
bleeding had stopped. After ten, she rose shivering from
the water.

A fire was out of the question. So she dressed with everything she had, curled up in the Space Blanket, and tried to
sleep. Unsuccessfully. But she did avoid freezing to death.

Jim Bobb made the river an hour before dawn, though
he was in such pain he didn't care at that point. Nor did
he care about catching the little girl, or about all the money
in the back of the van, or about much of anything else.
All he cared about was morphine, like he'd had over in
the Storm, and he couldn't remember why he didn't have
any now . . .

He watched the moon through a dim haze of pain while
drifting into a fitful slumber, better than no relief at all.

Chapter 47

SOMEWHERE A COCK WAS CROWING AS THE FBI task force prepared to move. Vests were donned, guns were checked, ammunition was doled out, coffee cups were crumpled, bladders were drained, pictures of family were put away.

"Now, you men know what to do. And you, too, Shirley," said Havershaw officiously.

"Yeah. Don't get shot," Agent Ib Blankenship remarked under his breath.

Shirley snorted.

"What was that?" from Havershaw, head swiveling.

"Uh, nothing," Shirley denied, giving Ib the evil eye.

"You all have the rendezvous coordinates. The sun will cleave the sky soon, so prepare to move out."

Shirley mouthed, *"Cleave the sky?"* at Blankenship, who shrugged and arched his brows. Shirley's bunions were killing her; she was too old for this kind of work. *To heck with strolling through the woods,* she thought. *Especially when there are mean dudes with guns in those woods.* But she was nothing if not game.

So she crossed the road.

• • •

Polly Petersen plucked a piece of pork from her biscuit and tossed it out the window. "Yecch," she exclaimed. "As if my fat intake's not high enough as it is."

She tried the biscuit—cold and hard and left over from last night. *Not too bad, though,* she thought, chewing the fat. Into the cassette deck went Creedence Clearwater Revival:

> ". . . Papa said, son, don't let the man getcha,
> And do what he done to me . . ."

Her mouth, though full of ham and biscuit, lip-synched the lyrics.

She *loved* John Fogerty.

Chapter 48

THE BORROWED TOYOTA AVALON WAS PARKED at the cabin. Facing almost due south and covered with a thin rime of frost, it refracted icily the early-morning sunlight. Connor's Mustang sat next to it, equally radiant. One was nearly new; one was two years old. Neither would be there long.

Connor Gibbs woke to a swelled head, a depleted blood supply, and a weakness such as he'd never known. He tried to get up. Couldn't. His crossed legs were asleep, his vision was blurred, and he was dangerously cold. How to attract attention? He could signal with his .45, but that might bring the wrong kind of attention. How about a fire—not only might someone spot it, he could get warm. Then again, there was a significant risk of attracting the wrong party. Still, he felt the risk was justified. He sensed that if he didn't do *something,* he was doomed, unless he was incredibly lucky.

He was right.

• • •

Henry Ritter and Mary Leigh were less than 250 yards from Gibbs, but had no way of knowing that, and it was beginning to look doubtful whether Henry could even continue to travel, let alone help anyone. His face was pale and drawn, both from strain and blood loss, and he was shivering uncontrollably.

Henry said to Mary Leigh: "Well, cutie pie, looks like you're gonna have to go on without me."

Strangely, Mary Leigh did not protest; she saw and understood the man's weakened condition. "Tell me what to do, Mister Henry," she said.

"Follow the river that way, in the direction the water flows. Stay on this bank. Don't try to cross, even if the water looks shallow in spots. If you come to a pile of rocks or something else that comes right to the river's edge, go around, but try to stay within sight or hearing of the river so you won't get lost."

"What if I see somebody?"

"You probably won't. But if you do, unless it's Connor or Aunt Bennie, duck behind something and hide till they're gone. That's very important, honey."

"What if it's Mister Matt?"

"If it's him, you can come out. But it won't be."

"How do you know?"

"Because he's way back on the east side of the cabin."

"You sure?"

"I'm sure."

Mary Leigh stood up, bedraggled, dirty, hungry. And resolute. "Don't you worry, Mister Henry. I'll bring someone back to get you."

She hugged him then, gently, so as not to hurt his leg, and left him there beside the cold river. She hoped he wouldn't die like her daddy had.

Benella was two hundred yards downstream from Mary Leigh, propped against a big piece of driftwood, tending her wounds. Her last apple had long been consumed, so she was hungry, but having lost far less blood than either

Henry or Connor, she was in much better shape. In fact, she was full of piss and vinegar. Her wounds were very sore but no longer seeping.

Life was good. Or at least bearable. So she folded up her Space Blanket, scooped up her shotgun, and followed the river. Less than three minutes after Benella had disappeared around a bend, Mary Leigh paused to remove a pebble from her shoe. She balanced herself against a big piece of driftwood and wondered who had left the apple core beside it.

Marvin Delaney had pretty much stanched the blood flow from his multiple wounds, though one of them was still a pain in the neck. He had never expected this situation to take all night. Chances were good that the cops would be moving in soon, especially if that dildo private detective followed the news and was able to put two and two together. Hell, they might be moving in right now—

He heard a noise over the din of the river, which flowed rapidly where he was. A rustle of dry leaves, maybe a twig cracking . . .

Something.

He moved, snatching up his rifle to melt into the undergrowth, silent and deadly and invisible.

Well, almost invisible.

Sure enough, Benella didn't spot him.

Jim Bobb's leg was numb all the way to his crotch because he was sitting on a flat rock by the river with the leg submerged. The relief was indescribable. His head still throbbed and the gaps where his swallowed teeth no longer were hurt like sin. But the knee had been the worst by far, and for the moment it wasn't.

He was 250 yards from the bridge over which the paved road meandered. When he felt like it, he was going to make it to that road, then flag down a car and make some-damn-body take him to the van.

Yep, that was what he was going to do.

When he felt like it . . .

• • •

Fifteen G-men (and one G-woman) stepped off the road and into the woods at 0800 hours on the button. They fanned out in a southerly direction, five of them west of the roughly north/south river, and eleven of them east of it. Half of them had shotguns in hand, the rest Uzi submachine guns.

A dangerous bunch.

Jim Bobb heard them coming a hundred yards away, one-legged it to a deadfall, and crawled under. Agent Blankenship passed within thirty feet of him, but was soon gone, which left no one at all between Jim and the paved road.

Except Mary Leigh.

Delaney had Benella Mae in his sights once again, this time at no more than eighty yards, and was taking up the trigger slack when he heard rustling sounds behind him and sucked in his head like a turtle. His camouflage clothing saved him; an FBI agent passed within a stone's throw.

Benella knelt behind a tree, spooked by a noise off to her left front. She thought quickly: *To hell with this sneaking around in the woods not knowing where anyone is. I'm heading back to the cabin.*

She did.

Marvin Delaney saw Benella leave, but was afraid to risk a shot; the fed was still around, somewhere. So Delaney followed her, waiting for his chance.

Shirley Tennibow was walking the riverbank just across the water from Henry Ritter, now sound asleep in the morning sun. She was being very careful not to twist an ankle on one of the slippery rocks underfoot, and didn't see him.

• • •

Polly popped open her purse. Should she call in a report to Hank Yarborough? She reckoned she might as well, and did. Within five minutes, Yarborough had alerted his counterpart up Polly's way and was going out the door, headed west.

Polly switched on her ignition and pulled off the grassy verge. Where to? *The best vantage point is the bridge,* she thought.

What if one of them was in the house, waiting? She could be spotted crossing the wide yard, no matter which direction. Then Benella remembered the cars. She could low-crawl to one of them, ease open a door opposite the cabin, slip in, and drive away . . .

Sure she could.

Delaney said aloud to himself: "Naw, it'd be too easy just blowing her up. Not after all the trouble I've gone through. I want to make the bitch suffer."

So while Benella was crawling sluglike on her flat belly—still half a football field from the nearest car—Delaney hit the switch.

Connor's car—on the far side of the Avalon—went up like a rocket, chunks of it flying everywhere, the hollow CRUMP! of detonation setting Benella's ears to chiming, pieces of metal raining down as she scrambled back to the tree line with acrid smoke filling her nose.

"Shit!" she said, and then the Avalon blew, even more spectacularly. "The son-of-a-bitch *did* booby-trap the cars!"

Then the cabin, BOOM!—splinters of wood, whole logs, glass, chunks of furniture, a sink, clumped masses of bricks from the fireplace—all flying high, spinning lazily and tumbling earthward. She covered her head as she moved deeper into the woods.

Every FB-ear in the forest heard the explosions, and despite their obvious lack of proximity, some of them hit the dirt. Not Havershaw. "Yo!" he called to Blankenship. "This way!"

And the two headed for disaster.

There she is, thought Delaney, and hove to his feet with his AK blasting, shooting too quickly to hit much. Bark flew, and rock chips, but not Benella meat. In seconds, his thirty-round magazine was exhausted.

When he stopped to reload, Benella made her move.

Oops, Benella thought, and hit the dirt, bullets impacting all around her as she rolled behind a rock for protection. Bullets ricocheted off its surface, then nothing.

He's reloading! she thought, and jumped to her feet, working the pump—BOOM! BOOM! BOOM! BOOM! BOOM! BOOM!—but the range was too far, at least ninety yards, so her singing pellets were ineffective, except in defoliating. No more shells, so she threw the Ithaca aside and drew the 9mm.

Delaney was coming.

He was charging, getting closer to ensure a kill, the AK at port arms, his boots pounding the earth, and the bitch was running at *him*! *Good for you, you got balls like coconuts,* he thought, blood pounding, mouth dry, adrenaline coursing, and suddenly she was *there,* forty yards, where he couldn't miss, and she was *still* coming straight at him, like freaking Dallas Stoudenmire right out of the history books, and up came his rifle . . .

Until somebody hollered, "HALT!"

Benella just didn't care anymore. This gob of spit had made her life miserable for far too long, and Connor might be dead, and Henry, maybe even little Mary Leigh, *So bring it on, old son!* and she went after Delaney, holding the 9mm in both hands, intent that one of them was going to DIE!

• • •

Havershaw heard the shooting and recognized the singular sound of an AK-47 and thought, *Fuck me,* and charged anyway . . .

A pompous ass, for certain.

But no coward.

Ib Blankenship wanted to duck, to hide, to run away . . . but he didn't. He should have; he had four kids and a wife, but when he saw the charging man, he yelled "HALT!"

It got him killed.

At the sound of "HALT!" Delaney didn't, he simply changed direction and charged the yeller. Two men actually, and the closer one had an Uzi, so Marvin blasted that guy with the AK, seeing his bullets strike, slam into the man's vest—which wouldn't stop a rifle bullet—and the man was suddenly spinning, opening up with the Uzi . . .

. . . into trees, the ground . . .

. . . the agent beside him.

Havershaw, having wisely stopped to kneel—thus making a steadier and smaller target—was about to jerk the trigger of his riot gun—with Delaney in his sights—when an Uzi stuttered over on his right and two bullets from it smashed into his brain and he was dead . . .

Benella took advantage of Delaney's averted attention and shot him three times in the body—BAM! BAM! BAM!—like that, so rapidly the reports blended together.

No effect, except to cause Delaney to turn his attention back to her, his AK stuttering, and she dove into a crevice, scuttled toward a rocky precipice, and took to the air. Sixty feet, straight down, but the branches of a mountain cedar broke her fall. She hit the ground so hard the breath was knocked from her, but Delaney suddenly appeared above with his damned AK, so she didn't have time to lie there, instead scuttling under a deadfall as bullets blew holes in things other than her while she crawled deeper under, then out the other side, where bullets couldn't reach because of the angle. Would he follow her down? She looked up at the sheer rock face.

No way, she thought.

Ha.

Hell, she did it, Delaney thought, and launched himself like Batman.

Here he comes! Benella thought, and opened fire, her bullets *whanging* off the sheer granite face, trimming needles from the cedar, but if any struck Delaney, there was no evidence of it. *I forgot, he probably has a vest,* she chided herself as she slammed home her extra mag, depressed the slide release, and heard Delaney hit the ground.

Zinging bullets were everywhere—one through the toe of his boot, another *whacking* into the protruding magazine of his rifle, silencing the gun for the duration. After tumbling down through the branches of the cedar, Marvin hit the ground hard, then rolled parachutist style quickly to his feet. Out came the Colt 10mm.

Now where is she? he wondered.

Not there.

Shirley Tennibow, due soon to be a grandmom, heard all the shooting and commotion, and headed toward it. Which was a mistake, though she didn't know it.

Polly placed a peanut on her tongue and chewed thoughtfully. All the shooting seemed to be coming her way. Should she abandon her spot?

And miss all the fun?

So she stayed.

Benella was moving in a semicircle, trying to get behind Delaney—or at least flank him—when she spotted movement in the direction of the river. Was that Delaney flanking *her*?

He was flanking her, all right, but from a direction other than where she was looking . . .

Shirley Tennibow had never been much of a shot. She was a thinker, not a shooter, or so she'd always told herself. She liked to use her head. So she used it now. Which way to go? The sudden silence seemed surreal—no birds chirping, squirrels chattering, twigs snapping, guns firing. Nothing.

There was, however, a pistol aimed at her left nostril, and from not far away.

Now, who is that? thought Benella. Then she saw the jacket clearly; it had FBI on the back in big letters. *Better not shoot this one,* she thought.

Should she signal? No. Any sound might bring Delaney running. Benella knew he was close; she could *feel* him.

So she lay low.

The shot was not a certain one, and Delaney knew it. Too far for a head shot, especially with all the intervening brush. He could barely make out her outline.

He took the shot anyway.

"Got her!" he yelled, and up he jumped.

The bullet took Field Agent Tennibow high, laying open her scalp above the hairline. Loss of consciousness was painfully immediate.

She never even heard Delaney's triumphant yell.

When Marvin Delaney popped up like a jack-in-the-box, Benella shot him six times. Or *at* him, anyway. Four bullets actually struck him—three in the vest and one through the upper arm, where the triceps meet the deltoid. Down he went.

Faking.

He dropped too fast, thought Benella. *I don't think I got his head. He's trying to sucker me. I better go check on the agent first.*

Benella low-crawled over to Shirley Tennibow, examined the woman's wound—bloody, but a gash only, no obvious penetration of the skull. Still, there was always the serious risk of concussion, and you couldn't put a tourniquet on a head wound. Delaney may or may not be dead, but this woman might soon be if she didn't receive medical attention.

So Benella Mae went to find some.

Delaney watched the tall bitch slither off, probably going for help now that she knew some was around. After five minutes, he walked over to the downed FBI agent. *Pretty nasty wound, lady. I have a feeling you won't survive it.* He raised his Colt.

Naw, where's the challenge in that?

So he went to the river, crossed it, hoofed it to where the van was hidden, and was gone from the area before Sheriff Yarborough even arrived.

Benella stumbled across an unconscious Henry Ritter, and tried to rouse him. No luck. She threw caution to the wind and began to yell for help.

Seven agents heard her and came to assist.

Jim Bobb heard her and them and headed for the hardtop road.

Mary Leigh heard her and for a moment was uncertain what to do. Then she, too, headed for the road.

No one found Connor Gibbs. He had passed out trying to light a fire.

Chapter 49

Mary Leigh had often gone to the firing range with her grandfather—who had been a black-powder competitive shooter—so the sounds of gunfire did not bother her. Nor did explosions; she had once been present when Mister Henry dynamited stumps on his farm down east. Nor did the cold vex her, for she was dressed warmly; nor hunger, at least not yet. What did bother Mary Leigh was disorientation. And she was disoriented now.

A while back, at a shallow place in the river, she had spotted some trout near the opposite bank and tippy-toed across a fallen log for a closer look. After squatting on the bank to watch for a time ("Hey, fishy-fishy"), she had gone back to following the flow of the river, just like Mister Henry had instructed. But she forgot that she had crossed over. After walking around a pile of rotting flotsam, then circumnavigating a briar patch, all of a sudden she couldn't remember where the river was . . .

Well, sa'sparilla. She steepled her fingers under her chin and tried to think.

That way? She turned her head . . . *Or that way?* She swiveled her dirty, pretty face . . .

And then smiled and went straight to the river.

For she had seen the bridge.

Jim Bobb was on the east bank, near the bridge, when he espied the brat over on the *west* side, walking purposefully, as if she knew where she was going. Using his sturdy makeshift crutch, he hobbled as fast as he could, aiming to head her off.

How he was going to cross the river was anybody's guess.

Mary Leigh stopped and looked up. There was *no* way she could go up *that* embankment. Too thickety. She looked across the river. Yep. The far side even had a path going up. Now to get across . . .

Not shallow here, but stepping-stones, some of which seemed pretty far apart for her short legs, but she gave it a shot. And made it—though she slipped twice, wetting the same shoe each time. Then she started up the embankment.

Come on. Come on across, Jim Bobb thought. And she did, hopping from stone to stone.

Right to him.

"Hey!" Mary Leigh heard someone shout, and she turned her head. *The troll!* She scampered up the hill, slipping, falling, sliding, then again, her slick-bottomed shoes digging for purchase but finding little, though she kept trying, frantically, with the squat ugly man coming behind her, mostly on one knee, grimacing as if in horrible pain, and she wouldn't quit, didn't quit, but scrambled, on and up and over . . .

With the troll right behind.

•   •   •

Polly Petersen was sitting in her car facing due east—heater on, with the sun in her eyes—when suddenly a child appeared.

A little girl. *The* little girl?

Probably, Polly surmised, since the poor baby was running hard, and—

A strangely misshapen man was behind her, hobble-running on a jerry-rigged crutch, a determined, nefarious look about him . . .

And he was gaining.

But the girl had a good lead—maybe twenty steps—so she would probably make it to Polly's car . . . just . . . in . . . the . . . nick . . . of . . . time.

Polly stepped from the car, held out an arm to pull the terrified child into her side, then covered the small face with a comforting hand. Jim Bobb, undeterred, advanced implacably. From her pocket Polly produced a High Standard .22 semiautomatic pistol that she often used to plink tin cans and pinecones.

This was no pinecone.

Drawing an ice pick and holding it menacingly in one hand, Jim Bobb said, "Let go the kid, fatso."

For this serious breach of etiquette Polly shot him nine times. Jim Bobb hit the ground writhing.

Polly said, "Who you calling fatso?" and shot him twice more.

When much later a medical examiner was called to examine, Jim Bobb's body was attached by its remaining teeth to a sapling six inches in circumference. "What do you make of that?" asked one of the deputies on the scene.

"Well," replied the ME, "given the extensive trail of blood and intestinal contents, and the dirt under his nails, I'd say he dragged himself to the nearest tree and chomped down, sort of like biting a bullet in order to bear pain. This man died in agony, and not quickly. Until the end, of course. That went very quickly."

"The end?"

"Oh, those bullet wounds didn't kill him. Small caliber peripheral hits? No, no, no."

"Then what the hell did?"

The ME knelt beside the stiffened, mephitic body, turned it half over, and said, "That." From Bobb's left ear protruded an ice pick, embedded clear up to the handle. "The pain from the bullet wounds—one of them to his scrotum—must have been more than he could stand," he explained.

"You mean . . . the guy offed himself?" asked the incredulous deputy.

"Indeed," confirmed the ME.

And so he had, old Jim Bobb.

But he'd had to do it twice.

Because the first time he'd lost his nerve at the last minute, and gotten only as far as the inner ear.

Which merely made him scream.

The second time he used the heel of his hand.

And finally got it right.

Chapter 50

WITHIN THIRTY MINUTES, FEDERAL AGENTS HAD removed both Henry Ritter and Shirley Tennibow from the forest and transported them in great haste to a local hospital. Both would live, though Ms. Tennibow would suffer severe headaches for the rest of her life, and Henry would never have quite the same jaunty gait of his younger days.

No one had found Connor Gibbs.

Mary Leigh was examined by a physician on the scene, plus a child psychologist, and once she had eaten, received a clean bill of health. Oh, she had a scratch here and there, from her brush with the briar patch, and a stone bruise on one heel, but there seemed to be no serious problems, mental or physical. The little girl was concerned, though, about Aunt Bennie (now heavily bandaged and chemically pain-reduced, but refusing to go anywhere until they found Gibbs), Mister Matt (whose body had not been found), and Mister Henry (too heavily drugged even to remember his encounter with Bachison, let alone where it took place).

The bodies of AIC Havershaw and Ib Blankenship were airlifted out by helicopter. The consensus among those present was that James Q. Bobb should go by garbage truck, but the medical examiner's Taurus station wagon served.

Polly Petersen promised the police a statement, preferably presented on the morrow, since currently she desperately needed forty winks and a back rub from her live-in. So she and Willie Nelson drove off wailing:

> ". . . and I ain't gon' let 'em catch me, no;
> I ain't gon' let 'em catch the Midnight Rider."

After what seemed forever to Benella, Sheriff Yarborough finally arrived, with Everette in tow. She greeted the sheriff: "We haven't heard from Connor. Mary Leigh said he fought the troll—"

"Who?" interrupted Yarborough.

"Jim Bobb, now deceased."

"Ah. Have they searched for Connor?"

"Halfheartedly, their reasoning being that first we take care of the walking wounded. One of them even had the gall to say maybe that Connor had sneaked back into the cabin and fallen asleep."

"Have they checked near the cabin?"

"Not since Delaney blew it up. By the way, Henry may have taken care of Bachison, but since he's soaked in painkillers, he's a bit vague. They're searching for Bachison's body east of the cabin."

Yarborough motioned to Everette. "Let's go find Connor."

And they tried.

But they didn't find him.

Connor Gibbs woke to the sound of a helicopter and staggered to his feet waving his good arm. No one saw him. He ran after the chopper—as best he could given the dizziness—but tripped over a stone and fell to his knees. Then he rolled under an overhang and passed out.

Which made him invisible except from the river. In a few hours, night would come. With it, the cold.

Connor could never survive another night of exposure.

• • •

Before driving off in the van, Marvin Delaney had booted Buster out. Stupid dog. He couldn't believe Matt had kept him around. Now someone else could feed him. Or let him starve to death, who gave a flip.

Buster did. So as soon as he was dumped unceremoniously at the side of the road, his brain said "hungry" and his smeller said "food."

Indeed it was. A rabbit, recently rendered roadkill by an FBI vehicle. Buster bellied up to brunch.

Later, while licking residue from his chops—in no great haste—Buster's brain said "thirsty" and his smeller said "water." Off he ran to get some.

For hours they searched, but no Gibbs. They did find and remove Mister Matt's body. Mike Everette was careful not to let Mary Leigh see.

Benella was on the verge of despair.

Until they heard it.

Does Henry have a dog?" asked Deputy Everette.

"I don't think so," answered Mary Leigh. "Not here. At his other house he does."

"Then whose dog is that barking?" Everette said.

They went to look.

Buster had lapped a surfeit when he heard something. His half-floppy ears half unflopped, and he tilted his intelligent head, first one way, then the other . . .

A groan. Faint perhaps, but still a groan.

Now, a groan didn't necessarily indicate to Buster what it might indicate to a human. It indicated a new friend. Maybe. (He'd become somewhat leery of humans after prolonged exposure to Jim Bobb.) So, with high hopes the little black dog diffidently traversed the river.

And found Connor Gibbs.

He let the world know.

Chapter 51

Bᴇɴᴇʟʟᴀ Mᴀᴇ Sᴡᴇᴇᴛ ᴡᴀs ᴘᴀᴛᴄʜᴇᴅ ᴜᴘ, ꜰɪʟʟᴇᴅ up, and had ten hours of sleep under her hat as she paced the waiting room for word on Connor . . .

Mary Leigh was back with her mom, now home from Charter and under heavy guard, since the slick but slimy Marvin Delaney was still at large. The child had adopted Buster, who was delighted to have a new pal and showed it by not peeing on the carpet. Much. Mary Leigh fed him Gravy Train, renamed him Mister Matt, and tickled his tummy a lot.

Henry was not only doing fine, but had pinched every female nurse within arm's reach.

And all the while, Benella waited. For word.

Around midnight, a very tired-looking doctor came and sat down beside her. Walter Gibbs, his grandson Cameron, and Blister McGraw were seated directly across from her. Holmes Crenshaw had gone for pizza. Braxton Chiles hovered inconspicuously near the water fountain, watching everything and everyone.

"Well?" said Benella.

"He'll live," said the doctor. "But it was touch and go for a while. The puncture wound is in a bad spot, and it became infected. His head is concussed, and there was a minor accumulation of blood under the skull, against the brain. We drained it off. The fractured collarbone was certainly painful, but not serious. It will mend nicely.

"Both of you were very lucky. I've seen your X rays, Ms. Sweet. A couple of inches to the right—or if the bullet had entered from a more acute angle—and you wouldn't be here. How're the wounds?"

"Back and side hurt like hell."

"And the arm?"

"Compared to the others, it's not even noticeable."

He nodded

"When can we see Connor?"

"He's still under anesthesia. Let him sleep for a while, then we'll see. He really did lose a lot of blood," said the sawbones, and took his leave.

Cameron came over, sat beside Benella. "Sounds like good news."

She patted his leg. "Yes. He's not out of the woods, but the sun is beginning to shine through."

The boy sighed. "He seems to spend more time in the hospital than an orderly."

Benella noted with relief that the lad retained a sense of humor even under dire circumstances. Like his father. After a moment, she said, "Wait here," and walked to the nurses' station. The shifts were changing, and one of the new nurses she knew; the lady had bandaged Benella's own wounds. After a brief discussion, she and Cameron were allowed to sneak into Connor's room, where she held the big man's hand, kissed his brow, and prayed. Cameron simply stood by the bed and watched his daddy sleep.

At three o'clock, Gibbs came around.

"Hey, babe," he whispered to his son, around cracked lips.

Cameron, too moved to speak, leaned over and kissed his father on the forehead.

"Hi, sugar pie," from Benella, smiling.

Connor said something unintelligible, so she leaned close to his mouth. "Water," he said again, very weakly.

She poured him a partial glass and helped him drink. "Better?" she asked.

He nodded and tried to smile. He was incredibly weak, incredibly pale, incredibly . . . *alive*.

"You find me?" he whispered, holding on to both their hands. She shook her head. "A dog. A stray, we think. Mary Leigh adopted him. If she hadn't, I would have."

"A dog . . ." He seemed amazed.

"You were nowhere near where we suspected, and you were under a sheltered edge of the riverbank. Only someone across the river could have seen you, and no one was looking for you over there."

"Miracle," he whispered.

Benella teared up then. "You're right," she said as he faded out.

She looked over at Cameron. "He's tired, and very weak. But he'll be okay. Let's go tell the others. They're all worried sick."

She kissed Gibbs once more and the pair ghosted away.

Hank Yarborough bullied his way into Connor's room around eight A.M., with a buxom nurse bristling behind him. "Ms. Sweet, I told him that sheriff or no sheriff, he could wait."

"It's all right, Phyllis." She smiled. "But thanks for trying."

Phyllis fixed Yarborough with a "you don't scare me" glare and took her mocha self back into the hall.

"Wonderful woman," opined the sheriff. "Takes her work seriously." He looked at Gibbs. "How is he?"

"Asleep right now. Mostly he's in and out. We talked some," said Benella.

"Know what's amazing? We worked it out from Mary

Leigh's limited story and the physical evidence at the site, plus an examination of Bobb's body. Connor beat the living crap out of the guy, and completely ruined his knee, probably with some kind of karate kick. The creep must have been in constant pain after Connor got through with him."

"Couldn't have happened to a nicer fellow."

"If Bobb hadn't had the ice pick . . ." Yarborough trailed off. "They tell me that Connor's going to be just fine."

"Appears so, though there could be recurring problems. The lesion on his brain is what worries me. What did that guy use on him?"

"A tree, we think."

"He hit Connor with a *tree*?"

"The other way around, actually. Bobb apparently slung him against the tree."

"Good grief! No wonder there's a concussion."

"Right. Well, let me go, I just wanted a quick look-see. Give him my regards when he wakes up."

"Hank?"

"What?"

She simply grinned at him and shook her head.

"Right," he said.

Chapter 52

KATELIN WAS FIXING BREAKFAST AND BUSTER a.k.a. Mister Matt was helping eat it; between the dog and Mary Leigh, nine pancakes had been consumed. So far. Katelin didn't seem to mind; she was whipping up another batch of batter when Benella joined them, yawning and favoring her back. She sat at the kitchen table, carefully.

"Pancakes?" offered Katelin, dropping the whisk in the sink.

"Just coffee, please. Too early to eat. It's still dark outside."

"Mister Matt woke me up," informed Mary Leigh. "He had to pee."

"And after that we couldn't get back to sleep," said Katelin. "So here we are. How about you, what's your complaint?"

"These bullet holes. It's hard to find a comfortable sleeping position."

A knock came at the back door. Katelin started across the kitchen.

"Wait," said Benella. She slipped the little .380 out of

a pocket in her robe and rested it on her thigh, under the table.

Katelin was horrified. She shook her head and opened the door. It was one of the FBI agents who were guarding the house around the clock, in rotating two-man, eight-hour shifts. There was also a deputy on duty, currently in the living room reading the newspaper.

The agent asked if coffee was ready, and Katelin said, "You bet," and handed him a thermos and two mugs, and the agent said thanks and shut the door. Cold air wafted through the room, stirring the cooking smells. Katelin brought Benella a steaming cup. As she placed it on the table, she whispered, "I refuse to live like this," and went back to the stove.

"We have no choice," Benella began. "Not with Delaney—"

Katelin held up a hand. "Mary Leigh, go to your room and play, or watch TV. I'll bring your pancakes up there."

"C'mon, Mister Matt," Mary Leigh said. "Grown-up talk."

After Mary Leigh left the room, Katelin said, "Don't tell me I have no choice, Bennie. I buried a husband recently, not to mention that horrible man coming here and making me—" She shuddered. "This house is half paid for, and far too large for just me and Mary Leigh. I've decided to sell it and move away."

"Where will you move?"

"Jackie Ritter stopped by after visiting Henry in the hospital. She invited us to come stay with them in Fayetteville until I have the house sold. There're two houses for sale on her street, both in the low hundreds, affordable and plenty big enough for Mary Leigh and me."

"But who do you know in Fayetteville, aside from Jackie and Henry?"

"I don't know anyone, but I've always made friends easily. We'll do fine."

"What about me?"

"What about you? You have lots of friends here in Wendover. And you have Connor, and JoAnn."

"They're not family, Katelin."

Katelin used the spatula to pile hotcakes onto a plate, covered them with syrup, and followed Mary Leigh. In a moment she returned, poured herself a second cup of coffee, sat across the table from Benella. She took a sip. "This may seem sudden to you, but it's all I've thought about lately. Mary Leigh's been having bad dreams, about being kidnapped, about wandering around the woods in the dark, about that man she calls the troll. It's all too much for her, and I've been having bad dreams of my own. And I refuse to have people with guns staying in and around my house, day and night."

She reached over and took Benella's hand to ease the sting of her words. "And that includes you, sister of mine. You are welcome in my home anytime, you know that. But your gun isn't. I always hated guns, and now a gun has killed my husband—"

"The man behind the gun killed Damien, Kate."

"Don't hand me that NRA bullshit! If the jerk hadn't had a gun to *begin* with, my husband would still be alive."

"Bad guys always have guns. Tools of their trade."

"But if guns weren't so readily available—"

"They'd make them. Or use spears, or clubs, or knives, or baseball bats. Or *ice picks*. Or simply strength of numbers. It's why they're called bad guys, Katelin. Guns give us good guys a chance."

"I've never bought that argument and I never will. Guns are *evil,* and so are the people who use them." Katelin poked out a determined chin.

There was nothing else to say, so Benella went upstairs, dressed, packed, and left. Maybe later, Katelin would come to her senses.

Then again, maybe not.

Chapter 53

Connor was much better. Benella could even hear him when he talked. So she finally told him about her conversation with Katelin—about the evil of guns, her plans to sell the house and move to Fayetteville.

"You can't blame her," Connor said. "Look what she's been through."

"How about what *you've* been through! And Henry. And those federal agents, three of them stone-cold *dead*. Not to mention me with holes in my back and side and arm."

"Kate didn't ask for any of this, or for that creep to come to her home."

"Right, and if she'd had a *gun* that day," Benella rushed on, "then maybe—just maybe—she could have held Amos Thorton at bay and *not had to cut his throat*!"

Gibbs changed the subject. "Henry came by."

Benella went over to the window. Breathe in, breathe out. Deep cleansing breaths; smell that spring air. After a moment, she said, "Not walking, I hope."

"In a wheelchair, piloted by the comeliest nurse in western North Carolina. Legs up to her ears, waist the size of my calf, rounded sensuous hips, upturned breasts with a hint of impertinence, eyes like liquid gold."

She turned to look at him, one brow arched. "Prettier than me?"

"Maybe not if you'd do something with your hair, highlight it to catch the sun. Maybe—"

She grinned, then crossed the room to lave his ear. After a moment, "What's this?" in mock surprise.

He looked down. "What do you expect, with all that talk about the nurse?"

"Nurse, hell. That was *me,* baby," she purred, and nuzzled.

Ten minutes later, Phyllis walked in.

She was shocked.

Chapter 54

"IT'S NOT A VERY GOOD PICTURE, I KNOW," lamented Tom Smithson. "Confounded disposable camera. But that's the finest Louis Marx I ever ran across."

"An ear of corn?" Benella was closely examining the blurry photograph that Smithson had mailed her.

"Yeah, riding a tricycle. See the windup key?"

"And the bell. You say it was in the original box?"

"Yes, and the box is mint. Dusty, but mint," Tom assured her.

Benella shifted the phone to her other ear. "Anything else come along?"

"I just swapped for a top-quality etching of three horses. On the back it says 'Mabel Tewksbury . . . Sep 1, 2, 3, 1912 . . . Laceyville Penn.'"

"No bigger stuff?"

"No, but I've got a line on a Mount Lebanon high chair, and possibly an elder's secretary, butternut and cherry. But I may not be able to buy them. This particular source is unreliable."

While Benella talked business in the other room, Connor sat comfy on the couch in a green-and-white cotton robe and sandals, no socks. Everette, fresh from church, had on a suit and tie and cordovan Weejuns; his shirt had broad blue stripes and a white collar. Spiffy.

"Since the 1930s," Gibbs was saying, "the price of milk has been determined by the distance dairy farmers lived from Eau Claire, Wisconsin, though that may soon change. A federal judge recently tossed out the system."

"What the hell does Éclair—"

"*Eau* Claire," Connor corrected.

". . . some *town* in Wisconsin have to do with milk pricing?"

"The upper Midwest is the nation's primary milk-producing area, and once shipped its surplus to parts of the country that didn't produce enough. A 'distance differential' was factored in to cover transportation costs. Over the years, most parts of the country developed the capacity to supply their own milk for local markets, so the system is antediluvian."

"What does that mean?" from Mike.

"Antiquated, outdated," answered Benella, fresh off the phone and carrying before her on a tray an array of potables. Then to Gibbs: "Tom may have a line on a maple snake-leg candlestand."

Before Connor could reply, the doorbell chimed.

"I'll get it," Everette said, and went to the door to peep through the peephole. "Sheriff," he announced, and released the dead bolt.

Hank Yarborough came in, placed his hat on the rack, his coat beneath the hat, and his hinder in the blue wing chair.

"Coffee?" Benella asked.

"I'd be obliged," Hank replied. She went to get him a cup.

"Mind if I smoke?" Everette said.

"Not if you do it in Eau Claire," Connor answered.

"Where?" asked Hank.

"Never mind," said his deputy, morosely tapping a cigarette back into its pack.

Yarborough squinted at Gibbs, then began: "First, the good news. Marvin Delaney has not been seen in the area."

"What's the bad news?" from Benella, returning with a steaming mug.

"He hasn't been seen anywhere else, either. Now, you're sure you hit him at least once, outside the vest of course?"

"I'm sure," she insisted. "I saw blood fly, like busting a ketchup bottle. From his right arm."

"Well, either he knows a tight-lipped intern, or an ex–army medic, or something. Or he fixed it himself."

"Probably the latter," said Connor. "He's resourceful. And even if he weren't . . ." He paused.

"What?" Yarborough prompted.

"I don't think he'd take a chance, either on being seen or being reported. If he did get treatment from somebody, I'd say start looking for a dead doctor."

Hank rubbed his chin thoughtfully.

"But," said Gibbs, ever the optimist, "no news is good news. Perhaps he's given up."

The three others just stared at him.

"Then again, maybe not," he conceded.

"Wouldn't be in character," from the sheriff. "He stuck around far longer than he should have, trying for Bennie. I doubt we've heard the last of Mr. Delaney."

Benella agreed. "Which is why we're going to Henry's cabin over in Hyde County just as soon as Connor thinks he's up to the trip. I can peddle antiques from there as well as here, and Connor can get back in shape, when he feels like working out again. We'll do fine. Besides, with Katelin gone . . ." She let it hang.

Yarborough segued for her. "How's Henry Ritter? I haven't seen him since he left the hospital."

"Walking with a cane and cussing a blue streak about his mountain cabin. And already drawing up plans for a new one." Benella smiled.

"What about the cars?" queried Yarborough.

"Connor settled with his insurance company, and the other car belonged to Triangle Toyota, so McDermott is handling it. I'll get my brand-new wrecked car back tomorrow. Connor's not ready to drive just yet. When he is, we'll get him something fast."

"I've got the van," Connor said.

"I said fast," from Benella.

Connor just grinned and drank his tea.

Three weeks to the day after their long, long night in Henry's mountain domain, Connor and Benella filled Connor's Sienna van to capacity and headed for eastern North Carolina. En route, they stopped in Fayetteville to check on Katelin and Mary Leigh. The little girl was delighted to see them, but Katelin was reserved. "Give her time," Jackie Ritter advised when she and Benella were alone.

"No problem. She can have all the time she wants." But Benella was deeply hurt.

Jackie said, "Henry had a couple of rifles and a shotgun here, in a gun safe. I had him take them over to Ed Humburg's. Kate couldn't stand knowing they were even in the house."

"What if Delaney were to trace her here?" from Benella.

"But what are the odds on that?"

"Don't underestimate him. He's extremely cunning."

And then Mary Leigh burst in and stifled the conversation.

Just before they left, Benella took Henry aside. "Here," she said, holding out her diminutive .380 automatic.

"Now, honey—"

"Don't 'now, honey' me. That's my sister and niece in there. If Katelin talked Jackie into making you remove your hunting guns, that's one thing. Your not having anything to protect my family is another. So take this. Keep it on you day and night. Don't let anyone know you have it, not even Jackie."

Henry took the gun.

"Marvin Delaney is like a burr, and there's no quit in the man. He jumped off that cliff like there was a giant pillow waiting, and without a second's hesitation."

"Honey, you jumped off the same cliff."

"But he was chasing me, Henry. I had to jump to survive. He didn't. He's got a screw loose."

"I'll keep that in mind," Ritter said, and stuck the .380 in his belt.

Chapter 55

AT HENRY'S EASTERN HIDEAWAY, CONNOR WAS back in training and Benella had set up her computer. It was much warmer near the coast than it had been in the mountains, and mosquitoes buzzed thirstily.

"Did you get the bear?" Benella said one evening, looking up from her keyboard as Connor clumped down the hall in muddy boots, with a camera around his neck.

"Got three, mama and two cubs. No telephoto lens, either. They sashayed right up to me."

"You're such a manly man," she trilled falsetto. "How did you get them to come so close?"

"I lay in the grass and made a sound like a jelly doughnut."

"Smart aleck."

"You expect me to yield my secrets of camouflage to a mere mortal?"

She gave him the full force of her startlingly blue eyes. "Come over here," she said. When he did, she ran a hand up his inner thigh, stopping juuust short. "I'll make it worth your while if you tell me," she promised, batting her lashes.

"There's a bunch of old tires in one corner of the field," he blurted, "where the bears regularly come out of the woods. I cut up this old Michelin radial and glued—"

"Never mind." She removed her hand.

"You're not planning to welsh on your deal, are you?"

She wasn't and she proved it.

They were in the shower when the phone rang. Henry Ritter.

"Yo," Connor said wetly.

"Hello, breeze."

"Hi, Henry. How's the leg?" Benella wouldn't release him.

"Great. I won a square-dancing contest yesterday."

"Good for you," Connor squeaked. She still wouldn't let go, in fact was washing him faster.

"Why does your voice sound funny?" from Henry.

"No reason," Gibbs lied. "Was it a close contest?"

Benella was using both hands now.

"What contest?" asked Henry.

"The dance contest," Connor said, squirming involuntarily.

"That was a joke. What's Bennie doing? I'd like to speak to her a minute."

"She has her hands full just now." Benella was pulling and kneading and beginning to breathe hard from the titillation.

She wasn't the only one.

"Can you disturb her? I won't keep her long," Henry asked.

Benella had replaced her hands with something else. "Tell him I'm simply too busy to talk," she whispered, easing onto him backward, then beginning to move rhythmically.

"I'm afraid she's indisposed," Gibbs croaked.

She moved more rapidly.

"Have her call me," Henry insisted.

Benella was moving with real urgency now, tossing her wet hair. He reached under with his free hand to stroke and probe, hoping she wouldn't moan loudly enough for Henry to hear. (Sometimes Bennie could be very vocal.)

"I will," Connor wheezed, and broke the connection. One of them, anyway.

Still in the shower, Connor scarcely able to breathe Benella had the water so hot. "Hey, cut back on the temp, will you? I'm not a dipnoan."

She did, and then it was his turn to wash her tanned expanse of hills and valleys.

He managed. For a while.

Priapism was often a curse.

Not always.

Toweling off, Benella said, "What's a dipnoan?"

"A critter with both lungs and gills. Hard to drown, in either air or water."

"Do they have—" she whispered into his ear, using the tip of her tongue more than necessary.

Back in the shower again . . .

Connor was dead.

Or soon would be.

"What do you want for supper?" Benella called naked from the kitchen.

"Six dozen oysters and a bowl of lime Jell-O," he groaned.

She came into the bedroom, all curves and plains, arms overhead to tousle her cascading hair. "What did you have in mind for the Jell-O? "

He showed her.

They were happy as clams.

Weeks passed and the geese came and went, northward bound, and swans, with their long graceful necks and regal bearing. Connor and Benella drove occasionally into Englehard for supplies, but for the most part lived and worked in solitude, reading and rutting and recovering. The days grew longer, the nights more cloying, and the wind bore a warm sense of salt.

Connor made photos, and Benella wrote an article on Shaker furniture, the two of them acting as if their lives actually belonged to them.

Even believing it . . .

And still no Delaney.
But they hadn't forgotten.
Nor had he . . .

And on one gray May day, a call came.

Chapter 56

As the search for Connor Gibbs had been taking place, Marvin Delaney was driving his van to North Wilkesboro, where Matt Bachison had previously stashed a legitimate Honda Accord (owned by an unmarried cousin stationed in Germany, who had no idea Matt had "borrowed" it) in an abandoned barn, along with six sets of stolen plates from three states. Delaney under the cover of darkness transferred three gym bags filled with unmarked bills (nothing smaller than a twenty); four handguns, a shotgun, and two AR-15 rifles; six hundred rounds of ammunition, in various chambering; two propane lanterns, with fuel; two dozen candles; a folding camp chair; three blankets; an army sleeping bag and folding cot; a two-man tent; assorted foodstuffs; instant coffee; five gallons of water; two tarpaulins and plenty of nylon cord; extra clothing; the collected works of Mark Twain.

He then drove just over one hundred miles to an isolated farm in Buncombe County, not far from Asheville. The farm was owned by a distant relative and had not been worked for a decade. He set up a campsite out of sight of the single dirt road traversing the property. There he stayed for twenty days, with no fires, no hot food, and no company, reading and carving recuperating. On the twenty-first day he packed up camp, dug a stack of twenties out of a gym bag before tossing it into the Honda, put the bills in his pocket, and drove away. He never returned.

His neck wound had begun to bother him more than the minor bullet laceration to his shoulder. He had originally treated it with an antibiotic, then dressed it carefully, changing the bandage every day. It had seemed to heal, as had the punctures in his leg and hand, but yesterday he'd experienced mild numbness around the bite. Today it gave off a sensation of cold.

So he went to an emergency center in Hendersonville. After a three-hour wait, during which he became increasingly agitated, a medical specialist finally escorted him to an examination room.

"This looks like a bite. Did a dog nip you, Mr. Lawrence?" she asked.

Delaney denied it, saying he'd fallen out of a tree and caught a limb on the way down.

"Well, these look like puncture marks to me. I'll be happy to treat this for you, but I have to report this as a possible animal bite. It's the law. I understand why you may not want to have your pet quarantined, but—"

He hit her in the mouth, and then, as she fell back against the wall, kicked her in the stomach. When she dropped to her knees, Delaney chopped her on the side of the neck and she collapsed. He bound her with adhesive tape found in a cabinet, gagged her with her own white coat and more of the tape, then left her there, telling the desk nurse that he needed to retrieve some insurance information from his car. She smiled and said sure.

In five minutes, he was on the interstate.

Rabies, wasn't that just his luck! He knew a doctor who had recently lost his license to malpractice, but he lived a long way from Hendersonville . . .

Still, better to be safe than sorry, so he drove more than 350 miles east, to New Holland, near Lake Mattamuskeet.

In Hyde County.

"Shit, Marvin. When did this happen?"

"About three weeks ago, give or take a couple of days. Why?"

The former doctor, whose name was Pilsner, said, "Because it's important, that's why. The incubation period for rabies is normally four to eight weeks, and sometimes up to a year, but not if the bite is in the head or the neck, or if there are multiple wounds. Were you bitten anywhere else?"

"No," Delaney lied.

"That's good news. Has there been any tingling, numbness, or sensations of either hot or cold about the wound?"

"No," Delaney lied again.

"Here, stick this in your mouth."

Delaney did, and in two minutes Pilsner removed the thermometer to check it. "No sign of fever, that's a relief. Okay, here's the plan. The method of immunization involves daily injections, and they're no fun. There are two vaccines approved for use in this country. The duck embryo vaccine, called DEV, and the rabbit nervous-tissue vaccine, or NTV. Neither of these is one hundred percent effective, but close enough if the treatment is started in time. The lower frequency of central-nervous-system reaction when using DEV makes it preferable to NTV, so that's what I'll use. Assuming I can get some.

"With mild exposure, fourteen daily injections would be required, administered to the abdomen, lower back, and the thighs. Rotating the sites, of course. With a bite to the neck, as we have here, we'll have to either give double doses or two shots a day. And for three weeks, not two. If we don't, and the raccoon actually was rabid, well . . ."

"Whatever," said Delaney.

"It'll cost you."

"No problem."

"Come back at four this afternoon. I'll have to go to Little Washington to get the vaccine."

"Right," said Delaney, slipping into his shirt. "You think we got it in time?"

"Probably. You said there's been no irritation around the wound site, and there's no temperature. Your pupils aren't dilated, you're not perspiring . . . have you been sleeping well?"

"Yes."

"Then let's hope for the best. We could do a full blood work-up, but it would take time. And blood work on the QT is dicey. Besides, no matter what the result, we'd still do the treatment just to be safe.

"Right," Delaney agreed.

And they went their separate ways.

Delaney crossed Lake Mattamuskeet to Fairfield, to have lunch at the town's only restaurant. He dug out Mark Twain (*The Innocents Abroad, Volume One*), before going in, and read while eating greasy barbecue and hush puppies, washed down with iced tea: "So far, good. If any man has a right to feel proud of himself and satisfied, surely it is I . . ."

The needle in his stomach did indeed hurt, but not as bad as being shot in the shoulder, or falling through a tree, or being attacked by a ring-tailed devil. After the treatment, Delaney checked into a motel in Fairfield and made his plans. After spending three weeks down here making like a pincushion, he would go to Mecklenburg County and hire a private dick out of Charlotte, or maybe Winston-Salem, and see what was cooking with Annie Oakley and her boyfriend. Marvin had been reading the papers—detailed accounts of the debacle in the mountains—so he knew who had survived and who hadn't. This time, no fooling around; fooling around had cost him too much—too much time, too much pain, too much irritation. The Sweet bitch was good; *too* damn good. This time, he would just sneak in, plant a charge, sit in his van down the street, and when the time was ripe, blow her to hell and gone. BOOM, just like that.

In the Honda he had enough C-4 to take out a bank building, let alone a house in the suburbs. So what if he took out a few neighbors? That'd teach them to be careful who they bought next to.

The next morning Delaney drove to Wilson to research his affliction. After twenty minutes of reading, he scurried to the bathroom to throw up. Then he reread the material.

Well, at least there'll be no more shots, he told himself, and left the library on wobbly legs. What he'd discovered was this: He was in the prodromal phase, characterized by increased irritability, restlessness, excessive salivation, insomnia and perspiration, not to mention the pupil dilation and stiff neck.

He was doomed.

And he hadn't long.

So he called an investigative firm in Raleigh and sicced them on Benella Sweet. Every available operative, around the clock, he instructed. He'd cover all expenses, pay double the going rate, he promised the office manager. But they must get to work immediately. He FedEx'd them a cashier's check and they did.

The phone call was from Hank Yarborough. Connor said, "Hello, Hank."

Yarborough got straight to the point. "Someone's been asking around about you and Bennie."

"Who?"

"I dunno. Time I got the word they were long gone. Not Delaney, though. Problem is, they got pointed at Henry."

"Lord no." Connor watched Benella through the kitchen window. She was out feeding the swans.

"Yeah, me, too," said Yarborough. "I called Henry to warn him."

"Yeah?"

"Too late. A pretty young thing in a postal uniform came

by with what she claimed were important papers relative to the sale of Benella's gym. Wouldn't let Henry sign for it. Said only Ms. Sweet could."

"Let me guess."

"Right."

"I'll go tell her."

"Y'all look sharp, now. You want help?"

"You've helped enough, Hank, but thanks."

And Connor went to inform Benella.

Delaney couldn't believe the investigator's report. He'd been living within a dozen miles of the bitch and her man for all those days. Who'da thunk it?

Now to catch them away from home.

He did. While the duo was in Swan Quarter looking for antiques, Delaney let himself into their cabin, looked around, then slipped into the cellar to plant his C-4.

All his C-4.

"They'll wake up on the moon," he told himself.

That night in his heatless tent, Marvin Delaney fought demons. He barely won, twitching nonstop in the sleeping bag, suffering mild convulsions, waking near dawn in a state of abject terror. As the sun climbed, his tension abated, but when he tried to eat breakfast, his throat spasmed and he couldn't swallow, in fact nearly choked. Even coffee wouldn't go down.

He spasmed at the slightest noise outside the tent, even the touch of his shirt on his skin. His neck was so stiff he could barely turn his head, so he compensated by swiveling his body at the waist. His nocturnal convulsions had produced a modicum of blood-tinged vomit, which he washed off his face and torso. Then he drove away in the Honda.

From a man who looked like Sheb Wooley, Delaney rented an ancient logging truck. Old but reliable, the man said of the truck. Into it Delaney loaded an AR-15, two pistols, a pair of binoculars, a can of Coke, and a short-range transmitter that would serve as a detonator. Then he drove to the bimbo's cabin and parked close by.

Within range of the transmitter.

There he waited, in constant torment.

Connor and Benella stopped in Englehard for supper. This would be their last trip until the Delaney situation was resolved, one way or the other. After shrimp and oysters and coleslaw and french fries, they hustled home.

Delaney tried to take a sip of Coke, just one sip, and went into a tonic convulsion. His temperature climbed through 102 degrees. He could barely breathe. He remained in stasis for nearly an hour, then slowly came around. Somehow he had wound up on the floor of the truck. As he laboriously pulled his sweat-soaked body onto the seat, a Sienna van sped by trailing a plume of dust.

Gibbs glanced at the logging truck as they flew past. Had he seen someone inside?

"Did you see anyone in that truck?" he asked Benella.

"I didn't see, we went by too fast. Remember, when we get home, we're going to dig in like moles and sit tight. Make Delaney come to us, right?"

"Right. We'll surround him." He squeezed her hand.

Delaney was frothing at the mouth, staving off convulsions, his finger on the transmitter switch. Just one flick . . .

. . . but he was about to go tonic again.

His temperature had reached 105 degrees and only a supreme act of will was keeping him from convulsion . . .

. . . and coma . . .

. . . and death . . .

Fighting the sun (actually painful due to his extreme dilation), he watched the couple arrive, then waited . . .

. . . *willed* them to go *into the fucking cabin* . . .

• • •

Gibbs climbed out and headed for the porch. Benella got out her side, slammed the door, hesitated, then said to his retreating back, "I'll lock up the car. At least make it harder for Delaney to plant another—"

She stopped midsentence . . .

"CONNOR! DON'T GO INSIDE!"

Too late.

Connor Gibbs was across the threshold when Delaney flipped the switch . . .

Epilogue

When authorities discovered Marvin Delaney's body, it was stiff as a board and wedged against the clutch and brake pedal of an ancient Ford logging truck. Delaney's face and chest were covered with a foamy pink froth. On the floor near his hand was a detonator/transmitter. It took but a few minutes for law enforcement officers to find the bomb linked to the device, since only one house was within range—a sprawling log cabin owned by Henry Ritter of Fayetteville. The local sheriff knew of Ritter, but not those residing at the cabin in Henry's absence, said to be a couple who kept to themselves.

A bomb squad—coptered in from Greenville—searched the cabin and recovered a sizeable quantity of C-4 with a radio receiver attached. When Benella Mae Sweet, present during the search, was told that a dead man had been found inside a nearby vehicle, she demanded to see the body, even though apprised of its unpalatable condition. Upon viewing the remains, she and a very large male companion were visibly relieved.

The sheriff wanted to know why.

They told him.

At the conclusion of the narrative, the sheriff produced from a satchel the detonator/transmitter found near Delaney's rigored hand, and held it out for examination. One of two exposed connecting wires was free of its mooring, probably the result of the horrific seizures obviously suffered by the decedent.

The toggle switch of the detonating device was in the "on" position.

"If that there wire hadn't come loose . . ." the sheriff said unnecessarily.